BEYOND THE STARS

Books by William Shatner:

QUEST FOR TOMORROW

Delta Search

In Alien Hands

Step into Chaos

Beyond the Stars

Published by HarperPrism

BEYOND THE STARS

QUEST FOR TOMORROW

WILLIAM SHATNER

HarperPrism

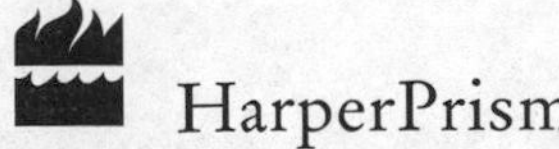

HarperPrism
A Division of HarperCollins*Publishers*
10 East 53rd Street, New York, N.Y. 10022-5299

This is a work of fiction. The characters, incidents, and dialogues are products of the author's imagination and are not to be construed as real. Any resemblance to actual events or persons, living or dead, is entirely coincidental.

For information address HarperCollins*Publishers* Inc.
10 East 53rd Street, New York, N.Y. 10022-5299.

ISBN 0-06-105118-7

HarperCollins®, ®, and HarperPrism®
are trademarks of HarperCollins*Publishers* Inc.

HarperPrism books may be purchased for educational, business, or sales promotional use. For information, please write: Special Markets Department, HarperCollins*Publishers*, 10 East 53rd Street, New York, N.Y. 10022-5299.

Library of Congress Cataloging-in-Publication Data
Shatner, William.
Beyond the stars / William Shatner. — 1st U.S. ed.
p. cm.
ISBN 0-06-105118-7
I. Title II. Quest for tomorrow
PS3569.H347 B49 2000
813'.54—dc21 99-42204

Visit HarperPrism on the World Wide Web at
http://www.harpercollins.com

00 01 02 03 04 ❖ 10 9 8 7 6 5 4 3 2 1

DEDICATION AND ACKNOWLEDGMENT

She defined love.
She was my passion.
I dedicate this book to my beloved.

To Bill Quick, who's become my friend.

INTRODUCTION

Through the first three books of the *Quest for Tomorrow* series, one of the main themes has been the destiny of humankind as our species moves into space. In the third book, *Step Into Chaos*, the vision of that destiny was revealed as the creation of the Omega Point.

The Omega Point theory, first invented and promulgated by the famous physicist Frank J. Tipler, postulated that humanity would, over millions of years, gradually expand to fill the entire universe and become, in effect, a superbrain.

By the finish of *Step Into Chaos*, young Jim Endicott, bearing the burden of his mother's gift of encoded DNA, became far more than human—in fact, he became one with the Omega Point itself.

He used the infinite power of that entity to set the universe back on its proper course by going back in time and changing one simple act: the coin his mother flipped to decide whether to alter his DNA.

Now, in *Beyond The Stars*, we return to Jim's tale at another crucial turning point: the moment when he killed Carl Endicott, the man he thought of as his father. In this new universe, Jim doesn't kill Carl. He kills Commander Steele instead.

The astute reader will notice other differences. In the first three books, humanity, constrained by Delta's paranoia and the necessities of the mind arrays, was not a race of colonizers.

Now humanity is. When Jim runs from Wolfbane, he flees into a galaxy throbbing with hundreds of Terran colony worlds, and the greatest obsessions of the human species are more expansion, more colonies, more people moving ever outward.

What happened to the old Jim, the Jim cursed by his own altered genetic heritage, dogged forever by his own self-betrayals? The universe he lived in, made a dead end by his own peculiar existence, still remains—but as an alternate dimension. When Jim restored the main universe, he didn't destroy his own first universe, but split it away. Yet all the universes are the province of the Omega Point, for the Omega Point is omnipotent and omniscient and omnipresent. And Jim is a part of it still.

Does the new Jim *consciously* know of the Jim he replaced?

For the answer to that, gentle reader, you must continue on with Jim as he moves into a universe the same, yet different, as a boy the same, yet different. It should be a wild ride. Enjoy it!

BEYOND THE STARS

CHAPTER ONE

1

The wrecked cabin stank of charred wood. The sun, its morning light filtered by a scrim of trees, leaked through a drifting haze of smoke. Jim Endicott licked his lips. His mouth was dry. His head ached. He could feel his pulse pumping in his ears.

He squatted next to Carl Endicott, the man who, up until a few days ago, he had believed to be his father, and said quietly, "Can you stand?"

"I think so. I'll need a hand." Carl levered himself into a sitting position. He groaned as the crust of blood on his chest split open. "No. I can't—" He gritted his teeth and sank back. Suddenly he seemed to shrink.

Jim's mother, Tabitha, until that moment seemingly calm despite the terror she had just survived, suddenly gasped.

"Oh, my God!"

"Mom, don't look."

Tabitha knelt next to Carl. She patted his shoulders, his head, his chest, as if her frantic touch could somehow heal him. Her hands came away streaked with red.

"Mom. . . ."

"Tab, it's not as bad as it looks," Carl said. He glanced at Jim. "Son, help your mother."

Jim put his hand on Tabitha's shoulder. She wheeled and glared at him. "Don't touch me!"

Jim pulled his hand back. "Mom, I—"

"You shot him! It was you, wasn't it?"

"I didn't mean—"

"This is all your fault! If you'd obeyed your father in the first place—"

"Tabitha!" Carl's voice snapped like a breaking bone. She turned back to him, her lips moving silently, an expression of utter helplessness on her face. Jim's stomach heaved. If there had been anything inside, he would have puked it up on the spot.

"I . . . I'm sorry," he said. He couldn't think of anything else to say.

I did all this. I caused it. My fault my fault my fault. . . .

He glanced over at the armored shape of Commander Steele's headless corpse, then quickly looked away.

Carl saw the glance. "Jim, stop it. Look at me!"

"Dad, I'm so sorry."

Carl shook his head, as if the apology were trivial, and Jim winced. "I brought a portadoc," Carl said. "It's in the large bag. If the explosion didn't damage it, I need it." He paused. "As for blame, there's plenty of it to go around. We can talk about it later, maybe. But right now, I'm bleeding. . . ."

A harsh, bright light seemed to explode Jim's skull, cutting through the film of shock that had leached all color from his world. The hues suddenly screamed at him: The crimson blotch on Carl's chest appeared to vibrate.

Blood. Too *much* blood . . .

He turned and ran, not noticing the tears that streaked silently down his smudged cheeks.

"Hurry!" Tabitha cried.

2

Jim lifted the compact square shape of the portadoc away from Carl's naked chest. Carl's eyes were closed, his face pale, but his breathing was steady. The wound stretched from just above Carl's right nipple almost to his shoulder, an angry red welt now closed beneath a glistening, transparent line of instant skin.

Tabitha had pulled all their bags and everything else she could salvage out of the shambles of the cabin and piled them on the front porch. Amazingly, the roof of the porch still stood, though the cabin itself was open to the sky. She looked up as Jim added the portadoc to the pile.

"Jim? I'm sorry. What I said before, I didn't mean—"

He realized his hands were shaking. He took a deep breath. "Mom, it's okay. We were all crazy. Everything was crazy."

Her face was as pale as Carl's, and now Jim noticed the livid purple-and-yellow bruise that began high on her forehead and extended up beneath her disheveled hairline.

He reached toward her head. She flinched away from him, her own fingers involuntarily flying toward the lump.

"It's nothing. That big man hit me. I'm okay."

"Let me look. At least let the portadoc—"

"We have more important things to worry about. Your father . . . he needs medical attention. Real medical attention. We have to go back. . . ."

As Jim listened to her, he felt something stir deep within his mind. Something cold, dispassionate, and hard. It seemed to operate like a computer, pulling up facts, examining them, weighing them, discarding some, and generating new facts from old ones.

"Mom. We can't go back."

She stared at him. "But we have to. Your father . . ."

He glanced at the unconscious man. "We can't stay here, either, but we can't go back. I don't know where we can go. Maybe he does. I'd better wake him."

"Don't you dare! He's hurt! He needs rest!"

He was shocked at her vehemence. Under ordinary circumstances he would have obeyed her without question. But that new, cold part of him wouldn't allow it. She was too close to hysteria, operating on the ragged edge of sanity, reacting to emotions he knew she was barely able to understand. He couldn't obey her, but it wouldn't do to push her over the edge, either. That would only create another problem he would have to deal with, and he had enough of those already.

"Mom," he said, keeping his voice as gentle and steady as he could, "I have to talk to Dad. Unless he told you what he wanted to do next. Did he tell you?"

She was staring at Carl. "He'll be fine, just as soon as a doctor . . ." Her voice trailed off. "What did you say?"

"Did Dad tell you what he wanted to do next?"

"Next?"

"Where he wanted to go from here. He couldn't have planned just to stay here. If they found us . . . "

Involuntarily, his gaze strayed to the three silent bodies arrayed in contorted positions around the clearing in front of the cabin. The one without a head, whom his father had called "Steele." Another one, impaled on a jagged tree branch. The third one, the big man, was nearly hidden in the underbrush, only his feet protruding into the clearing.

Two of them were women. Did it make a difference?

No, that cold part of him decided, it did not. All three had been doing their damnedest to kill him and his family. Now they were dead. But they had come from somewhere, for some reason, and there would be more.

There was no point in asking Tabitha about any of it, not when the man who knew everything was sleeping not ten feet away. The man he'd called "father" all his life.

Even the cold part of him cringed away from that. Carl wasn't his father, and that was somehow tied in with his own betrayal, and with these dead killers. He didn't want to think about that. It was too complicated, too frightening.

They had managed to survive the first attack. But he knew it was only the first attack, and there would be more. So they didn't have a lot of time. Some, maybe, though he had no idea how much. But his strange and surprising father, who wasn't his father, and who had turned out to know a hell of a lot more about the arts of death than Jim had ever imagined possible, might very well know.

"Mom?"

At the sound of his voice she blinked, as if he'd startled her.

"Mom," he said again. He reached out and took her hand. Her fingers were cold and felt thin, like sticks coated with ice. He tugged her up. She came without protest, evidently happy to be led. He walked her away, walked her around the end of the cabin, found a soft hummock where the grisly remains of the dead were no longer visible, and sat her down. She looked up at him, suddenly trusting as a child. For the first time in his life, he realized their roles were reversed. He would have to take care of her, not the other way around.

The thought scared him nearly senseless.

"Jim . . . is everything going to be all right? It is, isn't it?"

He patted her hand. "Yes, it is. I promise."

That was the most heroic thing he did that day.

3

As he rounded the corner of the cabin, Jim glanced back and saw his mother sitting placidly on the grass, her expression blank and helpless and weirdly expectant. He felt a knot just above the center of his breastbone, half in his chest, half in his throat, a knot it took him a moment to identify as terror. It was odd: He had never thought of terror as being a physical thing, a cold, almost fleshy mass that choked him as he forced himself to swallow it.

He went to his father and knelt near Carl's head, then slipped his left arm beneath Carl's neck and lifted him a bit.

Carl moaned. His eyes came open. His gaze was disoriented at first, but sharpened quickly.

"Where's your mother?"

"I took her around the cabin and sat her down. Where she couldn't see. She's not in good shape."

Carl Endicott's gaze went unfocused for an instant. "Your mother is one of the strongest women I've ever known," he said softly. "But this is too much for her. Maybe that's what I can't forgive you for. Causing something that even she can't handle. That nobody should be expected to handle."

"As you told me, we can discuss it later," Jim said, after consulting that new, cold part of himself. "Right now, I need to know. And don't lie to me or hold anything back for my own good, because if we are going to get away from here, I'm going to have to do it. You're too sick to depend on."

He looked down at the wound on Carl's chest. The portadoc had done as well as it could, but Tabitha was right. Carl needed more and better treatment, and he needed it as soon as possible. How soon that would be, Jim had no idea. Out on the edge of his awareness lurked the unthinkable: Carl might die.

Carl stared up at him. "You don't know it," he said, "but you just surprised me. Maybe I didn't do as bad a job with you as I thought."

"And we can talk about that later, too. In the meantime, I have to make sure there is a later. What are the chances that more of these killers will come? You said you knew this Steele woman. She's dead, but she came from somewhere. If more are coming, how quickly?"

Carl closed his eyes. "Steele liked to do things on her own, but the man who sent her watches everything. If he doesn't know what happened already, he will soon. And he'll send others."

"Who sent her?"

Carl went on as if Jim hadn't spoken. "There will be a mother ship somewhere. It will take them a while to put together a new team and send it out. We can't go back to the tube station, and we certainly can't go back home. So we'll have to go ahead."

Jim nodded. "Yes, I thought so, too. Where are we going?"

"Hannaport."

Jim had to think a moment before he remembered. "That little place. On the other side of the mountains from here."

"That's right. We need to get there. I have friends." Carl suddenly gritted his teeth. "Jim. The portadoc gave me enough painkiller to work under normal circumstances, but this isn't normal. I need more, enough to let me move around now. But that will be too much for me to function mentally. I'll be groggy, no use for anything. I'll be dependent on you."

"I'd tell you not to worry, that I'll take care of everything, but that would be a lie. I don't know what will happen. But I'll do my best, Dad."

Carl nodded. "Then let's hope your best is enough." He shifted his weight against Jim's arm. "Get me the painkiller. The quicker we get away from here and get into the trees, the safer we'll be."

4

Jim felt happy.

They walked along a narrow, rocky path, beneath an arch of bowed green pines that concealed the sky almost completely. The path was more an opening than a path, a trail for things with sure hooves or pads, and it wasn't meant for humans.

He was burdened with bags strapped down his back. Carl's left arm lay heavily across his shoulder. Carl could not really walk, but moved along in a halting, looping stagger, his head lolling, his eyes glazed and empty from the drugs. Tabitha supported her husband on the other side, and was similarly encumbered. She'd quit talking long ago, and her breathing sounded raspy and labored.

Jim was aware of all of this. He was aware of more: of the hopelessness of their position, of the danger of death, of the yawning inner abyss of his own betrayal. He was terrified, and numb with grief, and yet he felt happy. When he realized what he felt, he was amazed. Happiness? For a moment he wondered if he was going crazy.

The trail wound upward, following some secret fold in the land the animals had sensed but he couldn't. Now the trees pulled back a bit, exposing ground stony with loose, dark gray shale, and Carl's feet suddenly went out from under him. Tabitha let out a sharp cry as her ankle twisted. She stumbled and went to her knees. Jim listed toward her as Carl's bulk dragged him down.

"Whoa!" He barely managed to lower Carl to a loose sprawl on the hard ground, and then he reached for Tabitha.

"Mom!"

She was sitting, rubbing her left ankle with both hands. He

scooted around Carl, who began to hum tunelessly as he stared from one side of the path to the other, and squatted next to her. "How bad is it?"

She looked up at him. For the first time he saw, magnified by exhaustion and pain, the fine wrinkles at the corners of her eyes. Had they always been there? How little he had observed, how much he had always taken for granted! And still that odd, buoyant feeling of happiness would not leave him, even in the face of new disaster.

"It's not broken," she said slowly. She didn't sound sure.

"Let me see." Gently, he pushed the bottom of her pant leg back, to reveal a streak of discolored skin about an inch wide that began near the base of her heel and extended up over her anklebone. The patch was faintly blue, but darkening as he watched. Gingerly, he pushed at the spot where the knob of ankle protruded. Tabitha drew in a sharp breath.

"You're right, I don't think it's broken," he said. "But it's badly sprained, and you won't be able to walk on it."

Her lips began to quiver. Without thinking about it, he put his arm around her shoulder and pulled her close, suddenly realizing how *small* she was, this woman who had towered over his childhood.

"What are we going to do now?" she whispered.

She began to shake, and he squeezed her tighter, until the shaking stopped.

"The portadoc. I think we can get the swelling down, and maybe make some kind of cast. Or I can tear up a shirt, make a splint with sticks if the machine can't do that. Maybe enough for you to walk." He thought about it. "Enough to help with Dad . . . with Carl."

He knew she noticed the way he changed what he said, but she didn't say anything about it. *That* still lay between them, the mystery of mutual betrayal, but it was either too soon or too late to say anything about it, and so he was grateful for her silence.

5

Though it was very fast, the ship wasn't large, and as a consequence the comm section didn't have its own separate quarters but was merely two workstations on one side of the bridge, presided over by a chief petty officer named Hector Martens. CPO Martens noticed right away when the link between the ship and Commander Steele's kill team vanished, but he wasn't immediately worried. The ship had come to Wolfbane System on very short notice, and under strict orders to remain anonymous. They had not announced themselves to Wolfbane Ground Control, and had no intention of doing so. As a further precaution, the signal from Steele was being bounced off three Wolfbane weathersats to the ship, which was maintaining a position on the other side of the planet from Steele's current location. All this was unbeknownst to the operators of those satellites, and so the signal wasn't as stable as it might have been.

CPO Martens and his crew had been operating twelve on, twelve off, and he was nearing the end of his shift. Ship's time made it either very late or very early, and he was hesitant to wake the captain over something that could be a minor glitch. Captain Shelbourne was nearly as cranky as Commander Steele, and didn't take kindly to being roused over nothing.

It was therefore almost twenty minutes before CPO Martens realized that the link had been broken for good, not just the main link to Steele, but also the backup links to the other two members of Steele's team. Similar delays ensued while Captain Shelbourne was awakened, while further checks were made, while orders were requested from Terra, while orders were received, and while the ship left its orbit and repositioned itself over Steele's last known location. All in all, it took nearly six hours after the communications break for the ship to reach a stationary holding orbit thirty miles above the ruins of Carl Endicott's cabin—at which point CPO Martens discovered a further problem.

"Captain, they're socked in down there. Heavy cloud cover

over the entire region, and extending up about three miles."

Captain Shelbourne glanced irritably at her own screen. "I haven't gone blind, Martens." She leaned back in her seat, pursed her lips, and tapped the side of her chin. All these were recognized as signs she was unhappy with the general state of affairs.

"Very well," she said at last. "Send down some remotes."

The pilot, Lieutenant Baldocker, said, "We could take her down for a look, Captain."

This earned him a cold glance from the captain. "You may have forgotten, Lieutenant, that we are supposed to remain in strict concealment. So, unless you have come upon some way that I don't know of keeping our presence here a secret from Wolfbane ground radars, I'll have to reject your suggestion."

Properly chastened, Lieutenant Baldocker subsided.

"Remote comm units launched, Captain," Martens reported.

"Thank you."

After that, they waited.

6

The remote communications units, called "floaters," dropped beneath the cloud cover at five hundred meters, then homed like fat golden bees on the smoking rubble of the cabin in the clearing. The infrared signature of the cabin masked all other signals until the two floaters were actually on the site and humming busily about ten feet off the ground. From that height, the pictures they sent back to the ship were as sharp and detailed as human eyesight. Sharper, because these eyes weren't human.

Captain Shelbourne stared at the large holoscreen floating before her command chair and began to tap the side of her jaw more rapidly. Unlike the rest of her bridge team, she knew who had sent Steele and her kill squad, and she had a fair idea of how high up Steele's influence actually reached. Or had reached, because the headless corpse lying silently on the ground outside the cabin was plainly Steele's. The captain resisted her first impulse, which was to send notice of the disaster back to Terra immediately, and waited while the floaters examined the rest of the scene. It was during this process that the recording equipment on Heck Campbell's armor triggered a relay on one of the floaters and zipped the film of what had happened, at least from Heck's viewpoint, back to the ship.

"Privacy shield," Captain Shelbourne murmured, as the film began to appear on her screen. After she had reviewed this record of events three times, she left the bridge and went to her cabin, where she made an electronic package of all the data she had recovered and sent it to Terra.

The response came very quickly, so quickly that she knew the decision must have been made at the very highest level. Her new orders were short and to the point, though difficult to achieve: "Pursue and capture," Terra said. "Concealment no longer a priority. Use all available resources."

Captain Shelbourne shut down her private communications unit and returned to the bridge. The orders were clear enough, but how she would carry them out was not. Worse, she knew that her career was on the line. If she failed in her efforts to "pursue and capture," the black mark would remain on her personnel jacket for the remainder of her career—which might not be that long a time at all.

She had not liked Commander Steele when she had first met the dour and forbidding woman. Now she hated her.

"Lieutenant Baldocker, take us down," she said.

The pilot recognized the tone of her voice from past, painful experience, and began the ticklish process of bringing several thousand tons of spacegoing vessel into a landing on the side of a mountain without the aid of ground control or any kind of port facilities. The task was not unlike trying to park an elephant on a postage stamp.

While Baldocker sweated, Captain Shelbourne said, "Medical Officer. Prepare to take on three bodies." The way she said them, the words sounded more like a curse than an order.

7

From his vantage point higher up the mountain, Jim watched the ship settle toward the cabin below in eerie silence. It was unnerving that something so big could be so quiet. The sharp snap of trees breaking beneath its weight was the only sound it made as it landed, like a string of faraway firecrackers going off.

Tabitha squeezed his arm as they saw tiny figures emerge from the ship and busy themselves in the clearing.

"They came for the bodies," Jim said.

"It's so big," Tab observed. He could tell from the sound of her voice that she was badly frightened again.

"No, it isn't. That's a corvette, a small ship. Very fast, but small. Maybe it's a good thing for us."

"What do you mean?"

"You send a ship out like that because of its speed. Whoever sent it was in a hurry. So there probably wasn't much time. Maybe only enough time to get one kill squad together."

Carl grunted. They had seated him on a fallen tree trunk, and Tabitha was sitting next to him, holding him up. As heavily drugged as he was, he tended to doze off if they stopped moving. She was grasping his shoulder with one hand and rubbing the makeshift splint on her ankle with the other.

"Jim," she said. She began to cry.

He reached over and slapped her. Her dry, rasping sobs stopped instantly. He stared at the red marks his fingers had left on her cheek.

"*You hit me!*" she said. It was the most spirited thing he'd heard her say in hours.

"And now you're mad. Good, Mom. Get mad! You have to get mad and stay mad. You can't just give up, fight it! Get mad at me, why not? It's all my fault anyway, right? I'm just a little sneak, a disobedient brat. If I hadn't disobeyed my dad, none of this would have happened."

"I . . ." She looked away, then looked back, her eyes suddenly sparking. "Yes, damn it, that's true. Every damned word of it!"

The invisible knife buried in his chest twisted again, but he welcomed the pain. At least she was fighting again.

"That's right. It is. And none of it will matter if they kill us. That ship down there. It may be hard for them to find us. If they don't have another kill team set up and ready to go, they have to do it themselves. It's not easy to move a ship like that around. If we can keep going, maybe we can get away. But you can't give up. You can't! Or they *will* find us, and then . . . and then . . . "

"I don't hate you, Jimmy."

The knife twisted again.

"You should. Come on, let's go."

He took Carl beneath one arm. Tabitha took the other. Together they lifted him and got started again. Up ahead, the shadowy outlines of a break in the trees began to show. Jim hoped it was a pass. If they could get to the other side of the mountains, it would be that much harder for the ship to find them.

They heard a soft roar from below and looked back. The ship rose from the cabin clearing and floated straight up until it vanished in the clouds.

"Hurry!" Jim said.

He hated himself. But at least Tabitha was no longer crying. She was fighting again, if only fighting him, and that might be enough to save her life. He guessed that was worth it, although the cost was almost too high for him to bear.

But he would have to bear it. So he focused on the pass ahead. Tried not to think too much about the future because he had more than enough to worry about in the here-and-now. One foot in front of the next, lift Carl, pull him, and then one more foot, and one more foot again.

He didn't look back to see the four-man recon barge the ship had off-loaded rise silently into the air, hover a moment, then move briskly higher along the side of the mountain.

Higher. Toward them.

CHAPTER TWO

1

Jim, Carl, and Tabitha made it across the pass just after nightfall. Dusk had filled the woods with shadows an hour before full dark and made the going slow. The pass itself had not been obvious. The spaces between the trees had widened somewhat, and there were more rocky outcroppings, but otherwise the only real indication that the height had been reached and crossed was that they were moving downhill.

"Mom. We'll stop now." He wondered whether to risk using a light, and decided against it.

She heard him but didn't answer. She just quit moving when he did and stood, her head down, Carl's arm lying flaccidly across her shoulders.

"Come on," Jim said. "Let's find a place for him to lie down."

"He's heavy," Tabitha said. "I couldn't have carried him much longer."

Jim took a deep breath. Tabitha sounded disconnected, as if they were talking with each other but not *to* each other. And that bizarre, buoyant happiness had finally drained out of him. It had vanished suddenly, and he knew when and why. Left with his own thoughts as they climbed, he'd suddenly seen it for what it was: a false happiness based on his being the hero of this frightening little play. He had caused the trouble, yes, but now he would save everybody. His mom and dad would love him again. They would forgive him. Everything would be like it had been before. But as soon as he thought about *before*, every bit of his happiness disappeared as if it had never been. Because nothing was going to be the same again, no matter what he did. After that, he quit being happy and became numb. Now even that was wearing off. There was a chilly wind blowing, and the night was dark. Killers were hunting them. He shivered suddenly.

"Against this dead log. Where the leaves have piled up," he said. Together they wrestled Carl over and down. Carl was still half-conscious. He groaned as they lowered him. They had stopped two or three times to give him more painkiller, but now he was coming out of it again. Jim had to override manually the settings of the autodoc in order to dose him enough to kill the pain. He wondered if that was dangerous. If he gave Carl too much dope, maybe there would be permanent damage. To his brain, or his heart. Jim couldn't remember enough from his biology studies to know for sure. It was one more thing to worry about.

They got Carl settled as well as they could, wrapped in a foil camping blanket that seemed far too light to keep him warm. They sat on either side of him, their arms clasped about their knees, wrapped in their own blankets. When Jim looked at Tabitha in the starlight, her eyes gleamed out of the misty, pallid shape of her face.

"Well," he said. "I don't know."

Carl began to snore softly.

That seemed to frighten Tabitha. She inhaled sharply, raggedly, and when she spoke, her voice quavered so much he could hardly understand her.

". . . die," she said.

"What?"

"We're going to die."

"No. No, Mom, we're going to be okay. Hannaport isn't that far away. We made it over the mountain. It's all downhill from here. We'll be fine."

She shook her head. "Nothing will be fine. You're just a boy, how would you know? You don't know anything."

The recon barge floated silently across the tops of the trees. Light exploded from its belly like a sheet of lightning. A voice roared at ear-blasting level from its loudspeakers.

"*Don't move. You are under our guns. If you try to run, we will kill you. Repeat, do not move!*"

2

"One hell of a gun for a kid," the man said as he hefted Jim's Styron und Ritter .75.

The interior of the recon barge was crowded, what with the crew of three young men not much older than himself. They had picked up all the bags, and those were piled around, and they had laid Carl out prone on the deck, propped against the pile of bags. Carl was still groggy, but Jim thought he might be coming out of it a little bit. From where he sat, his butt on the floor and his back against a cold steel bulkhead, he could see Carl's eyelids flutter every once in a while. Not all the way open, but something was going on there.

"Where'd you get a gun like this? A kid like you?" the young man said.

"It's my dad's."

The young man hefted the weapon again. "Looks new."

"He just got it."

"Well, he won't need it now. I guess I'll keep it. Nice gun like this, it would be a shame for it to go to waste."

"Is that what you are? A thief?"

The young man stared at him. He reached up with his free hand and tapped the ConFleet patch on his shoulder. "You know what this means? It means I'm a gentleman. I'm a ConFleet spaceman first class and *that* means I'm not a thief. You little punk."

"What's wrong with you? Why are you doing this to us?" Jim pointed at Carl. "He's hurt. He got hurt trying to protect us from some of you gentlemen. Are you just going to let him lie there?"

The spaceman first class put the pistol aside. "Just so you know. I'm confiscating the gun. You are a prisoner, so I have that legal right. To confiscate it. Nobody's stealing anything around here."

"Where are you taking us?"

"Shut up."

"What?"

"I told you to shut up," the young spaceman said. "You're

under arrest. I don't have to talk to you at all if I don't want to."

"Hey, Carver, leave the kid alone," the pilot said. The pilot, though himself still young, appeared to be the oldest of the three crewmen. He had a small, spiky beard on the tip of his chin.

"What did you say, Hemmings?"

"You heard me," Hemmings said.

"Mr. Hemmings? Sir?" Jim said. A pilot would have to be an officer. There was no insignia on the pilot's shoulder, but he would have to be an officer anyway.

"What?"

"I told you to shut up," Carver said to Jim. He picked up the pistol again. Jim ignored him. Carver was a bully, and while he might not be afraid of Jim, Jim could see that Carver was afraid of Hemmings. And not just because Hemmings was a pilot and an officer.

The cabin of the small craft was roughly square. There was only a single pilot's chair, facing the ship's controls and, above the controls, the wide, glassy expanse of the forward observation port. To the left was the communications console, where the third young man was seated. He watched his screens and paid no attention to anything else.

Carver also had a chair, though he was standing next to it. It took Jim a while to figure out what Carver did. The instruments in front of his seat were uncomplicated, but didn't offer much information. A couple of screens and a wide touch pad on a narrow desktop. Probably weapons, Jim decided. Carver had the belligerent temperament of a gunner. Since a barge this size wouldn't have much in the way of weapons, the gunner's console wouldn't be large either.

Jim felt a slight mental pressure coming from his left, as if somebody was staring at him from over there. He looked over and saw that Carl's eyes were halfway open. Carl slid his gaze toward the pile of bags against which he lay. He licked his lips and blinked, once.

Carver said, "Yes, *sir*," to Hemmings.

Jim leaned across, unzipped one of the bags, and reached inside.

Carver swung around, and said, "What?"

Jim pulled out Carl's Styron und Ritter .75, a well-worn twin to the one Carver was now swinging up. Carl grunted and threw himself across the deck. He crashed into Carver's knees.

Jim aimed the .75 and pulled the trigger.

The sound of the weapon going off was like a hammer crashing into a huge bell. The air vibrated. The entire front window of the small cabin vanished as the huge .75 rocket slug smashed through it.

"Hey!" Hemmings shouted, as the small craft yawed violently.

Carver fell over Carl. His confiscated .75 went skittering into the corner, beneath a rack of equipment. Tabitha screamed.

Hemmings fought the controls as a vast gush of cold air filled the cabin. After a few hectic seconds, he got the craft righted again. He brushed a fine dust of shattered high-tensile plastic out of his hair and half turned. "What the hell?"

"If I have to, I'll kill him," Jim said. He stood up and pointed his .75 at the center of Carver's forehead. Carver, still tangled with Carl, looked up at the gaping hole in the end of the barrel, wide-eyed and shocked.

"Don't," he said. "Please, don't."

"Dad?" Jim said.

"It doesn't get you anything," Hemmings said. "You can't fly this thing. If you want to get down in one piece, you do it my way. Put the gun down."

Carl pushed Carver's legs away and slowly sat up. His voice was slurred but intelligible. "I can fly it," he said.

3

They used sticky tape from their packs to tie up Hemmings, Carver, and the comm specialist.

"Don't make it too tight," Carl whispered to Jim. "No need to kill them. They can get loose eventually. Just not too soon."

The three ConFleet men were arranged around the perimeter of a small clearing, well away from their vessel. Jim finished taping a gag across Carver's mouth and stepped away.

"Now what?"

"Go in and program the autopilot like I told you. Then disable the comm gear."

Jim climbed into the ship and looked around. With the air-conditioning system off, the small cabin smelled of sweat. He went to the pilot's chair, slid into it, and began to run his fingers across the control pads. He programmed the autopilot to take the ship at treetop level farther to the north and deeper into the mountain range. He checked a topographical map and arranged for the ship's last trip to end in a collision with a tall mountain so isolated it didn't even have a name. Then he got up, went to the comm system, unlatched the cabinet, and pulled out handfuls of fiber-optic cable. That would keep the ship from automatically broadcasting its position. Those in the mother ship would have to track it manually, by radar. They wouldn't know *why* it was heading north and not responding to their signals. They'd have no choice but to follow it.

"Jim? Are you done yet?"

He took a final look around, then climbed down and joined Carl, who was leaning on Tabitha for support. Carl looked drained and weak, but he'd summoned up reserves from somewhere. Jim thought he'd be able to go for a while yet.

"It's ready." Jim showed him a small remote-control module. "We can launch with this."

"Good. I gave all three of these guys a twenty-four-hour sedative dose with the portadoc. We'll have enough time."

"Enough time for what?" Jim asked.

"You'll see when we get to Hannaport. Which won't be long. It's only an hour's hike down the mountain."

Jim nodded. He didn't know how long Carl could keep himself together, but he was glad enough to let go of the responsibility. He even ignored the small flare of resentment he felt when Carl, closemouthed as ever, told him he would have to wait to find out their plans until they reached Hannaport.

"You want me to launch, then?" he asked.

"Yes, go ahead. I think we're done here."

Jim pressed a button. The dark shape of the tiny ship rose into the air, hovered a moment a few meters above the treetops, then sped off with gathering speed toward the north.

Carl grunted in satisfaction. "That'll give them something to think about," he said.

"And it'll give us about two days before they figure out for sure what's gone wrong," Jim said. "Assuming these guys here don't know how close they are to Hannaport."

"That's enough time," Carl told him.

4

Hannaport meant nothing to Jim, just a dot on maps he'd seen. Now he saw it from above, as the first morning sunlight streamed down at his back and illuminated the tiny port, which was cupped in a bowl of emerald foothills at the base of the mountains. His first glimpse of the port was from a ledge about three hundred meters above the bowl. There were maybe a dozen large buildings, their white walls turned pink and pearly by the dawn, and several dozen smaller structures, probably private homes. The street grid was regular and even, as if the whole place had been built at the same time from a blueprint.

The port itself was a broad expanse of gray concrete that filled the half of the bowl not covered with buildings. A control tower loomed over the side of the field farthest from the town. Three small ships were docked near the tower, looking like toys next to the huge globular shape of a modified freighter that dominated the center of the field. Even this early, Jim could see a stream of tiny cargo sleds moving around the freighter, like ants swarming around an apple.

Carl refused anything but a maintenance dose of painkiller because he wanted to stay lucid. It was a bad trade-off, because the pain dominated him, and no matter how hard he tried, most of his mind was occupied with trying to resist it.

"Dad?"

"Um. What?"

"We can rest for a while if you want."

"No, there isn't much time."

Off to the right of the ledge a two-lane concrete road snaked down a shallow canyon. This early, there were no travelers on it, and the aboveground grav-rail in the center was empty.

"There's probably a walkway along that road. It would make things easier; we could get down quicker."

Carl shook his head. The skin at the corners of his mouth was tight with controlled agony. "No, I don't want to go out in the open until we have to. This trail will get us there."

"Okay. If that's what you want."

Carl's gaze focused on him a moment, then drifted away, searching for Tabitha. She was sitting about ten feet away, her expression blank, her white fingers twisting like entwined worms in her lap.

"If I . . . if something happens to me. The man you want is named Carey, Nicholas Carey. I've got his address in my wallet. Everything's arranged. Just go to him, you and your mother, do what he tells you."

"You're going to be all right."

"I don't know that, and neither do you. Maybe I will. But if not, then you do what I tell you. This time you do what I say. You understand?"

Jim nodded. Carl exhaled, seemed to gather himself. "Help me up. We've wasted enough time."

Jim ducked under Carl's right arm, flexed his knees, and took his weight. Carl grunted as Jim lifted him.

He ain't heavy, Jim thought. *He's my father.*

It was a forlorn wish, not a truth. Not anymore. But it would do.

5

Hannaport felt bigger than it looked from above. Carl was fading fast by the time the path they'd been following led them out of the trees into a small park. It was much warmer in the sunlight. A few birds squawked, and bees that had been bioengineered for the Wolfbane environment buzzed among neatly manicured beds of bright orange flowers that had never grown on Earth.

On the inner side of the park a concrete walking path dead-ended, shaded by shaggy, dusty pines that looked a lot older than the small houses nestled beneath them. The air was filled with their heavy scent and the higher, sharper smell of the flowers.

"Find a public comm booth," Carl said. "By now our personal codes are being monitored."

They reached the end of the narrow concrete path, where it intersected with a broader street. In the center of the street was a small tube station, and on the apron there, a public booth beneath a luminescent green sign.

Carl fumbled in his pocket and brought out his wallet. He gave Jim a small piece of paper on which a name, address, and comm code were written in his neat, precise hand. "You go," Carl said. "We'll wait here."

Jim settled Carl on a bench at the side of the path. Tabitha, still silent and withdrawn, sat next to him. She was compliant, doll-like, and she scared Jim to death. She'd always been the optimist of the family, and now something inside her seemed to be broken. One more reason to feel guilty.

Nicholas Carey answered the comm on the second buzz. His voice was low enough to count as husky, but he enunciated his words with immense clarity. There was something reassuring about the way he spoke—a competence that reminded Jim of Carl. Jim explained the situation and told him about Carl's injuries.

"I know where you are," Carey said. "I'll be there in eight minutes. Look for a blue groundcar."

Jim hung up and returned to his parents. "He's coming," he said.

Carl sighed. "Remember, don't argue with him. Just do what he says."

"Dad, I said I would—"

Carl's head tilted to the side and his eyes closed. Jim reached for him, caught him as he slumped forward.

"Dad!"

Four minutes later a blue groundcar came to a silent halt three meters away. Jim didn't notice. Carl's lips were turning dusky purple, and his heart seemed to have stopped.

6

The groundcar was an older model, but it was freshly polished and neat as a pin on the inside. It was a two-seater with a hatchback opening into a larger space in the rear.

Nicholas Carey turned out to be in his forties, a tall man with the beginnings of a gut and heavy, thick muscles that had begun to sag just a little. His black, curly hair, touched with gray, had receded enough to make his high forehead look even more pronounced than it was. Bushy eyebrows arched over wide, dark blue eyes, giving his face a perpetually questioning expression. It was deceptive. A careful second look showed that Carey's eyes weren't questioning at all. They were cold and knowing, as if the man had seen too much he didn't want to see and forgotten none of it. He wore denim pants and a black turtleneck shirt beneath a brown-leather jacket, the pants tucked into ankle-high black boots.

Carey jumped out of the groundcar almost before it stopped moving. As he did so, his jacket dropped open, and Jim saw the butt of a pistol in a shoulder holster. With a swift, graceful economy that was almost magical, Carey crossed the distance from the car to where Carl was gasping on the bench.

"Let me," he said, pushing Jim aside and slipping his arms beneath Carl's butt and shoulders. He lifted Carl with no more effort than he would have lifted a baby, and Jim realized those big muscles weren't quite as soft as they looked. The hatchback of the groundcar slid open as he carried Carl toward it. He stooped slightly and slid Carl into the rear compartment as if popping a loaf of bread into an oven.

"What are you doing?" Jim said. He peered past Carey's wide shoulders into the interior of the vehicle. "Oh," he said. "Is that . . . ?"

"A full cyberdoc. Not the absolute latest version, but pretty good."

There were several silvery machines in the rear. One of them rose and floated over Carl's chest, painting his face with pale pink light. Clear tendrils exuded from another machine, and plunged into his chest. Suddenly Carl spasmed, his back arching. He relaxed, then spasmed again. This time when he collapsed he stayed unmoving, but Jim thought some color had come back into his face, and his labored breathing seemed to have steadied.

Carey reached into his pocket. The hatch door lowered with a soft *wheep*, cutting off Jim's view.

"I think we made it in time," Carey said. "There's nothing in this one-horse town any better than what I've got right there. A human doc, maybe—but you don't want that, do you?" He stared at Jim's taut, worried expression, then put one big hand on his shoulder. "It'll be okay. I've seen Carl in worse scrapes. He's tough. He's a survivor."

Once again Jim felt that air of tremendous competence, stronger now than what he'd sensed talking to Carey on the comm. It was enormously tempting just to relax, mentally lean back, and let Carey take charge of everything. But that would be a kind of betrayal, too, wouldn't it? He'd promised himself he would take care of his family. . . even if it wasn't really his family.

"Who are you?" he asked softly.

Carey smiled. It didn't make him look any friendlier, but it softened his broad, heavy features. "An old *compadre*," he said.

Jim vaguely recognized the word. Some Terran language, not English. *Friend*. . . .

Carey paused, as if remembering things he hadn't thought about in a long time, then shook his head slightly.

"Come on, let's get you folks out of here." He looked over at Tabitha, who had come far enough out of her daze to be staring at them with alarm on her face. "That your mom?"

Jim nodded. *I guess so. Maybe. Hell, I don't know if she is or not.*

He went to her, took her hands—her fingers were still like icy sticks—and pulled her gently to her feet. As he did so, he realized that it didn't matter. She had been his mother all his life. Whatever the truth was, the real truth was all those years when he had loved her, and she him. Just like Carl. Whatever had happened, whatever awful secrets were now spilling out into the open, made no difference. He had loved them as if they were his parents, and whatever they really were, he loved them that way still.

"Come on, Mom. We're okay now. We're okay."

7

"How do you know my dad?" Jim asked.

"It's not important," Carey replied. "A long time ago. Call me Nick, why don't you?"

Carl was stretched out on the sofa in the front room of Nick's small house. The room had that neat, sterile feel that Jim imagined the quarters of a military man would possess. Straight corners, neat folds, sparseness. A place for everything, and everything in its place.

We look messy, Jim thought. *We look out of place here. We* are *out of place here.*

Carl breathed softly, a sheet rumpled to his waist, his chest bare. Elements of the doc hovered nearby. A single cable stretched from one of them to his neck, where it merged seamlessly with his skin. A monitor, keeping watch. Guarding him

against the treachery of his heart. And in Nick Carey's bedroom, Tabitha curled in on herself like a shrimp, hands clasped together in unconscious penitence, sleeping on the bed.

"What happens next?" Jim said.

"You're all going away. As soon as Carl is well enough. It won't take long; he just needed decent medical attention and some rest. He's getting both. He'll be able to move around better by tomorrow. That's enough time."

Jim thought about the three ConFleet men lying taped and gagged in the clearing. Still sleeping from the effects of the sedative, but they would awaken. Early tomorrow morning, probably. And then enough time to wriggle out of their bonds, get oriented. But too much time otherwise. They hadn't left the spacers any way to use sanitary facilities. So they'd awaken smelling pretty bad, and maybe worse by the time they got themselves free of the tape. They'd be pissed. Jim smiled faintly at the sad-funny pun.

There was no way for them to communicate with the mother ship. They'd have to walk out on their own, find civilization, get in touch with their ship. ET, call home. The thought of that classic vid—one of his childhood favorites—made him smile again.

"Enough time for what?" Jim asked.

"For you to go away."

Jim gestured at Carl. "Tell me about that," he said. "I need to know."

So Nick did. Most of it, at least.

8

Nick drove them out to the port in his groundcar. They sat in the back with the windows smoked to opacity. Nick seemed to know everybody. He drove them through the gate, pausing only for a moment of cheerful conversation with the elderly guard there, then cruised out onto the concrete field itself. Bypassing the small ships, they drove right up to the huge freighter, parked beneath it, in the great blotch of its morning shadow, climbed out, and stretched.

He reminded Jim of a huge cat, luxuriating in strength, in a job well-done. Jim helped Tabitha clamber out, then Carl. Tabitha was better, but still too quiet, the flesh around her eyes gray and tired-looking. Carl was pale, trying to force an air of confidence. He chose humor, a bad choice.

Looking up at the vast hull arching overhead, at the flaking paint, the scars, the faded identification signs, he said, "Piece of junk. Probably won't fly at all."

Then why bring us here? Jim wondered. He knew it was only a joke, but for him, nothing was a joke anymore.

A middle-aged man in grease-spotted coveralls came up to them and sketched a sloppy salute. He turned to Carey.

"This my cargo?" he said.

Carey nodded. "Signed, sealed, and delivered."

"Well, I don't know about that. I'm the one taking delivery. It's my risk."

Something happened to Carey's face. Whatever it was, it changed the greasy man's face, too. Carey leaned forward and whispered a few words Jim couldn't hear. The greasy man flashed a nervous smile, showing yellow, ratty teeth. "No need for that," he said. "A man of my word, a deal's a deal."

Carey paused, let it hang, then nodded. The greasy man let his breath out. He smiled again. "Well, folks, let's get this show on the road."

Jim stood aside while Carl and Nick spoke quietly to each other, then shook hands. They'd been friends once, more than friends. It was obvious. Jim wondered where and when that had been. More secrets, more things he didn't know about the man he'd called "Father" all his life. He felt something hot sting at his eyes, but it went away quickly.

A small hovercart floated over. The greasy man piled their luggage, what was left of it, in the back, and they climbed on. The greasy man drove them toward a rickety boarding escalator that dropped like a tentacle from the belly of the ship.

"Good luck," Nick Carey called out. Jim waved at him, but couldn't think of anything to say. He watched Nick Carey climb back into his car, and knew he would never see him again.

He was right.

9

The passenger deck of the freighter smelled like boiled onions and fried fish. A thin film of grease seemed to cover every metal surface. There was none of the smartness, the spiff and polish of the great white ships he'd dreamed about most of his life.

"What's your name?" he asked the greasy guy who was lugging his bag as if it weighed half a ton.

"Uh." Greasy paused, as if he had to think about it. Finally came up with, "Sam. Call me Sam."

"Sure, Sam. Where are you taking me?"

They were walking down a long, narrow corridor. Closed, unmarked doors marched along with them, equally spaced. They had just finished getting Carl and Tabitha settled on another corridor, in a small, dingy cabin.

"Right here," Sam said, as he stopped, turned, and put his palm on the lock plate of a door. The door slid aside to reveal a cabin barely larger than the bunk it contained. Jim peered inside. A small washbasin, no refresher. Everything old, crude, dusty. Even some rust. Maintenance wasn't a priority here.

"Go on, get yourself strapped in," Sam said. "Liftoff in ten minutes. You can get together with your folks when we're off planet."

"And where are we going again?" Neither Carl nor Nick had told him their ultimate destination. He wondered if anybody would ever trust him again.

"Terra," Sam said. His eyes flickered. "A couple of stops on the way, but Terra."

Jim nodded. Sam was carrying the one bag he'd managed to pack in the frantic departure from their home. He watched as the man slung it into a space beneath the bunk, then stood and brushed his hands off as if he'd finished a major job of work. That bag was all he had left, that and whatever was inside him. Whatever he was *now*. He moved past Sam and entered the cabin.

"Low-gee liftoff?" he asked.

Sam raised his eyebrows. "You know the lingo, do you?"

"Yes."

"Well, then, yes to you. Low-gee. We got liquid commodities for cargo. Slosh around. Take better care of it than we do the passengers. As you can see." Sam cackled at that, amusing himself.

Jim sat on the edge of the bunk. "Thank you," he said. "I'll be fine."

No, I won't, he thought.

Sam backed out, closing the door behind him. Jim strapped himself in. A few minutes later, a huge, soft hand pressed down on his chest, his thighs. He closed his eyes and waited. When the pressure lifted, he knew he had left Wolfbane behind. Forever?

When he went to find his parents, their cabin was empty, and they were gone.

CHAPTER THREE

1

Three burly crewmen were draped around Jim like wet horse blankets, but he was still trying to wrap his fingers around Sam's scrawny, greasy neck.

"Where are they, damn it? You bastard, what did you do with them?"

Sam cowered against the bulkhead near the bridge gangway where Jim had found him, his yellow-tinged eyes wide. "Keep him away! Don't let him touch me!"

The ruckus finally attracted some new attention.

"What the hell's going on here?" a husky voice roared.

Sam whirled, his eyes going even wider. Then he sketched a sloppy salute. "Uh, Captain. . . ."

"I asked a question!" The tall man stared at Jim. "You, boy! Stop flopping around! Ed, let him go!"

Jim felt one set of bulging arms unwrap themselves from his chest. Then the rest slowly fell away. At least he could breathe again. Panting, he paused a moment, his hands on his knees, then straightened up. Ouch! A few more bruises for his growing collection.

The captain moved closer, reached up, and brushed a thumb lightly across Jim's forehead. Jim winced.

"That's going to be a shiner, boy. Now what the hell is this all about?" The captain glanced at Sam, then back to the three deck jockeys. "You three, go on, back to your stations. I think I can handle this—is that right, boy? Are you done now?"

It felt like somebody had half crushed his larynx. The words hurt coming out. "Yes, sir. I guess so."

"Good." The captain watched the others go, then roared again: "Where the hell do you think you're going, Mr. Cavetts?"

Sam froze.

"Uh, Captain. Sorry, I was just—"

"Not another word. Just get your ass back here."

Even more resembling a weasel dipped in lard, Sam slunk back.

"Good. Now. First, you, boy. Who are you?"

"My name is Jim Endicott."

"Ah. Well, Jim. I'm Captain de Moot. Jan de Moot." He stuck out one large, oddly smooth hand. Jim took it. They shook.

"Pleased to meet you," Jim said.

"I don't know if I feel the same way, but at least we're properly introduced. Which means you'll now tell me about whatever burr it is you've got rammed so far up your youthful ass, hmm?"

Despite de Moot's gruff manner, there was something about him Jim liked. He didn't know him, but he trusted his own instincts. Given the events of the past few days, maybe *that* was a mistake, but—

"Him," Jim said, and pointed at Sam. "He did something to my parents. *With* my parents. They're *gone*, and *I want to know what the hell he did with them!*"

Captain de Moot transferred his forbidding gaze to Sam, who seemed to wither a bit beneath it. He rubbed his palms across the greasy front of his coveralls.

"I didn't do anything with them," he muttered. "It was all arranged beforehand. Soon as I got the boy away, they left. Just like they'd planned all along, I guess."

He fumbled inside his coverall and drew out an envelope. "Here," he said. He handed it to Jim. "Your dad said to give this to you after we were in space."

Jim took the envelope. Sam's fingers left dark smears on one side.

"They left? You mean they left the ship? Left me here?"

His mind whirled. He couldn't get his thoughts around the idea. *They just* left *me?* Abandoned *me*?

He knew he'd screwed up, screwed up badly, but . . .

Did Carl and Tabitha hate him *that* much?

"Well, boy, maybe you'd better read that. I don't know how

you got aboard, your name isn't on the passenger manifest." He glared at Sam again. "But I can *guess*."

Jim's fingers were numb as he tried to get the envelope open. It took him two tries, and he finally just tore the end off. He lifted the few sheets he found inside and tried to read Carl's neat, steady script, but it was hard. Something was in his eyes, something liquid and burning.

Probably some irritant in the air. He was too old to be crying.

2

Dear Son,

Yes, I call you that, even though you believe it isn't the truth. Well, the truth is, I don't *know* what the truth is. You could be my son. Or maybe you aren't. I just don't know, and the reason I don't know is that I've chosen not to know.

There are tests that could be done. I haven't had them done. I had my reasons for this, reasons I'm not going to go into now. But you should know there is at least the *possibility* I'm your real father. There's also a possibility I'm not.

As for Tabitha, she is not your real mother. Your real mother is dead, and has been for a long time. You needn't concern yourself with her, although when you sent your genome report to the Space Academy at Solis, you stirred her ashes without knowing. And you stirred up something else, too, something evil. Some*one* evil.

Jim, if only you'd obeyed me—but that's not worth discussing either. What's done is done. Now we all have to live with the consequences, and that includes you as well.

I won't tell you everything, but you need to know some of the things that happened in the past, so you will understand why I've done what I've done. Long ago, because of your mother, I made a deadly enemy out of a powerful man. That man is still alive, and he is probably the most powerful man

in the ConFederation today. You felt a taste of his power in the reaction after you sent your genome report. No hesitation, hardly any time lapse, just a kill team. I have tried to hide us for most of your life, and until a few days ago I was successful. Now that is all changed. Changed for the worse, because that man knows not only that I am still alive, but that *you* exist. I would have given anything, even my own life, to keep him from finding out about you.

Jim, this man will never stop. He won't stop until I am dead, and he won't stop until he finds you. Now he knows, if he had forgotten, that I am harder to kill than most people. That won't stop him, but I won't make it easy for him. Nevertheless, in the ConFederation, his power is nearly absolute, and he will eventually find me, I guess. He would find you, too, if you stayed.

So I will stay, and give him something to look for. I don't know how long it will take, but I guess a while. I have resources he doesn't know about, and I will use them. I have Tabitha to protect as well.

But looking after her, and you as well, it would slow me down, lower the odds. And in the end he would have us all. I can't allow that to happen.

Tab and I have discussed it. You have your life in front of you. If you remain in ConFederation territory, I fear it wouldn't be a very long, or very happy life. So you must leave. Go somewhere beyond this evil man's reach, somewhere he won't think to look. He will chase me, and by the time he finds me, you will be far away.

In the short time I had, this was all I could think of. I know you must think I'm a monster, but I had no choice. By the time you read this, you will be well on the way to your final destination.

Whether I'm your real father or not, Jim, I've loved you all your life as if I were. And Tabitha has been the only mother you've ever known, and she loves you that way, too. However hard this is for you, remember that it's just as hard for us. We both love you very much. If we didn't, we would not have done what we have done.

I've raised you as well as I could. You are a good boy, Jim, well, maybe not a boy anymore. Now you'll have to grow up

faster than I anticipated. I'd hoped for better things, but we play the hand we're dealt. You have resources you don't realize, because you're still young. Use them. And forget about us, because we are gone, and there is no going back. Not for me, not for Tabitha, and not for you.

I love you, Jim. I always have, and I always will. Take care of yourself, son. Because whether the gene code matches or not, that's what you are—my son. Never forget it.

Love,

Dad

And, scrawled beneath this in a shaky hand:

Jim, I love you!

Tabitha

3

Jim realized what he must look like when he saw the expression on Captain de Moot's broad, flat features. De Moot glanced at Sam.

"Beat it," he said. Sam ducked his head and scurried away, looking more than ever like a potbellied rat. De Moot turned back to Jim. "I take it the news isn't good, boy?" he said, his gruff voice soft.

Jim ran the back of his hand across his nose and sniffled heavily. "We have to go back," he said. "Turn this ship around. Right now."

The captain blinked, then shook his head slowly. "Pretty quick with the orders, aren't you, boy? Especially standing on another man's deck?"

Jim blinked. Suddenly it sank in. Off to his left was the hatch with the word BRIDGE painted on it. He was standing on worn steel plates, and at his back was more of the same. The air still reeked of onions and sweat, a stench alien to his nostrils. This wasn't home, this wasn't even Wolfbane. This was *somewhere else*, and he was right in the middle of it. Alone.

"You don't understand . . ." he said, shocked to realize how weak and quavering his voice sounded in his own ears. He took a deep breath and tried again. "My parents, they're back on Wolfbane. I have to go back, you have to take me back."

But de Moot was still shaking his head. "No," he said, "it is you who doesn't understand. What'd you say your name was? Jim? Well, Jim. This is a freighter. At the moment you're a stowaway, because I don't have you on my passenger list." He raised one big hand, palm out. "Don't worry. I know what happened. Sam did some kind of deal, and there's money in his pocket. But none of that matters. I own this freighter. It's my business, the way I earn my living. Do you have any idea how much it would cost to turn her around and make planetfall again, just to drop you off? When as far as I'm concerned, you're not even supposed to be here?"

Jim swallowed. One part of his mind was a whirlwind, battered by the contents of the letter he'd just read, dodging and ducking amidst the chattering rubble of everything he'd once taken for granted. But the other part seemed above or maybe beyond the fear and disbelief. That part was cooler, even rational. It stood back. It listened. It surprised him about as much as anything that had yet occurred, because he hadn't known it was there.

Was this the way adults thought? He swallowed again, glad that the impulse to run to the nearest corner and squat with his arms wrapped over his head seemed to be passing.

"It would cost a lot of money, I guess," he said.

"A lot more than the cost of your passage," de Moot agreed. "I don't suppose you have a lot of money?"

Jim stared at him. It was a perfectly logical question. He had no idea of the answer. He still had a credit chip, but Carl had warned him against using it, said it could be traced. As far as cash, he had no idea. He remembered packing a few small gold coins from his collection when they'd left home, but how much could they be worth?

It would probably cost hundreds of thousands of ConFed creds to turn the ship around, take it back to orbit, launch a landing lighter.

"No," he said. "I don't have a lot of money."

De Moot nodded. "Somehow that doesn't surprise me." He paused, then suddenly seemed to make up his mind. "So here's what we'll do, young Jim. The matter of your passage fee will be between me and Mister Sam Cavetts. You don't need to worry about it." He rubbed his grizzled chin thoughtfully. "And when we reach our destination, you can try to make whatever arrangements are possible to return to Wolfbane, if that's what you still want to do. Although I have to tell you, I don't think any such arrangements will *be* possible."

"Really? Why? I mean, wherever you make planetfall, surely there'll be some way to get passage to Wolfbane."

"Well, that would be true. If we were making planetfall. But we aren't."

"What? But . . ." Jim stared at him, unable to take it any further. This was a freighter. Freighters carried cargo between planets. What else could they do?

The captain reached out and placed one hand gently on Jim's shoulder. "We aren't bound for a planet this time. My cargo is several different kinds of valuable liquids. Water, kerosene, high-energy liquid fuel. You understand?"

Jim shook his head.

"Our destination this trip is the *Outward Bound*," de Moot said.

Jim's mouth shaped the words but nothing came out. The captain nodded. "That's right. The colony ship. I don't know what arrangements have been made for you there, if any. But unless you have the cost of your return fare, you won't be coming back on my vessel. As I said, I run a business."

His dark gray eyes hardened slightly. "I'm sorry. I'm sure you understand. I'm stretching things as it is. In other times, stowaways were jettisoned."

"But I didn't . . . "

"Sorry," de Moot said again. Then he turned around and walked away.

4

Jim sat cross-legged on his tiny bunk, staring down at the heavy, glittering pile in his lap. Once again he ran his fingers across the greasy metal. Forty-five of them, each one about two and a half centimeters wide, half that thick, and seven and a half long. Each one of them apparently solid gold.

He had no idea how Carl had gotten them into his pack without him knowing, and wondered why he hadn't noticed the extra weight when he carried—wait a minute. He *hadn't* carried the bag. Sam had been insistent. He must have been in on it . . . no, that wouldn't work either. Sam didn't look like the kind of guy anybody in his right mind would trust with the knowledge of forty-five gold bars. Certainly Carl wouldn't be that stupid.

It was a *lot* of money.

Too much.

And it changed everything. Jim stared at it, trying to fit everything together. Only now, in retrospect, did he understand how little he knew about things. About his life, about his parents' lives, about how and why they'd lived the way they had, about—about *everything*, damn it!

These gold bars, for instance. He'd never thought of his family as wealthy, but this was a lot of money. A *lot.* Carl must have had it squirreled away, ready for use at a moment's notice. Which meant that Carl, at least, had not assumed they were safe hidden away in their small house on Wolfbane, light-years from the hustle and bustle of Terra.

How much more was there? Jim picked up one bar, hefted it, let it fall back into the pile with a dull *clunk.* Suddenly, as clearly as he knew his own name, he knew there wasn't much more. This was most of it, most of the escape money Carl had put aside. And Carl had sent it with him. Knowing this somehow made his predicament even more final.

There was no doubt he had enough here to pay for his passage back to Wolfbane. Ten passages, maybe even a hundred. But what then?

When he got back, they would be gone. Either the mysterious *evil man* his father had feared would have caught up with them, and he'd already seen sufficient proof of that man's intentions. There had been three armored corpses, two of them headless, in the clearing around the cabin. If things had gone just a little differently, those corpses would have been him and his parents instead of three killers trying their best to execute their boss's *intentions*.

So he might go back only to find Carl and Tabitha dead, though if that were the case, he doubted he would ever see, or even know about, their bodies. Or they would have managed a successful escape, using whatever resources Carl had kept for himself, and he wouldn't find them in that event either. So either way, if he returned, he'd find nothing. Maybe Nick Carey would know. . . .

No, he'd already tasted that one's mettle. He was too much like Carl. He might disappear also, and even if he didn't, if Carl had told him not to say anything, he'd be as tight-lipped as any sphinx.

Which left what?

Exactly what Carl had intended. Go on, follow the path he'd laid out, take the gold and use it to start a new life. A life in a new galaxy, because that's exactly what the *Outward Bound* meant. A colony ship, bound for a new world in the Taurus Sector, millions of light-years away from Terran space. A vast ship, a small world in itself, stocked with everything it needed to make the slow, lumbering trip to . . . where? He couldn't even remember the name of the new world. Not that it was immediately important. Because of its size, the *Outward Bound* couldn't use the most powerful methods of travel, not without ripping its gigantic bulk apart. Maybe that was what Carl was counting on. Once the voyage got under way, the *Outward Bound* would be cut off from the rest of the universe. Oh, no doubt it would have a couple of exploratory ships hidden away somewhere, and there would be infralight communication systems, but in any practical sense the ship would be isolated.

No killers chasing him. In fact, nobody even knowing who he was. He picked up the other items mixed in with the gold bars. A dark green unichip, one no doubt containing his vital medical records, perhaps his education and training files, all the other informational baggage anybody picked up as they passed through their own life. But the name on the chip wasn't Endicott. It was James Evanston. Evanston . . . well, that made sense. Carl had once told him that if you wanted to change your name, pick something that sounded like your old one. Easier to remember.

At the time, he hadn't thought much about it. But now he realized there had been many odd nuggets like this one. Strange bits of esoteric knowledge no normal sixteen-year-old boy would ever find a use for. Not unless he was on the run, hiding from . . .

A new life.

Jim looked down at the gold, at the chip, at his new life.

Damn it Carl, damn it Dad.

Damn it!

I hate you!

I love you. . . .

CHAPTER FOUR

1

The freighter was far too big to shake as it docked, but Jim felt a sort of masslike tremor that reminded him of the microquakes that plagued Wolfbane. A huge movement too quickly gone really to notice, but leaving him with the disquieting feeling that something big had happened.

The red light on the dilapidated comm panel above his rusty washbasin wavered, then turned green. He unstrapped himself, sat up, and put his feet on the floor. His bag was packed, his cache of gold safely hidden in the bottom. He stared at the bag as he waited for someone to knock on his door.

Last chance. He could buy his way back to Wolfbane, squandering a part of what his parents had sacrificed so much to give him—and then most likely dissipate the rest in a futile search for them. And probably get himself killed into the bargain. Or he could do what Carl wanted him to do, had paid a great price to *allow* him to do.

He could go away. Far, far away. To a whole new world, in fact.

Doing that felt a whole lot like cowardice. *Running away.* Abandoning Carl and Tabitha. But was that really what it was? His dad had told him many things. One was the dictum that it wasn't cowardice to run away in order to fight another day. And then the idea of abandonment. Was he abandoning them? Or they him? Or were they *sending* him away, to save his life, neither one abandoning the other?

Carl had made it plain that was what he thought *he* was doing.

And certainly it was true, if Carl believed it so. At least it was true for Carl.

Then why did it *feel* so much like being abandoned?

If only—

Somebody knocked softly on his door.

"You in there, boy?"

"Yes, Captain."

The lock clicked. The door slid back into the wall with a soft screech. Captain de Moot stood there, an unreadable expression on his wide, flat face. "You ready?"

Jim nodded and stood up.

"Need any help with that bag?"

Jim shook his head. "No, I can carry it." He reached down and picked it up. It took an effort to make the lifting look easy, but he managed. De Moot stepped back into the narrow passageway to make room as Jim walked past him.

"Down to the end, and to your right," de Moot said.

Jim started trudging along, conscious of the captain's footsteps behind him.

"Boy."

Jim stopped, turned. De Moot eyed him. "I've thought some about it. I don't think any of this is your fault. And there are some programs, the Red Cross, Traveler's Aid . . . I could get the money for your passage out of them, I guess."

"My passage . . . ?"

De Moot's jaw twitched, a small, irritated motion. "You a little slow, are you? What I'm trying to say is, if you want to go back to Wolfbane, we'll make planetfall there in about six weeks. If you want to go, I'll take you."

Jim stared at him, then slowly shook his head. "No," he said. "I'm not going back."

De Moot opened his mouth, closed it, shrugged. "Suit yourself."

"Right," Jim said.

2

After that, Jim just kept on walking, de Moot trailing behind. He couldn't help but look around a little, though there wasn't much to see. He'd spent all of the trip in his room. The gold was there, and he was afraid to leave it unguarded. He wasn't sure about Sam.

All his life he'd wanted to go into deep space, and now that he had, everything about the experience was sour and bitter. No great white ConFleet ship, just a rusting, greasy freighter. No heroic quests, just ignominious flight. No proud family.

No family at all.

However large Captain de Moot's ship was, it was a cargo ship, and not much space had been allotted for passengers. The passageways were barely wider than Jim's shoulders, though there seemed to be miles of them. Finally, de Moot grunted, "Through that hatch on your right."

Jim undogged the plain steel door and found himself looking out into a tall, echoing space full of light.

"Main cargo transfer bay," de Moot said. "We're off-loading the passengers there. Follow the crowd."

Jim stuck out his hand. "Thanks, Captain."

De Moot took it, shook once, let go. "I don't know what's going on with you, Jim Endicott, but good luck. Fair skies and willing women." He grinned.

Jim smiled back. De Moot was the first man he'd had an adult relationship with, meager though it was. Just him and the captain, no Carl or Tabitha or anything else to fall back on. *Fair skies and willing women.* Suddenly he realized he liked the sound of it. It was a man's farewell, a spacer's farewell. He rummaged in his memories and found what he was looking for.

"Bright stars, Captain," he said.

"Yes," de Moot replied. "Those too." He nodded, turned, and walked away. Jim watched him vanish back down the narrow passage. Then he lifted his bag and stepped through the hatch into the transfer bay. Across the echoing, metallic space a large, noisy group of colonists were clustered. Jim headed toward them. As he walked, his slumped shoulders began to rise. A certain jauntiness crept into his stride. By the time he reached the edge of the crowd and melted into it, he was almost smiling.

Maybe this wouldn't be so bad after all.

3

The passage from the freighter to the receiving bay of the *Outward Bound* was simpler than Jim had expected. A few men and women wearing dark green coveralls organized the restless crowd into a line and began to shepherd it forward. Jim found himself about midway back, shuffling along, carrying his bag, then setting it down for minutes at a time as some unseen problem was unknotted at the front of the line.

After an hour or so, he passed through a large, gasketlike flexible tube about three meters high, and found himself in a chamber with lower ceilings and less harsh light than the freighter's cargo transfer bay. The smells in the air changed also. No more boiled onions, but there was the faint, formless tang that hinted at lots of people in an enclosed space not quite large enough to hold them.

Finally, he reached the checkpoint, which turned out to be three more of the green coveralls, two women and a large, dark-skinned man, all three sitting behind impromptu desks made of aluminum panels resting on packing crates. Jim found himself in front of the man.

"Name?" the man said, without looking up.

Jim had no idea what would happen when he answered. How far had Carl's arrangements extended? He took a breath. "Jim Endicott."

The man looked up. He had large brown eyes. "What? Speak up, kid."

"*Jim Endicott.*"

The man nodded, lifted a microphone, and repeated Jim's

name. Then he looked at Jim again. "Hang on."

He spoke into the microphone again, waited, then shook his head. "Shit. Half this roster is screwed up." He pushed a palm plate toward Jim's side of the desk. "Put your right hand on it."

Jim did. He realized his heart was pounding.

The man glanced at a screen on his left.

"First name?"

"Jim. . . ."

"Okay. Got you. Jim Evanston, right?"

Evanston . . . ? "Uh, yeah. That's me."

"Thought you said it was Endicott."

"Uh . . . sorry. Endicott's my middle name. Doesn't it say that on your records?"

"Shit. No, it's not entered. Like I said, half this roster's worthless." He spoke again into the microphone.

"Okay, Jim, it's entered. You're all fixed up." The man reached into a box and withdrew a large envelope. "Here's your info packet. Rules, regs, keycard to your dorm and storage locker—you're in with the other single males—and a bunch of FAQs. Welcome to the *Outward Bound*. Intake's just ahead. Good luck."

Jim took the envelope. Was that all there was to it? Evidently so. The dark-skinned man had already turned to the next person in line. Jim lifted his bag and walked on.

Intake was a smaller room, much more crowded. People with the half-bored, half-anxious expression of new arrivals, strangers in a strange land, milled around. The noise level was deafening.

Jim pressed forward, aiming for a long counter he could barely see against the far wall, where more clerks worked busily. He was trying to peer over the heaving shoulder of an enormously fat woman when somebody bumped him hard enough to knock his grip loose from his bag.

"*Hey*!"

He turned, just in time to see his bag vanishing into the mob, firmly in the grasp of a bald man whose shoulders looked almost as broad as he was tall.

Jim didn't even think. He flung himself after the thief, not realizing that he was shouting at the top of his lungs.

The man didn't look back, just kept on going, plowing

through the crowd like a very fast, compact bulldozer. Jim flailed along in his wake, bouncing off startled, angry colonists like a crazed pinball.

"Hey! Asshole! *Watch it, kid!*"

Jim ignored them, closing the distance step by step, until—

As soon as he landed on the thief's back, he knew he'd made a mistake. It was like belly-flopping onto a mattress filled with bowling balls. The man's heavy shoulders jerked once, and Jim went flying through the air. He slammed down hard on his left elbow, scrambled to his feet, and waded in again.

Once again, his father stood him in good stead. Carl had insisted that he become proficient in the martial arts, and Jim had trained five days a week since he'd turned ten years old. The collision with the deck had shaken his initial rage out of him, and now he fought with cool, icy efficiency. A hand-ax strike to the older man's bull neck that bounced off with no noticeable effect, a twisting back kick to the belly that brought a startled *oof!*, and then a series of straight-ahead right and left jabs.

For a second, Jim felt a wild thrill of triumph. He had landed twenty or thirty punches, he was a *lot* faster than the older guy, and then a hand grenade exploded beneath his jaw.

A moment of intense pain, then whirling white fountains of light, then darkness, then . . . nothing.

When he woke up, he was lying flat on his back, staring up at a circle of onlookers. It took him a second or two to focus, and in that time he realized that the right side of his face felt as if it had somehow become a large, numb pillow. One of the onlookers was the bald man. He was staring at him angrily, his lips moving. After another few seconds, Jim's ears began to work again.

". . . got no idea," the bald man was saying. "Minding my own business, and then this young punk just jumps me."

Jim tried to protest, but his mouth didn't seem connected to his brain. He tried to speak, but nothing came out. Another face swam closer. A female face, dark hair, hard blue eyes. Another green coverall, but this one with some sort of official patch on the biceps. A stunner in her hand.

"You're under arrest," she said. "Don't try to get up." The stunner in her hand hissed softly as electricity crawled between the two electrodes on its business end.

Something clicked, and Jim realized he could speak again. "He stole my bag!"

He tried to point at the bald man, but as he raised his arm, she raised her stunner. He froze, then carefully lowered his hand. "He's a thief," he said.

She glanced at the bald man, then back at Jim.

"What bag?" she said.

4

It wasn't like any of the holovids he'd ever seen. No fingerprints or genome-identification samples, no rooms full of gruff cops, no clerks or paperwork. They just marched him down a wide, green-painted corridor, opened a heavy steel door, and pointed.

"I have a right to a lawyer," Jim said.

The blue-eyed woman stared at him, glanced at the tall, skinny man with her, then made a short, barking sound deep in her throat. "Kid, do you ever have a lot to learn. Get your ass through that door."

She gestured toward the open door with her stunner.

"Listen, I'm a citizen of the ConFed, I've got rights."

The woman sighed. "You can either walk in, or we can carry you in. Your choice."

Jim turned and walked through the door. It swung shut behind him with a dull, heavy thud. He stood there, waiting for his vision to adjust to the dim light. The air was rank with the stink of unwashed bodies. Just as he was beginning to make out some shadowy forms in front of him, somebody laughed.

"A newbie," a voice cackled. "Welcome to the brig, newbie."

That was bad enough, but a moment later it got worse. Another voice, deep, masculine, hoarse. "Hey, he's mine, you assholes. I think he's just the *sweetest*-looking little thing. . . ."

Jim clenched his fists. He knew about such things. Homosexuals were no longer treated as second-class citizens, stripped of common rights or otherwise persecuted. Sexual distinctions no longer existed in the world of the ConFed, though sexual awareness did. But it was still a crime to force sex on an unwilling partner, no matter what the sexual status of either the victim or the attacker might be. Rape was still rape.

And the guard had laughed at him. "A lot to learn . . ." she'd sneered. Was this part of it, part of what he had to learn?

He balled his fists tighter. *Not while I'm still conscious,* he promised himself.

His vision finally cleared. He was in a room about ten meters on a side. On his left was a series of fold-down bunks, three high. A dozen of them. On his right, two 'fresher units that looked as if they'd been added as an afterthought. A scattering of rickety wire chairs, two tables, around which sat several men. It was from the table on the right that the laughter had come. And now, as he turned to face them, one of the men stood up. The man loomed over the table and the other men seated there. They leaned back, watching him, expectant grins on their faces.

He was in his forties, waves of dark, curly, grease-encrusted hair falling to shoulders like gravcar fenders. His belly bulged over a thick, chrome-studded belt. There were tattoos across his scarred knuckles. In his right ear, a silver earring shaped like a skull.

He looked like a cliché out of a bad holovid, but he was real. About three hundred pounds of reality, Jim guessed.

He stepped around the table and moved toward Jim, smiling to reveal yellow teeth. His lips had a liverish tinge, looked like two thin slabs of raw meat.

"You gonna fight me, sweetheart?" he rumbled, his grin growing wider. "That's nice. I like that."

Jim planted his feet and raised his hands. Liver-lips chuckled and lumbered forward.

"All right, Honeg. That's enough."

The voice came from his left. Jim slid his gaze in that direction and saw a tall, thin, blond youth, maybe four years older than himself, lounging spraddle-legged on one of the chairs. The guy weighed maybe half of what the gorilla in front of him did.

No help there. But when he looked back at the gorilla, the gorilla had stopped.

"Stay out of this," he said. "Isn't any of your business."

The sound of chair legs scraping suddenly across the deck. Jim looked again. Now the thin youth was standing. There was a lazy elegance about the way he moved. Lazy . . . but somehow threatening.

"Hey, Honeg," the young man said as he slouched toward them. "Since when did you start telling me what my business was?"

Honeg's gaze, half-hidden behind pouchy bags of swollen flesh, began to skitter back and forth between Jim and the other guy. And his voice, once thick with choked anticipation, now sounded thin and whiny.

"Korrigan, look—"

Korrigan, a dreamy smile on his face, reached them. He stopped, looked at Jim, and then his right eye closed in a quick wink.

Whack!

Jim had never heard a sound quite like it. Sort of a cross between a meat cleaver slamming into a frozen roast and a busy cook snapping a stalk of celery. Nor did he see the move that had caused it. But the effects were immediate and obvious.

Honeg staggered backwards, his huge hands going to his face, covering the whole middle of it. Blood spurted, then leaked through his fingers and dribbled down his wrists. His liverish lips contorted into a round oh! of agony.

"Uh, uh, uh," he grunted, still stumbling backwards. The rear of his massive calves made contact with the edge of a chair, and he sat down hard.

The tall, thin youth fluttered his right hand languidly up and down, as if he were shaking drops of water from his fingertips.

"Ooh," he said. "Ouch. That hurt." He looked at Honeg. "You hurt my fingers, Honeg. That wasn't nice of you."

Honeg let out an amazing sound that was half anguished blubber, half gasp of terror.

"No. . . ."

The tall youth stared at him a moment longer, then nodded, evidently satisfied. He turned to Jim and stuck out his hand.

"Hi," he said. "I'm Kerry Korrigan. What's your name?"

5

"Don't mind Honeg," Kerry said. "His brains, such as they are, are all in his crotch. I think he enjoys getting himself tossed in the brig. It's the only place he can get a date." Korrigan chuckled softly. "How about you? You don't look like you needed to come here to improve your social life."

Jim explained how he'd ended up incarcerated. Kerry listened attentively, nodding encouragement. When Jim finished, Kerry grunted.

"Bald guy? That would be Bertie Huff. He works with one of his daughters, usually. Did you see any little blond-haired girls hanging around?"

Jim shook his head.

"Well, take my word, one was probably there. Oldest scam in the world. He heists the bag, then if trouble starts, passes it on and stands around looking innocent. You were suckered from the start, my friend. Sad story. Happens all the time."

They were sitting at the left-hand table. Some unspoken signal had passed from Kerry to the others, and everybody had left them alone. Honeg was laid out on one of the bunks, his friends trying to stop the bleeding from his shattered nose by ramming bits of shredded pillow stuffing up his swollen nostrils.

"So there's nothing I can do?" Jim said.

Kerry leaned back in his chair, the dreamy look back on his face. "Nothing *you* can do," he murmured.

Jim heard the inference plainly. "But there's something you can do?"

Korrigan shrugged. "Maybe."

"Why would you help me?"

Korrigan tilted his head further. "You mean do I have designs on your tender young flesh? Like Honeg?" He uttered a short, barking laugh. "No, Jim, my tastes run in the majority direction, and I don't change them because of a little bit of brig time. Not that there's anything wrong with other preferences, they just aren't mine." He turned his head slightly. "In other words, don't worry about it."

Jim nodded. "Then why?"

Kerry let his chair tilt forward with a soft crash. He put his elbows on the table, propped his thin, high-cheeked face on his fists. "I like to help my friends," he said.

"Am I your friend?"

Korrigan turned his head farther, until he was staring directly at Jim's face. His pale blue gaze was direct, piercing, mesmerizing. He remained motionless for almost five seconds. "That would be up to you," he said.

Jim returned his stare. Finally, he nodded.

"Okay," he said. "I'm your friend."

Thirty minutes later, a guard came and whispered to Kerry. Ten minutes after that, they were out.

Kerry, it seemed, had connections.

6

"Men's B dorm," Kerry said, with a theatrical sweep of his hand. The room was the size of a gymnasium. The ceiling, which was fitted with a Venetian-blind pattern of softly glowing light strips, was about ten meters above the floor. They stood on an entrance balcony halfway up one wall, looking out over the huge expanse of the dorm.

From there they could see the general layout. The room was divided into dozens of cubicles, some large, some smaller. One large cubicle housed a dining area, empty at the moment, but filled with tables and chairs, and food and drink dispensers along the walls. Another area for public 'freshers, with ten of the units surrounding a central area that housed a good-sized whirlpool bath. A third large space housed the recreation facilities, including three large holoscreens, all dancing with silent images. The rest of the space was a maze of individual cubes, each one slightly larger than the cabin Jim had used aboard the freighter.

"Home, sweet home," Kerry said. "At least for the next couple of years." He paused a moment, gazing out like a monarch surveying his kingdom. Then he clapped Jim on the back. "Come on, Mister Evanston. Into your personal chunk of cube heaven. What's the matter?"

Jim blinked. "Huh? Oh, nothing." Jim realized his new name was going to take a little getting used to. He'd missed it when Kerry called him "Evanston." *Jim Evanston,* he told himself. *Remember it. It's who you are* now.

He followed Kerry into the maze. After a thoroughly confusing trek back, forth, and back again, they came to a door in the middle of a corridor, indistinguishable from any of the other half dozen doors on either side of it.

"Well?" Kerry said. "Aren't you going to open it?" He sounded strangely expectant.

"Oh . . . right. The keycard." Jim fumbled for the envelope folded in the back pocket of his pants. They'd returned it when he was released from the brig.

He opened the envelope and took out the slender piece of plastic. Pushed it into a matching slot on the door. The lock emitted a short, soft hum and spit the key back out. When Jim withdrew it the rest of the way, the door slid open. As it did so, a movable spotlight built into the right-hand wall lit up, illuminating the single bunk.

Beneath the bunk was a locked storage space. To the right, a narrow desk, a comm unit with a dark holoscreen, a single chair, and a waste chute built into the floor. Spartan, but adequate.

In front of the locker was his bag. Jim stepped into the room, stared at it, then turned and goggled into Kerry's grinning features.

"My bag! How did you . . . ?"

Jim couldn't be sure—he'd always thought it was a figure of speech—but there almost seemed to be a twinkle in Korrigan's eyes. "Oh, you know . . . things just happen sometimes."

Which was warning enough. Ask no questions, and be told no lies. Whoever—or whatever—Kerry Korrigan was, he seemed to have a very long arm aboard the *Outward Bound.*

"Go ahead," Kerry said. "Check it out."

As soon as Jim lifted the bag to his bunk, he knew the gold

was gone. Quickly he opened the bag up and thrust his hands through the rumpled clothes and personal effects. The cloth bag that had held the small, heavy bars was gone. Something must have shown on his face. So was his .75.

"What's the matter?" Kerry said. "It's your stuff, isn't it?"

"Uh . . . yeah, sure. It's mine." What was the use? The gold was gone. And the gun Carl had given him. At least he had the rest of it. Clothes, a few holopics of himself, Carl, Tabitha in better days. His cherished scale model of one of ConFleet's white ships, reminder of yet another shattered dream.

To hell with it. He hadn't counted on the gold in the first place, so why cry over it now that it was gone?

"Kerry . . . thanks. I really appreciate it."

Korrigan relaxed. "Anything for a friend, Jim." He began to back out of the cube. "Okay, you probably want to get settled. Listen, I'm in Seven B. Just ask anybody."

Jim started to repeat his thanks, but before he could speak, Kerry vanished, leaving only a Cheshire-cat-like vision of his dancing blue eyes and wide, white grin in his wake.

Jim closed the door, then turned around, leaned against it, and luxuriated in a moment of silent solitude. For the first time in a week he was alone and unafraid.

That was when it hit him, slammed into him full force, and sent him stumbling to the bunk where he flopped facedown, his shoulders heaving silently.

Seven days ago he'd been Jim Endicott, with a father, a mother, a home, a past, and a *future* on the world of Wolfbane. Now he was Jim Evanston, with no parents, a past he couldn't talk about, and a future of utter mystery.

What do I do? he wondered hopelessly. *What the hell do I do now?*

CHAPTER FIVE

1

Jim spent the rest of the day unpacking and putting his things away. He placed a holopic of himself, Tab, and Carl, taken a year ago on his previous birthday, on the desk. He remembered that Tabitha had taken some pictures of his last birthday party, and was glad he didn't have any of those. That party had been the beginning of the series of disasters that had destroyed his family, his past, his future, and brought him to this bare, unfamiliar cubicle. No good memories there.

When he finished unpacking, he stretched out on his back on the bed and stared up at the ceiling high above. There were no roofs on the cubicles, but anybody trying to climb over the walls would set off alarms. He wondered why they hadn't simply gone ahead and enclosed the cubes entirely. Then he realized there were most likely cameras hidden in the ceiling along with the lights. Somebody would be watching. This was the young men's dorm, one of them, at least. He knew his history well enough. Unmarried young men were the single most dangerous group in any society. No sane leader ever gave them a chance to start trouble, not if he could help it. He bet himself that the family cubicles would be completely enclosed. . . .

In a way, the lack of privacy was comforting. It signified limits, rules, a framework within which to live. Somebody would be watching, but maybe that also meant somebody would be taking care of him.

Exhaustion thrummed in his bones. He considered getting up, going to explore his new home, but the thought of climbing out of bed was distasteful. The thought of everything was distasteful . . . life sucked.

His eyelids grew heavy as he considered just how much life currently sucked, his life, at least. Why had he sent his damned genotype to the Solis Space Academy? Carl had told him not to, but he had gone ahead anyway. And now look. Could the results of his disobedience have been any worse?

He sighed, thinking about it. Sure they could have. For a moment the chaotic memories of the firefight at the cabin replayed themselves across the back of his eyelids. Tabitha screaming, Commander Steele moving, an impossibly fast killing machine, him standing, pulling the trigger of his S&R .75 over and over again, the deep, bell-like explosions hammering at his ears. Another couple of inches to the right, and one of his slugs would have blown a basketball-sized hole in Carl's chest. When he thought about how close he'd come to killing the man he'd always thought was his dad, his forehead was suddenly slick with icy sweat. What would his life have been like *then*?

It was that thought he took with him as he drifted away, and it was that thought that filled the nightmares that followed, nightmares so awful they might as well have come from a different universe. But when he awoke to the sound of a loudly clamoring alarm the next morning, he didn't remember any of those terrible dreams. Not consciously, at least.

2

"Rule of thumb," the cheerful voice behind him said. "Don't eat the brown food."

Jim turned, found himself staring into Kerry Korrigan's infectious white grin, and smiled in return. "Oh, hi." He shifted his tray to let Korrigan step up next to him in front of the food dispenser he'd been perusing with some puzzlement.

"Brown food," Korrigan repeated. "Just check the holos after you punch the DISPLAY button. If the picture is mostly brown, give it a pass. Green's okay, pink's usually pretty good, gray is usually at least edible, if not much better than that. And orange, of all things, generally tickles your taste buds right into heaven." He shrugged. "Naturally, we don't see much of the orange."

Jim swallowed. "What is this stuff they're feeding us?"

"Reprocessed krill, mostly. Some soy concentrates. Vitamins and minerals. All very healthy, I'm sure." Kerry punched a button and eyed the resulting holopic dubiously. "What do you think? Would you call that brown, or orange?"

"Burnt umber," Jim said.

"Huh? Is that a color?" Kerry checked again. "Never mind. Better safe than sorry." He tried several more buttons, until he got a combination he approved of. Then he slapped a larger button marked DELIVER. The machine's innards grumbled a moment, then extruded a shelf on which rested a plate, a couple of covered bowls, and a tall cup of dark, steaming liquid. Korrigan transferred all this to his tray.

"Join me?" he asked Jim.

"Sure," Jim said.

He finished with his own selection and followed Kerry as he wove his way through a raucous crowd of young men—the youngest, Jim estimated, in their early teens, the oldest around twenty-one or two—until they reached an empty table in the opposite corner. Unlike most of the rest of the tables, which were square and seated four, this one was round and looked easily able to accommodate twice that number. But it was empty, though just about all the other tables had at least one diner busily shoveling it away.

Reserved? No sign there. But empty anyway. He glanced around as he put down his tray. Nobody was looking directly at the table, but he had the oddest feeling that everybody in the room was aware of who was seated there.

The mystery of Kerry Korrigan was growing deeper.

"You nod out a lot, is that it?" Kerry said, looking up at him.

"Huh?"

"I asked you how you liked your bunk, but you were doing your zombie number again."

Jim felt his cheeks go hot. "Oh, sorry. It's just that—well, everything's so new. Takes a little getting used to." He sat down quickly in order to cover his embarrassment. Kerry must think he was an idiot.

But Kerry just started to dig into his breakfast, occasionally lifting his head, rolling his eyes, and announcing in exaggerated tones, "Yum, *yum! My*, this is delicious!"

"Oh, stop it," Jim said finally. "It isn't that bad." He lifted his fork and examined the orangeish mass balanced on the tines. "I admit, it doesn't look like anything I ever ate before, but still . . . "

Kerry laughed. "Beware of any food that looks about the same going out as it did going in."

"Thanks, nice thought. And while I'm eating, too."

Kerry grinned and went back to work.

When he was finished, he pushed his tray aside, leaned back in his seat, laced his long-fingered hands behind the back of his head, and uttered a resounding belch.

Jim grunted. "Didn't your mother teach you any manners?"

Something happened in Kerry's eyes. Jim couldn't tell exactly how, but they changed. "My mama wasn't exactly big with her teaching skills," he said.

Leave that one alone, Jim thought to himself. *Damn. All I seem to do is put my foot in it.*

"You know," he said aloud, "it's hard."

"What's hard?"

"This." Jim lifted his fork, pointed. "You."

"*Moi?*"

"Well, not just you, all of it. I grew up on a little planet, in a small town. Went to school with the same kids all my life. I always pretty much knew where I stood, what my place in things was. Now I don't know anything. I'm feeling my way, and I don't even know how to do that. So if I say the wrong thing . . ." His voice trailed off.

Kerry's expression grew serious for a moment. "Yeah, I hear you. It can be tough, trying to fit in." He paused. "A small world, huh? Which one?"

"Wolfbane," Jim said.

"Wolfbane? Never heard of it."

Something wrong with that, Jim thought. But no, it made perfect sense. ConFed had been colonizing from the very beginning.

Expanding Terra's growing confederacy was the prime objective of the world government. There were dozens of little worlds gathered beneath Terra's skirts, most of them relatively near to the home planet, but some farther away. And now Terra was reaching out with a longer arm, sending out the huge colony ships into sectors far away from her own. Why should Kerry know the name of one insignificant frontier backwater out of so many?

Still, *something wrong.*

"Where are you from, Kerry?"

Once again, that imperceptible change in the way Kerry's eyes looked. Maybe a trick of the light, but . . .

"Terra," he said.

Jim waited, but Kerry didn't add anything to the one short word.

"That's it? Just Terra?" He paused. "I came from a planetary version of a mudhole. By Terrie standards, I'm a hick, green behind the ears, crap on my shoe soles."

"Huh. By *Terrie* standards, you say?"

Jim grinned. "Well, maybe by any standards. But I always wondered what it would be like to live on Terra. My dad was from there. . . ." *No, don't think about that.* "All the great cities, the museums, the historic places. Everything shiny and bright. Things *happening.*"

Kerry's eyelids drooped to half-mast. "Yeah, lotta things happening on Terra," he said finally. "Not all of them shiny and bright, either." He chuckled sourly. "I used to dream about going to some shitkicker place like—what did you call it? Wolfbane?"

Jim nodded.

"Right. Someplace with a lot of open space, not too many people, diddy-wop schools where everybody said 'Yes, sir,' and 'No, ma'am'. . . . "

"You're kidding."

"Not even a little bit," Kerry replied. The somber expression on his face said he was telling the truth. He sighed. "Someplace where you didn't have to fight all the time."

"Fight?"

"Yeah. Fight for anything. For everything."

He fell silent, and for a moment Jim saw on Kerry's features the hint of a sadness so deep, so *uncomforted* that it was almost impossible to imagine. He wanted to reach out and pat the older boy on the shoulder, but—

"Hey."

The moment vanished. Jim looked up to see two more boys standing next to the table, each holding a tray. The shorter, stockier of the two, his expression carefully serious, said, "Got room for two more?"

Kerry didn't say anything, just waved one hand in assent. The two new boys quickly sat down. Kerry leaned forward and put his elbows on the table. His mercurial features changed again, seemed washed with a glossy kind of tough camaraderie. Friendly, yet distant.

The general relaxing with his troops, Jim thought.

"The one that looks like a chocolate fireplug," Kerry said, pointing at the stocky boy, "is Ferrick Autry. The skinny, ugly one is Darnell Cota. Guys, meet Jim Evanston."

Two pairs of eyes—one set dark as raisins, the other resembling corroded copper lightly dipped in lead, regarded him.

"Hi," Ferrick said. "How you doing?" Darnell added.

Not shy, but standoffish, Jim thought. No real friendship offered. Not yet. Only the possibility of it, because Kerry Korrigan decreed it so.

I'm on probation here. But probation for what?

"Hi," Jim replied. He thought about offering his hand, but then let it fall back into his lap. Having spoken, the two new arrivals promptly put their heads down and began to shovel breakfast into their mouths, ignoring him.

Kerry watched them chow down, a faint grin flickering on his lips. "Good guys, Jim. Real troupers. Real Stone Cowboys."

He sounded proud as he said the last.

Stone cowboys? Jim wondered. *Is that a description . . . or something else?*

3

Jim finished his meal in silence. He was conscious of Kerry's frank, appraising stare. But since he had no idea what the other boy was looking for, he ignored the inspection as best he could. Finally, he pushed his tray away, only for a moment sadly remembering his mom's cooking.

"You can have seconds if you want to," Kerry said. His tone said that only maniacs or fools would consider the notion.

"Thanks, I'm full," Jim replied.

Kerry was still eyeing him. His frank gaze began to make Jim feel uncomfortable, even angry. Who was this guy to stare at him like he was a piece of meat or something? But just as he opened his mouth to voice his thoughts, Kerry's pale blue eyes shifted away from him.

"Ferrick, Darnell," Kerry said softly.

The other two looked up. Kerry inclined his head an inch or so in the direction of the dorm's main entrance. Jim turned. On the entrance balcony stood three young men, all of the same approximate age as those who surrounded him now.

"Injuns on the horizon," Kerry said.

Ferrick pushed his chair back and stood up. "I'll handle it," he said. He wiped his lips on his napkin, tossed it to the table.

"Darnell, go with him," Kerry said.

Darnell stood. The two boys walked off toward the stairs leading to the balcony.

"What's going on?" Jim asked.

"Housekeeping," Kerry said absently, his pale gaze riveted on the trio waiting just inside the entrance. "Don't be obvious about it, but watch."

Jim shifted his chair to the side, so that by turning his head slightly he could keep an eye on the visitors without appearing to stare at them directly. He could also see Ferrick and Darnell weaving through the tables and approaching the bottom of the stairs. So could the new arrivals. As the two boys mounted the first steps, the trio at the top shifted into what looked like a prearranged formation: the biggest one in front, the other two flanking him.

Evidently Darnell or Ferrick said something, because Jim could see the larger boy's lips move, though he couldn't hear anything over the din of the cafeteria.

Something flashed in the big one's right hand. Darnell and Ferrick stopped at once, not retreating, but no longer climbing, either.

"Shit," Kerry said. "You'd think the assholes would catch on."

"Who?" Jim asked, confused. "Darnell . . . ?"

But Kerry was already out of his chair. "Stay here," he said abruptly, then whirled and began to stride rapidly toward the confrontation at the entrance.

Jim felt his mouth drop open. He snapped it shut, even angrier now. Stay here? Some kind of trouble brewing, the only person even close to a friend he had on the entire ship heading right into the middle of it, and he was supposed to *stay here*?

What the hell kind of friend did Kerry think he was?

As he sat there, cheeks flaming, mulling it over, the tableau frozen at the entrance suddenly broke apart. Darnell, thin and wiry, obviously much faster than Ferrick, took the final three steps to the landing in a single leap. A moment later Ferrick lumbered on up and began swinging fists like small hams.

Jim came to his feet without thinking about it and headed toward the fray. Around him the large room fell silent, as the battle began to draw everybody's attention.

Kerry was running when he reached the stairs. He took them three at a time, bounding up like some tall, narrow human pogo stick. He blended into the melee, which was now a whirling gavotte of kicks, fists, grunted curses.

Jim crossed the last of the distance to the stairs at a dead run, leaped the first step, and galloped on up. The fight at the top had separated a little by the time he gained the top. Ferrick was faced off against a smaller lad who, by dint of superior speed, was landing blow after blow to Ferrick's broad, blunt face. Already his left eye was nearly swollen shut, and blood streamed from his nose. Nevertheless he fought on, launching blow after ponderous blow, as if the fists of his opponent hadn't affected him at all. Darnell was in better shape. He had his opponent down and was gleefully holding his ears and banging the back of his head on the steel floor.

Kerry and the big kid were faced off, both in a half crouch, hands wide before them in a classic guard position. Jim didn't understand at first. He'd seen what Kerry could do, and the boy opposite him was nowhere near as big or ugly as Honeg had been, back in the brig. Although there was something weird going on with the big guy. He looked nuts. His eyes were bugged out, his cheeks red as beets, and a thin trail of drool leaked from the side of his mouth. But just because he looked half-berserk, Jim couldn't understand why Kerry was being so cautious. Honeg hadn't been a walk in the park either, and Kerry hadn't hesitated then.

Then the big kid moved, and Jim figured it out. Kerry leaped back, sweat shining on his face, barely dodging the low, sweeping blow. The force of it spun the big guy half around. His right hand brushed near the steel rail that guarded the balcony. There was a sharp hissing sound, a fountain of white sparks. Kerry stepped in, trying for an advantage, but the big kid fell back until the stalemate resumed.

Jim stared at the railing. It was cut cleanly all the way through!

Monomole knife, Jim thought. *That's what the flash was I saw earlier.*

A monomolecular knife was a simple, deadly little instrument. It consisted of a unit about five inches long and as big around as a broomstick, which contained a battery that generated a static charge that held a piece of wire exactly one molecule wide, extending stiffly from one end of the unit. The wire could be almost any length. Monomole knives came in all sizes, from units that were effectively swords all the way down to units with wires only an inch or two long. But no matter how long the wire was, all monomole knives shared one essential characteristic: Kept stiff by the static charge, the length of wire was far thinner than the sharpest standard knives ever made. The "blade" was only a single molecule wide! A monomole knife could slice butter, flesh, or case-hardened steel with equal ease.

Jim estimated the blade on the weapon the big kid held in his right hand was about two inches long. Not a sword by any means, but capable of inflicting wounds two inches deep with no effort whatsoever. A belly wound that deep would leave your guts spilling out onto the floor, or a quick slice across the jugular would drown you in your own blood.

No wonder Kerry was so wary! A single slip could be his last. Jim froze a moment, staring at their straining poses. He'd been trained for years in all kinds of martial arts, against all kinds of weapons. But he'd never faced the real thing in a real hand-to-hand fight. The knot in his belly told him his body understood the fatal possibilities, even if he hadn't quite got his mind around them yet.

So he didn't try. Thinking about it might paralyze him. He couldn't let that happen. Instead, he took a couple of steps for a running start, leaped into the air, caromed off the still-sizzling railing, took a rolling fall, and bounced to his feet behind the big kid. He spread his arms wide for balance and then, putting the full weight of his thighs into the motion, wheeled like a ballerina on the ball of his left foot and rammed the heel of his right as hard as he could into the big kid's right kidney.

The force of the blow straightened his opponent up with a gasp of agony. His hands lost their defensive position and spread wide. Kerry stepped forward, his own hands a blur. Once again Jim heard the meaty solid *thwack*! as Kerry's fist met flesh.

The big guy flew backwards as if kicked in the chest by a mule. The back of his head slammed into the steel bulkhead behind him with a dull *crack*. He froze a moment, as if stuck to the wall. Then his eyes rolled back in his skull. He slowly sank to his knees, then pitched over onto his face. Kerry bent down and picked up the monomole unit that had fallen from his hand.

"Thanks," he said, glancing at Jim, who was staring at the unconscious hulk before him. Then he spun around, light as a boy at dancing class, and launched himself at the rest of the melee—just as Ferrick finally connected with one of his own haymaker punches.

Two down, and now the third one cowered back as Kerry, Ferrick, and Darnell surrounded him. His face went pale. "No," he said. "It's cool. I'm done."

Kerry stepped forward. His right hand darted out, fast as a striking snake. He wrapped his long fingers around the smaller boy's throat. He pushed him back against the wall and rapped his head on the metal a couple of times. The smaller boy's eyes bugged out.

"Pepper, you little weasel," Kerry said. "What the hell you think you were doing? Even with Hump over there"—he nodded in the direction of the unconscious big kid—"you had to know we'd kick your worthless ass. B dorm is *our* turf, and you frigging well know it's gonna stay that way. Right?"

He rapped Pepper's skull against the metal again. "Right?"

"Yeah, sure, Kerry. B dorm's yours. Stone Cowboy turf. No problemo."

Kerry stared into Pepper's terrified eyes, then suddenly grinned. He dropped his hand and stepped back. "Just so we understand each other. Go back and tell that asshole Tabazz we *do* understand each other, okay?"

Pepper nodded frantically.

"And tell him that if he sends somebody over here with a 'mole blade again, I'll send the guy back in a box. And come looking for your boss myself. You got that?"

"Yeah, Kerry. I'll tell him."

"Good. Now drag this worthless garbage out of here. It's messing up my entrance. And if it stays messed up much longer, I'm gonna clean it up with your tongue."

Pepper didn't say anything more, just bobbed his head, leaned over, and began to drag Hump's unconscious carcass toward the hatch. Kerry watched for a moment, then nodded.

"Come on," he said curtly, and started down the stairs. The rest followed him, Jim bringing up the rear. He looked back as he reached the bottom of the steps, but Pepper was already gone. No trace remained of the unwelcome guests.

When they got back to their table, Kerry stopped. "Saved my ass there, Jim. Took some balls to go up against a 'mole."

Jim felt himself blush. He hadn't really thought about it yet. Now he did, and his blush turned chilly. What if he'd jumped wrong? What if Hump had been just a hair quicker? What if . . . ?

Kerry looked at Darnell and Ferrick. "I say Jim's shown us his balls, and I say they're good enough. What about you guys?"

Ferrick glanced at Darnell. Darnell nodded. "Yeah," he said.

"Me too," Ferrick added.

Kerry turned to Jim. "There's a few more formalities,

but . . . welcome to the Stone Cowboys, Jim. If you want to, that is."

Jim stared at the hands of all three boys, stretched out toward him. He took a breath and nodded. "I want to," he said, and gravely shook each outstretched hand.

"We'll show you the codes and the hand jive and all the rest of the secret bullshit later," Kerry said. "But you're one of us now, brothers in the blood."

Brothers in the blood, Jim thought. *Sounds like a vid-kid game. Except somebody could have gotten killed back there. . . .*

"It's not a game, is it?" he asked softly.

Kerry seemed to understand. "No," he said, equally softly. "It's not a game."

4

Ferrick's face was cut and bruised. Kerry sent him off for a visit to the dorm's autodoc. Jim, still wondering what he'd just got himself into, watched him go.

"What was that all about?" he asked.

"Not much," Kerry replied. "D Street Dudes," he added cryptically.

"Somebody could have gotten hurt," Jim said. "A monomole knife. Those are illegal where I come from."

"But you're not where you came from, are you? The rules are different here."

"Okay, what *are* the rules here?"

"For us? There aren't any," Kerry said. He paused, searching for words. "That's not exactly right. There are rules. A few. But they only stay rules as long as we can enforce them."

Jim thought about it. "Might makes right, is that it?"

Slowly, Kerry grinned. "Now you're getting it."

Jim shook his head. "That's wrong."

"Maybe. But when has it ever been any different?"

"So, are the . . . Stone Cowboys the mightiest? Is that what that was about? These Dudes from D Street were testing us? You?"

"Yeah, pretty much. Hump's their best fighter. If he'd taken me, things would have changed."

"Changed how? What things?"

Kerry shrugged. "Oh, just things. Changed, you know?" Suddenly, he seemed preoccupied. "You'll figure it out. Anyway, listen. It's time to show the flag."

"What does that mean?"

"Well, the Dudes took a shot at us. But we kicked their asses. So now we show up, rub it in their faces. We're the Cowboys. Nobody screws with us."

Kerry pushed his chair back and stood up. "Come on, new boy. We'll give you a tour, Cowboy style."

Darnell chuckled. "That's right, Jim. The way we do everything. *Cowboy* style."

CHAPTER SIX

1

A generation ship.

Jim was familiar with the general idea: You build a gigantic vessel, really a small world, and start it off on a very long journey with a minimal crew. A seed crew, because those first crew members would have children, and those children would also have kids, and eventually, many generations later, the ship would be full. Presumably by the time this happened, the ship would be approaching its destination.

It was an old concept, one from the dawn of spaceflight, before a workable method of faster-than-light travel was discovered. Now man could move distances in days that once would have required centuries, even eons. But there were some exceptions. If you wanted to move a *lot* of people, you had to go more slowly. You couldn't take something the size of Detroit and squirt it a few hundred thousand light-years in just a jump or two. The stresses would tear it apart. So you did it in microjumps, a few light-years at a time, and you recalibrated after each jump. Which meant that a journey from Terran space to, say, the Taurus Sector could take as long as three Terran years.

Three years is a long time to feed, house, and maintain that many people. So the generation ships made a comeback. Not as long-haul ships with a slowly growing population, but relatively short-time journeyers with a huge population. A city of folks willing to uproot themselves and take off for a new world thousands of parsecs from their previous lives. The sort of citizens who, for one reason or another, would take that sort of risk. Wanderers and adventures, yes, but also failures and crooks, misfits and losers of every stripe imaginable.

Every stripe imaginable. That was the human cargo of *Outward Bound.* A multitude of people uprooted and rootless, the foundations of their previous lives shattered beyond repair. Broken families, dysfunctional families, the human wreckage of bankrupted businesses, obsolescent careers, the socially halt, the lame, the discarded. Their home world was happy to see them go, happy to put their useless lives to some good use. Many of them not happy at all to go, but going anyway: out of fear, out of desperation, even out of legal fiat.

Such exoduses were nothing new in human history. Penal ships had helped colonize Australia for the British Empire, and poverty and terror had sent the dregs of Europe flooding to the New World for two hundred years.

Now, as always, another of humanity's great leaps outward was being fueled from the corroded underbelly of society. Jim had never seen the hundred-meter-tall statue in the Terran harbor of New York City, but he knew the inscription on it well enough: "Give me your tired, your poor, your huddled masses yearning to breathe free. . . ."

Huddled masses. That was as good a description as any for the *Outward Bound.* He began to understand just how huddled those masses were as Kerry led him up to the inner surface of the ship.

He'd remained in his room during the voyage to the *Outward Bound*, guarding the hoard of gold he'd lost immediately on his arrival. He hadn't watched the docking procedure from space, and so had no idea what sort of ship was now his new home. He hadn't paid much attention, in his previous life, to the colony ships as they were designed. He knew only that they were of different types and sizes, the specifications dictated by the sort of colonies they were built to establish.

He knew that the most popular design for a colony ship was a Bernal Sphere, a hollowed-out globe or cylindrical shape designed to spin so as to provide Terran-normal gravity along its inner surfaces.

Kerry led his small crew out of B Dorm and into a maze of winding passages, steel-walled corridors all painted the same institutional green. Most of the walls were so encrusted with layers of crude graffiti it was almost impossible to determine what their original color had been.

Darnell reached into his pocket and withdrew a small laser unit. In less than thirty seconds he etched a series of blackened letters on an unmarked space, sweeping his hand back and forth in quick, sure motions.

COWBOYZ ROOLZ!

When he finished, he glanced at Jim. "Well? Not bad, huh?"

There was a certain crude artistry to his efforts. The bulging shapes of the letters throbbed with energy. Darnell had added so much detail and shading the script looked oddly formal. It reminded Jim of hieroglyphs or runes.

"What does it mean?" he asked the other boy.

"Huh?" Darnell stared at him as if the answer was obvious.

"Several things," Kerry broke in. "It's our mark, first of all. It shows we own this territory. It means we rule it. Second thing, it means it's our rules that apply here." He grinned. "It's our joint, and we run it our way. Somebody doesn't like it . . ." He shrugged.

"Oh," Jim said. Something more to think about. Evidently the social structures here were more complicated than he'd imagined. Then he realized Kerry and his friends probably didn't even know what a social structure was, or that they were part of one. His knowledge gave him an advantage. Best to keep it secret, though. His new friends might not take kindly to such an objective view of their lives. And even a small advantage might come in handy down the road somewhere.

They walked on. Eventually their corridor debouched into a larger, circular area, lined with elevator doors. Kerry walked to the middle door of three and pushed a button. A moment later the door slid open, and they entered. Jim looked up. The ceiling of the elevator car was transparent. Far overhead he saw blue sky. And clouds.

Jim's mouth fell open. "Clouds?" he said slowly. He tried to get his mind around it. "How many . . . how many people are on this ship?"

Kerry shrugged. "About ten million," he said.

Ten million people . . .

It wasn't a ship. It was an entire world.

"Then it's not really your territory. Not all of it," Jim said.
"Not yet," Kerry replied.

2

The elevator reached the inner surface of the sphere and stopped at ground level. The tube containing the car continued up, now completely transparent above the "ground." The door opened, and they stepped out onto a broad plaza made of concrete paving blocks. The first thing Jim noticed was the foliage. There were trees and bushes everywhere, set into pots, growing from sections cut into the pavement, or planted in nodding emerald ranks above broad swaths of pool-table lawn. Moonflowers and trumpet-horns blossomed in popcorn profusion, scenting the faint breeze with sandalwood and rosemary and dense, drowsy lilac. Jim took a deep breath.

"Wow. . . ."

"Yeah, it gets you, doesn't it? The first time?" Kerry grinned cheerfully. "Best place I ever lived," he added. "Except for those freaking dorms. They're lousy."

They strolled to the edge of the plaza. Jim kept stopping, just to look around. But it was when he looked up that his stomach jumped into his throat. He felt a surge of vertigo, though he barely noticed when Kerry caught his arm and steadied him.

Up, up, up! For a moment he didn't understand just what it was he was looking at. Small, fluffy clouds floated a couple of thousand feet up, and far above them, the harsh blue-white glare of a sun.

Well beyond the other side of the sun, a dark haze. He squinted, trying to make out what that distant panorama might be. Then, with a heart-wrenching jerk, it suddenly came into focus. Roofs! Thousands of roofs, multicolored, pink, mauve, light purple, white, tile red. And streets, some straight, others meandering like the veins in a slab of marble. And . . . *rivers*, sapphire traceries that connected lakes like scattered translucent jewels!

That was when his belly heaved, as his mind tried to encompass what he was seeing. Except for a few short orbital flights, Jim had never been off planet. Even his subconscious reactions were keyed to the norms of planetary life. The ground was *down*, the sky *up*. So when he saw the ground floating miles above his head, his mind made the necessary connection, and started sending danger signals roaring along his nervous system.

High in the air . . . upside down. . . .

Falling!

"Hey. You okay, buddy?"

Jim swallowed hard, tasted a wad of bile that had burned into his throat. He closed his eyes, shook his head, and waited.

"Whoa. . . ."

Somebody, Darnell maybe, laughed. "He's got the wobblies, man. First-timers, it always hits that way. Stand back, he's probably gonna puke." He laughed again.

"You gonna heave, Jim?" Kerry asked, genuine concern in his voice.

Jim kept his eyes closed. He swallowed again. No, he wasn't going to vomit. Maybe. . . .

"I'm okay," he said, and took a deep breath. He opened his eyes, but didn't look up. It was too soon for that. Instead, he focused on what looked like a six-story apartment complex that fronted one whole side of the square. Nothing out of the ordinary about it, a ferrocrete structure painted light blue, wide windows and glass doors facing out onto filigreed balconies. It could have been anywhere on Wolfbane, but it wasn't. It was inside a spinning tin can trillions of miles from any planetary surface. That this building was so ordinary only emphasized the strangeness of its location.

Jim blinked, staring at it, as it finally hit home on some level his awareness had not yet consciously penetrated. He was far away from his old life. His old life was gone, and he was now in a new life. He had severed all the connections he'd once understood completely and trusted without thought. He was alone.

One more member of the lonely crowd. Just like everybody else on the *Outward Bound*.

3

"How big is this place anyway?" Jim asked, as Kerry led them into a street crowded with people. Small jitneylike buses, open to the air, floated down the center of the street, crowded to the gills with passengers. The walks on either side of the jitney track were also crowded. People of all shapes, sizes, and ages strolled, ambled, jogged. They chatted or shouted or laughed. They gestured with mad abandon, almost as if their waving hands, fluttering fingers, and mobile expressions constituted a voiceless language all its own, a communication of signs rather than sounds.

Jim noticed out of the side of his eye that as they passed a group of four boys on the far side of the street, Ferrick raised his right hand and did something complicated with his fingers. One of the distant group immediately responded with a similar gesture.

Secret codes? Was this the hand jive Kerry had mentioned earlier? If so, then those four must also be members of the Stone Cowboys. He made a mental note to keep an eye out for things like that. He still didn't know what sort of group, or club, or gang he'd joined. He didn't even know what Kerry's role in it was. Or what his own role was supposed to be.

Hell. Supposed to be? Why should there be any "supposed to be" about it? Whatever rules he'd once thought he knew, they wouldn't apply here. He was on his own. "Supposed to be" didn't count any longer. On the *Outward Bound*, kids carried monomolecular knives and tried to use them on other kids. Maybe that was what was "supposed to be" around there. Or maybe not. But it wouldn't help to pretend that anything he'd learned before about the way Wolfbane worked would do him any good now. Just the opposite, in fact. It could get him killed.

He'd thought he knew the proper order of things on Wolfbane, too, and look where that had gotten him. He'd assumed he knew what was up with his own family, his own safe, secure life. Knew enough to act on his own, make his own decisions. Disobey his father. And so he'd followed his own flawed understanding of the world and destroyed everything he'd thought he understood. There were no safe moorings, no magic key of comprehension. Only a thin veneer of normality over yawning chaos, where one false step could lead anybody to a final endless fall.

Be careful, he warned himself. *Just be careful.* He realized Kerry was speaking to him.

"How big?" Kerry said. "It's a cylinder four miles thick and about twenty miles long."

Automatically, Jim did the equation and came up with a result that shocked him. The inside of the cylinder wall covered about *250 square miles*! He groped for an analogy. The city of San Francisco, on Terra, was on a peninsula and couldn't expand. It held about a million people in fifty square miles. That made the population on the *Outward Bound* only twice as dense as an entire Earth city! Dense enough by Wolfbane standards, but nothing compared to Hong Kong or Manhattan Island.

"Jim? You're doing it."

He came out of his mental fog with a start. "Huh? What?"

"Buzzing off. And you look kinda pale again."

He forced himself to grin, though his gut was still churning almost as badly as his thoughts. "Hard to get used to, is all," he managed. "All . . . this."

Kerry seemed to understand what he was trying to say, because his blue eyes flickered and seemed to go out of focus for an instant.

"I bet one thing isn't much different from what you're used to," Kerry said suddenly.

"What's that?"

Kerry pointed. Up ahead, seated around a table that fronted a tiny restaurant, were three girls. All of them had turned to face them, watching them as they approached. One girl—a thin, pretty blonde, waved suddenly.

"The women," Kerry said. "The pretty little girls. They're the same everywhere."

Darnell laughed. "Yeah," he said. "Crazy. Every damned one of them. Rip your heart out, spit on it, throw it on the ground." He sounded strangely proud of this as he spoke. "Real Stone Cowgirls."

And he's proud *of that?* Jim thought.

"Watch yourself, Jim," Darnell added. "They're gonna love you. Probably never seen green eyes like yours before."

"I'm not worried," he said, trying to fake a confidence he didn't feel. Did these boys treat their girls as some kind of possessions? Or some kind of enemy? None of it made sense. . . .

He grinned inwardly, feeling the sour taste of it in his mind. His entire life now made no sense at all. Why should these girls—or anything else—be different?

4

"Samantha, call me Sam," she said.

"I beg your pardon?"

"Ooh, Kerry. Where'd you find this one? Listen how pretty he talks."

Jim took his hand back from her cool fingertips. Her skin was the color and smoothness of melted chocolate mixed with warm honey. He imagined he could feel a faint tingle in his own fingers from where he had touched her. Her voice was rough and raucous and lilting. It reminded him of a flock of birds, happy starlings, maybe, conversing beneath a distant wind. He put his hand on the tabletop and stared at the dusty blue veins on the back. The same color as the soft shadow that throbbed in the hollow of her throat. Her brown hair, the same gleaming brown as the shell of a snail, was a mess. A confusion of curls and braids and odd protruding tails with bits of shiny plastic mixed in. A don't-give-a-damn magpie's nest perched in an untidy sprawl atop her heart-shaped face.

"Would you marry me and have my children?" he said. He had no idea if he was serious or not. He felt a mild chill as he waited for her answer.

"Oh, you," she said. "Silver-tongue devil."

"Tongued," he said.

"Oo*wee*! I like that better," Darnell said, laughing. "Tongued."

He draped his arm over the cute blond girl's shoulder and nuzzled at her ear. "How about you, babe? You want tongued?"

Cleopatra, Jim thought. He knew Cleopatra had actually been ugly, a short woman with a huge nose, but the idea of Cleopatra was beautiful. That was what Samantha-call-me-Sam looked like. The idea of Cleopatra.

"So, will you?" he asked her.

Lips like cherry wine. It was an old, old line, one he'd studied in a classical music class that had otherwise bored him to death. But that line had stuck in his mind. It made no sense. Cherry wine? What color was that?

It was the color of her lips, that's what. She stopped laughing and looked at him, really looked. Her eyes were like bits of polished anthracite, lightly veined with silver.

"Marry you?" she finally said. "No. But if Kerry says it's okay, I guess I could sleep with you."

Kerry let out a giant whoop. Jim felt his cheeks go crimson, felt his ears begin to glow. Darnell pounded on the table. The blond girl tinkled like a bell. Even the phlegmatic Ferrick allowed himself a dark, mocking grin.

Jim didn't realize he was standing. He didn't hear the soft crash of his chair tipping over. He looked back and forth, the laughter thundering in his ears, and tried to remember how to get back to the dorm. Get away from *there*, anyway.

Kerry reached for him, but Samantha got to him first. She planted herself in front of him, so close he could feel the heat radiating off her body. She tilted her head up and stared directly into his eyes.

"I'm sorry. Look at me. Okay. I'm sorry. You hear me, Jim? It was just a joke. No, look at me. Don't look away. You weren't ready for it. Now you'd like to smack me in the mouth. Okay. Go ahead. Smack me."

It all came out so fast it stopped him. He couldn't move until he processed all the dissonant input. Her eyes, her words. The smell of her breath, hinting of raspberries. Her lips.

"No," he said. "No, I can't do that."

"Then sit down."

Somebody had replaced his chair. He felt the edge of the seat against the back of his knees. He sat as if somebody had cut his strings. She looked down at him.

"I apologize. You're new around here. Everybody will take advantage. But I shouldn't have. My firepower is different from these apes with you. Too much for you to handle, so it wasn't fair. You understand?"

"No, but I accept your apology."

Kerry leaned in. "How about you accept another beer, buddy? You look like you could use one."

More laughter, but kinder. More inclusive. He was one of their own. They'd stung him—she'd stung him, and now they were laughing. But with him, not at him.

Somehow, she'd changed all that.

As he watched her go back to her seat, he realized that he'd passed another test. But he didn't know what the questions had been. Or understand just what answers he'd given.

He didn't know how much longer he could survive this school of hard knocks. The education was wearing him out.

5

"So what did you think of the girls?"

"They're girls. Especially that Sam. She's really a girl. Is she your girl?"

"They all are, in a way. All the Stone Cowgirls are mine."

"*Droit du seigneur*," Jim said.

"What?"

"In medieval times, on Terra, it was a custom that allowed the feudal lord first crack at the women on their marriage night. Most of them took money instead, but if they wanted, they could have the bride."

Kerry's jaw dropped. "Just walk in and take her, with her husband standing there? You mean like do the old in and out, right on the spot?"

"Sure."

Kerry mulled it over. "No, me and the girls, it's not like that.

But it isn't a bad idea. . . ." He slapped Jim's shoulder. "You're more valuable than I thought you were."

"How valuable did you think I was?"

"Hard to say, Jim. Hard to say. It's a moving target."

They were walking down a tree-lined street. Jim's eyes told him they were climbing a hill. But when he looked back, a hill was rising there, too. His brain kept telling him he was constantly in the bottom of a gently sloping valley that rose both before and behind him. His mind told him that he was walking around the inside of a cylinder, but his brain wasn't having any of that. *Valley,* his brain kept insisting. *Valley.*

Of course, his brain also thought he was strolling along upside down, four miles above the woods, lakes, and houses on the other side of the cylinder, ready to fall headfirst out of the sky at any moment.

"Okay, if you don't have screwing rights to all the Cowgirls, and Sam isn't your girl, how come she has to ask your permission?"

"To sleep with you?"

"Yeah." He felt uncomfortable talking about it that way. As if discussing Sam in such terms was insulting. Hell, it was insulting.

Even Kerry seemed mildly uneasy with the discussion. "She doesn't, really. It was mostly a joke. Yank your chain a little, see what happened. Sam's a piece of work. Darnell wasn't far wrong about our women."

"Pull your heart out, spit on it, that stuff?"

"Uh-huh."

"You say she doesn't really. So what does she do, really?"

"Well, it's sort of. . . . I run the Cowboys, you know? And the Cowgirls, too, when it gets right down to it. So everybody tries to keep me informed."

"Informed?"

"In the loop. If you're gonna do something major, you let me know about it. So I don't get surprised or nothing."

"Ah," Jim said. "I get it. Because you're the leader. You take care of everybody, they take care of you."

"There you go."

They came to an intersection. There was no jitney rail down the middle of the streets here. An occasional bicycle hummed down the center of the road, but mostly people walked. Jim noticed that most of the walkers seemed to amble without much purpose, as if a destination was the last thing on their minds. Everybody stopped to smell the roses, of which there were an abundance in the hedgerows that fronted the lawns on either side.

"How come all the shrubbery?" Jim asked. "This is a spaceship, not a greenhouse."

"It's both. All this weedy stuff pumps out a lot of oxygen. And soaks up a lot of carbon dioxide. Ten million people run through a bunch of that stuff, both ways."

"Oh. That makes sense."

"Everything on this tin can makes sense. The mechanical stuff, at least. This damned thing is pretty much self-sufficient. These big ones were designed to be self-sustaining colonies in orbit around some star. And that's what this will be, eventually."

"A colony? I thought we were going out to *start* a colony."

"We are. But you don't just dump ten million city folks—Plebs is what most of us are, and you don't get more city than that—down on some bum-fragged virgin planet and tell them to start plowing. The *Outward Bound* will take up orbit and start the heavy manufacturing. Prefab housing, small factories to make use of the local natural resources, build farm equipment, light industry, stuff like that."

"Okay, that makes sense. Do all the heavy stuff in orbit, and just drop it down the gravity well. Efficient."

"Yeah, it would be. If most of the people here weren't total assholes, it might even have a chance."

Jim stared at him. "What do you mean?"

"Didn't you hear me say just about everybody was Pleb?"

"Yeah . . . ?"

"Well, Pleb. I'm a Pleb, so I know. Can't find a bunch of more useless people in the whole galaxy. Half of them are wireheaders, and the rest are just plain lazy. Plebs are useless by definition."

Jim thought about it. "You aren't real big on history, are you?"

"That's what I've got you for."

Again, the odd feeling that he was missing something.

Something important. "Is that what I'm for?"

"Among other things."

"You seem to think you know a lot about me."

Kerry stopped, turned, looked at him. "Oh, Jim. You're an open book, my friend. Green as this freaking grass. But don't worry. You've got me in your corner. That's all you need. You've got a great future with the Stone Cowboys."

They turned left at the intersection, began working their way down a new street. This one was less residential. They passed several small shops, places that sold garden implements, sausages, holovids, spirit crystals, beer, cheap clothing, and one place that, as far as Jim could tell, specialized in inflatable animals. He wondered if the sheep he saw floating outside the shop door was anatomically correct.

"What, exactly, do the Cowboys do?"

Kerry shrugged. "We're entre—entreper—we're business people."

"What kind of business?"

"A little of this, a little of that. Don't worry about it. I'll fill you in later."

Bingo, Jim thought.

Kerry took a hard right toward a small beer stand. "Buy you a brew?"

Just before they entered the shop, Kerry stopped. When he glanced at Jim, his light blue eyes seemed to have acquired a faint glaze, like fine china.

"I know you're smart, Jim. Got a lot of education. Know stuff like that *droit du seigneur* shit. But don't make the mistake of thinking I'm a dummy." He clapped Jim on the back. "Just a friendly warning."

Funny, Jim thought. It didn't feel friendly at all.

"A beer would be good," he said.

CHAPTER SEVEN

1

"Where you going?"

Darnell seemed to materialize out of thin air. Jim stopped on the bottom step of the dorm stairs. "Just out. Take a look around."

"Want some company?" Darnell was already moving up the steps. It wasn't really a question.

"Uh, sure. I guess."

This time Darnell didn't stop to etch any new graffiti. He seemed preoccupied as they rode the elevator up to the surface. His copper-lead gaze was withdrawn, focused inward.

"Something wrong?" Jim asked.

"Huh? No. Why?"

"I don't know. You seem like you're not here or something."

Darnell ran one hand through his dusty blond mop. His thin features were stark. He looked like he hadn't been eating well. Or sleeping much, either.

"You know. Got things on my mind. Stuff."

Jim waited to see if he'd say more, but he didn't. They stepped out of the elevator together onto the plaza. Jim stopped, closed his eyes, took a deep breath, then opened his eyes and looked straight up.

The vertigo and nausea hammered at him again, and the screaming need to *grab hold of something*, but he forced himself to keep looking. Darnell saw what he was doing.

"Yeah, you have to fight it," he said. "It's quicker that way. If you try to pretend it's not there, it'll keep sneaking up on you."

Jim nodded, swallowing hard. "How long does it take?" he managed.

"Depends. Some people, just a few good doses, they get used to it, and they're fine." He chuckled. "And some never adjust at all. That's what those things are for."

Jim looked at him. Darnell pointed at a square green post about five feet tall that rose from the pavement to their left. "That's for them."

"What is it?" A horizontal slot bisected the top of the post. From the slot hung a flap of brown paper, like a tongue.

"Barf-bag dispenser," Darnell said. "If you see somebody running toward one, get the hell out of their way."

Jim nodded. Then he turned his face up again.

"You gonna do that all day?"

"I think it's getting better. I *know* what it is, but my reflexes don't. Not quite." He gave it up. "I'll keep working at it."

"If you decide you're gonna toss your cookies, let me know, okay? So I can duck." Darnell laughed.

Jim didn't quite catch the humor of it. Of course, he hadn't found anything very funny lately. "Which way was that little restaurant?" he said.

"The one where the girls were?"

"Yeah."

"This way." Darnell veered off to the left. They walked a bit. Darnell kept sneaking glances at him.

"Something wrong? Toilet paper hanging off my ass or something?" Jim asked.

"Nah. Just never met anybody quite like you. You look . . . uh, I don't know. Clean, I guess."

"Clean?"

Darnell groped for it, his high forehead furrowed with the effort. "Like wherever you came from, people cared about you. There was somebody who worried if you didn't show up where you were supposed to. Gave you shit if you didn't brush your teeth. Like that."

"I don't get it," Jim said.

"Nobody ever gave a damn about me. Anything I did."

"What about your parents?"

Darnell uttered a short, harsh bark. "Parents? You mean like two of them?" He barked again. "Never did know my old man.

Neither did my mom, I bet. She was a wirehead, did some hooking, more out of boredom than anything else. But when she wasn't screwing or jizzing her brain, she used to take me for walks sometimes. When I was a little kid. And she'd point at every blond-haired mothra-fracker that came along, and she'd say, '*There's your daddy, Darnell. Wave hi to your daddy.*' And me, the dumb little shit, I'd wave, and she'd laugh like crazy."

"Jesus."

Darnell's grin was just a little twisted. "I don't think He had much to do with it either. How about you?"

"How about me what?"

"You know. How'd you end up on this oversize tin can?"

"You mean Kerry didn't tell you what happened when I got here?"

Darnell's eyes flickered. "Kerry. No, he doesn't talk much if he don't feel like it. And he usually don't feel like it."

"I thought you guys were friends."

"Well, sure. Of course we are. But it isn't one of those buddy-buddy things, okay? More like . . . hell. I can't really explain it. You'll figure it out."

"That's what everybody keeps telling me. I'll figure it out. But what am I supposed to be figuring out? What's the big secret?"

"There aren't any secrets, man. It's all laid out on the table, if you know what you're looking—*shit!*"

Somebody bumped Jim's shoulder, hard.

"*Run, you dumb mother. Run!*" Darnell hissed.

Jim froze, staring into the face of a monster.

2

The monster was no Honeg in retro biker drag. He was about six feet tall, maybe 250 pounds, wearing a conservative banker's suit that might have been tailored for an armored personnel carrier. He looked like he could smash bricks with his face. Under the best of circumstances he would have been an ugly, frightening guy. Somebody the bank used to foreclose on widows and orphans.

He didn't look ugly now. He looked nuts. His eyes were streaked with pink and bulged like a pair of hard-boiled eggs in a microwave. Thin, blue-tinged lips stretched across yellow teeth like overstrained rubber bands. Purple tongue protruding, neck veins like bridge cables, drool foaming at the corner of his mouth, face the color of radiation burns.

A nightmare with hands like meat hooks reaching for Jim's throat.

"Aargghhh," the monster said. His right claw snagged on Jim's shirt and tore it away. He paused, staring at the ripped cloth in his hand as if it might be skin. As if maybe he would eat it.

"Jesus Christ!" Jim shouted.

"Urgggh!" the monster replied, and reached for him again.

Jim's paralysis vanished. He whirled. Lightning bolts of terror shocked his thighs and calves as he leaped away. A vise clamped on the back of his neck. He felt his spine creak, and realized that his feet were no longer on the ground. Running in thin air, kicking like a rabbit raised for slaughter.

A hammer smashed into the back of his skull. Everything went loose and gray and silent. He tried to raise his arms, but the connections seemed to be shorted out.

I'm going to die, he thought. *He's going to kill me. . . .*

Darnell kicked the guy in the back of his right knee. Jim heard a soft snapping sound. Then the guy toppled over. Jim hit the ground with a thump that jarred the cobwebs out of his skull.

"Run!" Darnell shouted again. He grabbed Jim's right arm and yanked hard. Jim got his feet under him and came up sprinting. Twenty feet away he risked a glance back. The monster lay on the ground, trying to rise on his shattered knee but falling back. His lips were streaked with red as he gnawed on his left hand. He looked up, grinned, and spit out a finger.

3

"Ouch!"

They were sitting at the table in front of the restaurant where they'd met the girls the day before. Jim had stripped off what was left of his shirt. Darnell's fingers prodded gently at the back of his skull.

"That's a nasty cut, and it's gonna be a real bad lump, too." He squeezed the thick muscles where Jim's neck joined his shoulders. Jim gasped.

"One solid bruise, man. You're gonna be stiff as a board."

"*What the hell was wrong with that guy?*"

Darnell left off his ministrations, sat down, and lifted his beer. "The bleeding's stopped, but you better see a doc when we go back to the dorm. There's a med station on the way." He gave Jim a worried look. "We ought to go back now, really. You don't look so good."

"I don't feel so good."

"All right."

Jim fought back a wave of dizziness. "But I don't feel like walking much, either."

Darnell's worried expression grew more pronounced. "Hey, man. Maybe I better get somebody. You could have a broken head or something. That mother popped you pretty hard."

"Yeah, maybe I . . . "

It was the weirdest feeling. He knew his lips were moving. He could feel them, feel his tongue moving sluggishly against the roof of his mouth. Could even feel the faint vibrations of his voice buzzing in his tender skull. But he couldn't *hear* a damned thing. And there seemed to be some kind of bright halo around Darnell. Bright and growing brighter. He was perfectly aware of what was happening. He was falling forward, sinking into that light. Then he wasn't aware of anything at all.

4

"Are you gonna live?" Sam asked him.

Her face hovered above his like a honey-colored moon. She leaned forward and blurred out. He felt her lips touch his forehead. A kiss of coolness against the heat. Then she moved away.

Kerry's face swam into view. He looked worried and angry. "The proctors took that guy down. Good thing. They got to him before we did."

None of it made any sense.

"What guy?"

"You don't remember?"

Jim shook his head. Thunder rolled in waves behind his eyes.

"Hey, take it easy," Kerry said. "Doc says you got a concussion." His blue eyes had that porcelain sheen again. "Nobody screws with Cowboys. We'll pay the guy a visit when he gets out."

"What happened?" Jim asked.

Kerry smiled. "Don't worry about it now. Doc says you need rest, so you rest." His grin widened a little. "Sam will watch you. That'll be okay, won't it?"

"Okay," Jim said.

5

He didn't know how much later, but when he woke up again, he knew it was later. He was flat on his back, staring straight up. He was in a dimly lit room. Formless shadows were printed on the ceiling. He stared at them and tried to put it together. Something had happened. He couldn't remember what, but his head and neck hurt like hell. He discovered this when he tried to move. He groaned softly.

"You awake?"

A darker shadow against the shadows moved above him. He smelled a whiff of raspberry. "Is that you, Sam?"

"I'm here, hardhead," she said. "How you doing?"

"I'm alive. I think I am."

"You lucky to be that way. Don't move, now. You want a drink of water?"

He ran his tongue across his lips. His tongue felt swollen, his lips felt like sandpaper. "Yeah," he husked. "That would be nice."

He listened to the clink of glassware, then smelled raspberries again.

"I'm gonna put my hand under your head. I'll try to miss the bandage, but if it hurts, say so."

It did hurt, but he didn't say anything. He felt the rim of the glass against his lips, and then his mouth filled with blessedly cool liquid. He tried to swallow too quickly and began to choke. She held him until he stopped.

"Not too much," she said.

He kept at it until she said, "That's enough." She took the glass away and gently lowered his head. His vision had adjusted to the dimness, and he could make out her eyes gleaming in the faint light. When she smiled, he thought of the Cheshire cat.

"Where am I?"

"In bed, dummy."

It was a weak joke, but he found it incredibly funny. Until he laughed.

"You just supposed to lay there," Sam said. "Doc told me not to let you move around. And wake you up every four hours or so, make sure you still got all your brains working."

She was very close, sitting on the edge of the bed, leaning over him. He could feel the heat radiating from her body.

"Something's working," he muttered. Suddenly he realized that he was wearing only underpants beneath the thin sheet that separated them.

She moved slightly. He heard a soft gurgle of laughter. "You don't look like you're gonna die."

"Oh, God," he said, when he realized just what embarrassing signs of life she'd noticed. "I'm sorry."

"For what?" she asked. "My favorite is probably chocolates and roses, but as compliments go, this isn't a bad one." She gurgled again. "Not bad at all."

"Sam. . . ."

But she was moving away. "Get you well first, boy. Then we'll see."

Jim closed his eyes and concentrated on getting well.

6

When he woke again the ache in his skull had subsided to a dull throbbing that was almost bearable. He pushed himself up against the pillows, wincing at the pain that shot through his neck and shoulders. Felt like something was torn in there. Definitely at least a sprain. He sighed. Even with the doc, it would take a while before he was one hundred percent again.

"You're awake. Good."

He blinked and waited for the morning fog to dissipate. The little blond-haired girl with the tinkling laugh was on the other side of the small room, next to a window half-covered with a lacy curtain. Sunlight streamed through the window, picking out the flowery pattern of a thick carpet. She was fiddling with a small kitchen unit.

"You hungry?" she asked, not turning.

He realized he was starving, and said so. She turned around and smiled at him. Still as cute as a button, her white-blond hair a smooth cap on her egg-shaped skull. Her eyes were some indeterminate color that might have been gray or blue or green. Her thin, high-arched nose had been broken sometime in the past and badly set. That was strange. Medical care was universal. It wasn't ugly, though. It gave her otherwise ordinary features character. She looked tough and no-nonsense underneath her cuteness.

Her body wasn't bad, either, Jim thought. She wore a white

blouse with a frilly collar that exposed the soft curve of her belly. Her jeans looked as if it took her a lot of effort to squeeze into them. The cuffs were tucked into fake ostrich-skin boots. She saw him staring and struck a hipshot pose. "Thanks," she said. "I know I'm not Sam, but it's still nice of you to notice."

He looked away, blushing, and she chuckled. "A boy with manners. I can tell you, Mister Evanston, you're going to be a big hit around here."

Evanston. Damn, it was still hard getting used to that.

"Do I smell waffles?" he said, his mouth suddenly watering uncontrollably.

She fiddled with the cooking unit some more, then swung it open. "Yep. Hope you like your eggs scrambled, and your sausage in links instead of patties."

She brought it to him on a tray. He set the tray on his lap, grateful that it covered up the customary morning evidence of what Sam had taken as a compliment. It was an effort not to ignore the silverware and shovel the food in with both hands. When he'd done everything but pick up the plates and lick them, he sighed and leaned back. He felt human again, for the first time in—

How the hell long had it been, anyway?

"I'm sorry, but I forgot your name," he said.

She had been sitting on a fat, chintz-flowered chair on the other side of the room, watching him eat, her expression composed and serious.

"That doesn't do much for a girl's ego," she said.

"Look, really, I'm sorry, but I don't even remember much about what happened to me." Then he realized he recalled more than he thought he did. A big guy, well dressed, ugly . . . and nuts. Murderously, outrageously nuts.

Her face changed. "Oh, gosh, I'm sorry. I forgot about that. Well, I didn't, but I got all wrapped up playing little miss nursey. It's Jenny. My name's Jenny."

"Pleased to meet you again, Jenny. I do remember meeting you before."

She smiled. Seen head-on, it transformed her face. For a moment, battered nose and all, she looked beautiful. Jim grinned back at her. He couldn't help it. Nobody could resist that smile.

"Well, look at us," she said. "Googling at each other like a couple of monkeys."

"Googling?"

She laughed. "I guess I can tell Sam you're gonna live."

"Sam? Is she here?"

Jenny waved one hand vaguely. "Oh, she's around somewhere."

"Where is here, anyway?"

A barely perceptible pause. "The clubhouse. The Cowboy club."

He almost laughed, caught himself in time. Clubhouse. It was too much like some hokey holovid, but he doubted if they saw it that way. *When in Rome . . .*

"Well, I owe whoever brought me here."

"It was Darnell. Lugged you into a private cab and brought you right here. Then he called Kerry and"—she waved again—"we all came running."

They all came running. They hardly knew him, but he was hurt, and they all came. No questions, they just came. He felt a soft glow in his chest. He'd never felt anything quite like it before.

"And Sam? She came running, too?"

Jenny stared at him, then sighed. "You've got it bad, don't you?" When he started to reply, she waved him off. "Never mind. I'll tell her you're awake."

She headed for the door.

"Jenny."

She stopped, turned, looked at him. Her eyes glistened. "I'm not so bad-looking, am I? And I'm a nice girl, really I am."

He didn't know what to say. "The nicest," he said finally.

She nodded. "But not like her." She closed the door behind her with a soft click, leaving him to stare at it while he considered how much of an idiot he was. Nevertheless, she was right.

Not like her. Not like Sam. Nobody was.

7

Jim stayed in bed for two more days. Both Sam and Jenny kept an eye on him. He gave Kerry the keycard to his room and locker, and Kerry brought back fresh clothes.

On the second day, Kerry pulled a chair close to Jim's bed and sat down. The sunlight slanted through the lace drapes and laid a spidery pattern across his tall blond crew cut. His blue eyes were hooded in shadow.

"That guy," Kerry said. "We're not going to be able to do anything about him. Sorry."

"The guy? Oh, that guy."

"Yeah. He messed you up, we were gonna mess him up."

"Hey, man, you don't need to do that. Really. Somebody said the cops—what do you call them, proctors?—got him. Am I going to have to go to court or something?"

Kerry shook his head. "No. That won't be necessary."

There was something in Kerry's tone, a chilly offhandedness.

"I don't know," Jim said. "I think you're scaring me. What happened to the guy?"

Kerry sighed. "He died."

"What!"

"It's not a big thing. Just some half-assed suit. He went nuts and ended up in a restraint tank. And then he hung himself with his expensive tie."

"Jesus, Kerry. That's awful. He's dead?"

Kerry nodded. "So he doesn't have to worry about us. He doesn't have to worry about anything."

Jim had a sudden, terrible thought. "Kerry? What's this restraint tank? What's it like?"

"It's just a big holding cell. Padded and stuff. For drunks and nutballs and wireheads that burn too many synapses and go wacko."

"He wasn't by himself, then?"

"I don't know all the details. Probably not, though."

"So he killed himself in front of witnesses? Why didn't anybody try to stop him?"

Kerry eyed him quizzically. "This ain't Saint Teresa we're talking about here. The guy was a beast. Look what he did to you. If he decided to tighten his necktie a little too much, would you want to be the one to stop him?"

"But . . . they could have called somebody. Or—" The thought wouldn't go away. "Or maybe somebody else was involved? Were . . . any of the Stone Cowboys in that tank with him?"

Kerry looked away. "I don't know. I guess anything's possible."

"Oh, man, don't tell me that. Don't say a guy is dead because of me. I don't want that on me. Jeez, Kerry. What a hell of a thing to do."

Kerry stared at him. "Look. We didn't—I didn't—have anything to do with that guy croaking himself. Nobody strung him up. None of the Cowboys were involved. You get it? It ain't on you, because none of us had anything to do with it."

Jim locked eyes with him. Neither moved for several seconds that felt longer than just seconds. Finally, Jim looked away.

"All right," he said.

"Okay." Kerry leaned forward and slapped Jim on the knee. "Doc says you can get out of bed tomorrow. Got to take it easy, but you aren't an invalid anymore. So that's the end of you pounding your pile driver and drooling all over yourself every time Sam walks into your room."

"It's that obvious?"

"Huh." Kerry scooted the chair back, then stood up. Ran one hand through his crew cut. "Got things to do, man. I'll get back to you later, or see you tomorrow. Somebody will stick around though. Somebody's always here."

"Kerry?"

"Yeah, man?"

"Thanks. Really. For everything. And tell Darnell."

Kerry nodded. "All part of the package, man. You're a Cowboy. All we got is each other. Don't ever forget it. Your turn will come for payback. Somebody will need you. And you'll be there for them, just like we've been for you. Right?"

"Right."

"Well, then." Kerry flicked him a half-assed two-fingered salute, grinned, and left.

Jim lay back and closed his eyes. He thought about the dead

guy for a long time. He wondered why Kerry had lied to him about it—and what the lie was. He thought about Carl, too, and Tabitha. And about the mystery man who'd sent killers after them. He thought about being alone, and lonely, and afraid.

But the weirdest thought of all was the overpowering idea that this was all familiar. That somehow he'd done it all before, or something a lot like it. What was that feeling called?

Déjà vu.

CHAPTER EIGHT

1

All Jim could think about was Sam.

He thought he heard her name in the popular songs that wafted from public speakers in shops and restaurants. In crowds he would see her, rush up, and find some other girl who only vaguely looked like her. The scent of raspberries on his morning cereal—he always ordered it that way now—left him dazed with longing. He kept the memory of the way she'd leaned over his nearly naked body in his mind like an emotional lottery ticket. Replayed it over and over, the rough honey of her voice, the laughter. He went to sleep dreaming of her, woke wanting her, and spent his days mooning over her.

He felt foolish as he carefully arranged his time so he would just happen to be in her favorite haunts, but not foolish enough to stop. The table in front of the small restaurant where he'd first seen her had become his home away from the dorm. He would sit and drink gallons of coffee, hoping she would show up. Often enough, she did. She would always pretend surprise at finding him, though he was obvious enough about it that Kerry, Darnell, and Ferrick had made a running joke of it.

"How many cups is that?" Kerry said as he pulled a chair away from the table, spun it around, and sat down spraddle-legged. He rested his chin on the back rung and surveyed the littered table-top. "Ten? Fifteen? You're gonna need a kidney and bladder transplant any day now. All that coffee."

"Maybe I should switch to decaffeinated," Jim said.

"Maybe you should ask Sam if she wants to sleep with you."

Jim felt his cheeks go red. "No, I can't."

"Why not?" Kerry seemed genuinely curious.

"I don't know. I just can't."

Kerry shook his head. "Why don't you just shoot yourself and get it over with?"

"It's a thought," Jim agreed.

"Look. We need to talk."

"About Sam? I thought we were."

"No, something else. You remember when I said the Cowboys were a business?"

"Yeah, sure."

"That's what we need to talk about. The business. And you, how you fit in."

"Do I have to fit in?"

Kerry pursed his lips. "I think so. You can be a help. I spotted that right away about you. In the brig. That's why I stepped in with Honeg. I thought you had possibilities. We don't see many people like you. Not available, at least."

Jim set down his coffee cup. The caffeine was fizzing along his nerves. He knew he was sweating, but it was only the coffee. *Sure it is.*

"There's so much shit in what you just said I hardly know where to start," Jim said.

Kerry blinked. "What?"

Jim spit it out in a nonstop rush, without pausing for breath. "Whatever you're seeing about me isn't what I'm seeing. For instance, what possibilities? Why? And if I am whatever it is you think I am, why am I available? And how does all of this mean I should join up with your business. What the hell *is* your business anyway?"

Kerry raised both hands. "Whoa, slow down." He leaned forward. "Okay, here's what I see. You're not a Pleb, first thing. Second, you're educated. You know stuff I don't. Third, because you aren't a Pleb, you don't look like one. You look clean, if that makes any sense. You talk different than we do. Fourth, we need somebody like that, to handle marketing. You'd start at the bottom, of course, but you'd work your way up fast, if my guess is any good. Why should you join the business? Because we helped you, because you owe us, and because I'm asking you to." He settled back, but kept his eyes locked on Jim's face.

"And as for being available"—he spread his hands—"what else you got going? No family, no plans, no nothing as far as I can tell. Or am I wrong?"

Jim lifted his cup. The cup was empty. Just like everything else. Kerry had him cold, and it hurt. He set the cup down. "You forgot to mention just what your business is."

"Heat, Jim. We sell Heat."

"What the hell is Heat?"

"It's dope. That's what the Cowboys do. We deal drugs." He interlaced his fingers, cracked his knuckles, and smiled. "So how about it, Jim? You want to become a dope dealer?"

2

Jim and Sam walked along a side street in an industrial sector, well away from the residential and shopping areas where the crowds were thickest. Even here there were trees and bushes, and a few scraggly flower gardens. Her amazing hair was concealed beneath a red-and-white-checked bandanna scarf. It only made her eyes look bigger.

"Kerry wants me to deal dope for him," he said.

"I know," she replied.

"I can't do that."

"Why not?"

"Well . . . it's wrong," he said slowly. "It's illegal, I think."

"Actually, it isn't. Not Heat. Not on board this ship."

They came to an intersection and paused beneath a young oak. Starlings quarreled in the leafy branches above their heads. A wooden bench leaned invitingly against the rough trunk. Sam settled herself on the bench, patted the empty space beside her.

"Sit with me," she said. "We need to talk about this."

He was so conscious of her nearness. Raspberries. And the

swell of her lightly freckled breasts beneath her loose white shirt. "We sure do," he said.

She turned to face him. She let her left hand fall to rest on his knee, where he felt her touch through the fabric of his jeans as if her fingers were red-hot. It was amazingly distracting. He swallowed and tried to remember what he'd been going to say.

She waited a moment. She seemed to have some understanding of what she was doing to him, because her faint smile seemed wise beyond her years. Or maybe, he thought, it was just something women automatically knew. Maybe they were born knowing the power they wielded over men.

"So let's talk," she said, and he gave a little mental start. Drifting away again. *Come on, focus.*

"Well, I just think dope dealing is wrong."

"What do you know about Heat?"

He shrugged. "Nothing. I didn't ask Kerry."

Her fingers moved. He tried not to look down. "It's a sex drug," she said. "Are you one of those prudes, those people who don't like sex?"

Jesus!

She wasn't smiling. Her expression was dead serious. So why did it feel like she was laughing at him?

Because she probably was.

"Uh . . . I'm fine with sex. I'm very okay with it." *How about you?*

For a moment, from the expression on her face, he thought he'd spoken the last aloud, and he felt the heat rise into his cheeks. Doing a lot of that lately, too: blushing.

"Well," she said, "that's good to hear."

He looked away.

"It makes sex great. I mean, sex is great anyway, if it's with"—her fingers moved again—"the right guy. You know?"

He nodded, feeling like a flounder laid out on the table for gutting. "And this Heat stuff makes it better than great?"

"Yeah. I can't explain it. The only way would be to show you."

He just about fainted.

3

The clubhouse was empty. That was so unusual that Jim wondered about it, but not for long. He had other things to think about.

"You've got some of that stuff, that Heat?"

She reached into her pocket and took out a small plastic envelope. Inside was maybe a quarter teaspoon of fine-grained pinkish powder. She shook it, held it up to the light. "This is it."

He stared at it as if it were some kind of magic talisman. Hell, maybe it was. "Do you take it? Or me?"

"Both of us," she said. "It works both ways."

"And it makes sex better?"

She pulled off the bandanna and shook her hair free. Then, holding the envelope in one hand, she took his hand with the other, stood up, and led him toward the door to the bedroom where he'd recovered from his injuries.

"There's only one way to convince you," she said.

"Sam, we don't . . . you don't . . . "

She glanced over her shoulder, a silver light dancing in her black-ice gaze. "But I want to," she said.

"Okay."

4

"It wasn't your first time," she said later.

"Almost," he told her. "I'm not very experienced."

"You did fine," she assured him.

He felt absurdly proud when she said that. In the dim light, she was a mass of honey-pale curves and shadows. "You have the most beautiful . . ." He touched her.

"I know," she said.

The Heat was wearing off. He couldn't explain, even to himself, what that had been like. Nobody could explain, not unless they'd felt it. Not unless they'd shared it. Fire and ice, a great silent vaulting of time and space.

"Is it always like this?" he whispered, watching the pattern of his fingers against her skin.

She sounded drowsy, sated, almost complacent. "Pretty much." She sighed. "It's a little different each time, but you get the general idea."

"Jesus."

"It's pretty major."

"Yeah," he said, thinking about it.

She waited a while, then said, "So, do you still think dope is a terrible thing? No socially redeeming qualities? Nothing for you to get your hands dirty with?"

"You must think I'm a prissy asshole," he said.

"No, I think you just haven't had the same experiences I have. You come from a different place, you know? A different kind of world. Maybe where pleasure is a little easier to find, and you don't need to pour it out of an envelope."

He took a deep breath. "If I joined up, would you be my girl?"

"No. But we could do this again, if you wanted to."

"Are you trying to bribe me?"

"Only if you want it."

He reached for her. "I want it," he said.

5

"You've got ten packs, okay? The way it works is, you do the deal with somebody, then you send them to the place you've got one stashed. Never hold your stash on you. When you've got the money, you signal Darnell, and he'll stash the packet for the john to pick up. That way, if you get busted with the cash, you don't have the dope."

"I thought this wasn't illegal."

"It isn't. Not technically. Not to use. But it's illegal to sell it and illegal to buy it."

"That doesn't make any sense."

Kerry shrugged. "It's dope law. Who says it's supposed to make sense? Anyway, if it wasn't illegal to sell, we'd be out of business. I make a lot of contributions to the right places, to make sure it stays illegal." He grinned. "I've got a lot of overhead."

Jim nodded. "All right. So Darnell will stick with me?"

Darnell was standing at the end of the block, watching them. He was a few feet away from one of the barf-bag dispensers. When Jim signaled that a deal was done, Darnell would put a bag in the dispenser. Either the john would already know about the drop, or if he didn't, Jim was supposed to direct him to it without saying anything actually incriminating.

"And never actually use the word Heat or dope," Kerry had told him. "If a john asks for it like that, walk away. Nothing on tape that could hurt you, right?"

"Okay."

"You gonna be okay, Jim? Listen, I was serious. You won't be doing this shit long. But you gotta start at the bottom, just like everybody else."

Jim nodded. "I guess."

Kerry slapped him on the shoulder blades. "Do your ten, that's it for the day. I'll see you later. If anything comes up, check with Darnell."

Jim glanced to where Darnell was standing. When he turned back, Kerry was already several strides away, moving out, not looking back.

Well, Jim thought, *my first real job. I'm a dope dealer. Not exactly what I had planned for the future, just three weeks ago. . . .*

Darnell whistled softly. A woman was coming, dragging a little kid along by one hand. He watched as she approached. She reminded him of Tabitha. A housewife, a mother. Surely not?

"Mister? I ain't seen you before. You new?"

"Yeah," Jim said.

She seemed uncertain. "Maybe you can help me out? I'm looking for a vitamin shop?"

"Ten creds for directions, ma'am," he said, still not quite believing he was doing this.

She carried a small tote bag. Now she rummaged inside, while the little kid stood looking up at Jim. She brought out a small, copper-colored chip and handed it to Jim. He swiped it across his encrypted reader and handed it back.

She looked around. "The directions?" she prodded.

Jim signaled Darnell, keeping his hand resting discreetly on the side of his leg. He saw Darnell nod and move toward the barf-bag dispenser.

"You want to be careful of those vitamins," Jim said. "Sometimes they can make you sick to your stomach." He tilted his head in the direction of the dispenser. She turned, saw it, smiled.

"Oh, yes," she said.

That was the first time. It also marked the first night he began to have nightmares, but he didn't make the connection till later.

6

Late at night, long after the overhead lights in the dorm had dimmed, Jim lay on his bunk and stared up at the distant ceiling. He thought about peer pressure. In his studies of gang culture, back in a previous life when he studied such things instead of living them, much was made of peer pressure. Now he thought that was probably wrong. At least partly. Because not everybody belonged to a gang. Everybody didn't demand that you join a gang. It wasn't something everybody did. Or could do. He had already learned that much. Kerry made a big deal of it, that not just anybody joined up with the Stone Cowboys. No, you had to want to join, and the Cowboys had to want you.

Peer meant equal. It didn't necessarily mean *like*. He wasn't really like the other Cowboys. They were mostly Plebs, raised in a subculture he had no experience with and understood in only the most cursory fashion. But he was equal to them. The Cowboys came from dysfunctional families, or no families at all. Most of the boys lived in the youth dorms, rootless and unconnected. The gang was their family.

And he had no family either. He'd once thought he did, but they had abandoned him. Oh, Carl could put as pretty a face on it as he wanted, could even mean it. It might even be the truth, that he'd sent Jim away to keep him safe. But in the end Carl and Tabitha had left him, no more and no less than Darnell's mom had abandoned him.

A few weeks before, he had possessed a home, a family, a past, and a future. Now he had none of these. There was no clear, clean path to the Solis Space Academy, with his mom and dad behind him all the way, applauding his success, loving him.

Now there was nothing but today and, with luck, tomorrow. If he wanted a family, he would have to find his own. As it turned out, it had found him.

Peer pressure? No, peer acceptance. They thought he was a little high-and-mighty. He could see it in Darnell's cautious reserve, and in Ferrick's more obvious suspicion.

But Kerry liked him, and so did Sam. Like any family, though, you had to prove yourself. Live by the rules. Do the necessary chores.

For some reason that comforted him. Rules, chores, obligations, loyalties. A structure to replace the structure he himself had shattered forever.

He wondered if Carl or Tabitha would understand. Probably not.

And did it matter, if they understood? He had betrayed them, but they had also betrayed him. The points were even, and he was alone. If he wanted a life, he would have to make it for himself. By himself. That was his own punishment.

On my own, he thought. Life was messy. You did the best you could with what you had. Peer pressure? No, more like peer longing. He *pined* for what the Cowboys could give him. For the balm they offered to his bruised soul. Friendship, loyalty, structure—and Sam. How great a price would he pay for this? Almost anything.

He closed his eyes. The sense of déjà vu was so strong he

wanted to scream. Instead, he gritted his teeth and thought of Sam, even though thinking of her made the feelings worse.

No wonder they called it "Heat."

7

My name is Harry, he thought. He hung on to it. The identity. He knew who he was. As long as he knew who he was, things couldn't be completely gone, could they?

It was a better life than he'd known back on Terra. Better than any of them had known. He didn't even have to think about *that.* All he needed to do was look around this nice apartment. Bigger than the old one, plenty of space for Doris and the two kids. The kids loved the trees, all the open space. Eight-year-old Sally picked flowers and dried them, had fifty or sixty of them frozen in little plastic cubes. Jimmy had taken up sky-kiting, riding the big plastic gliders that looked like batwings, up in the center of the ship where gravity dwindled to nothing. Only ten years old, and floating like a bird. . . .

A better life than they'd had when he was only a tech third grade, working for OmniComp. Now he had his own section, or would, when the new colony finally got going. Something to look forward to. . . .

Damn. Crying again. The Heat had worn off, at least the first great rushing fling of it. That was something new, too. The Heat. There hadn't been anything like that back in SoCal Region Six, North American Population Unit, Greater Western Hemisphere, Terra. And he'd always had a little bit of a problem with that. He knew he was a man. Had two fine kids to prove it, didn't he? But Doris, something about her. About the way she was after. Sort of blah, not really excited. He could tell it wasn't everything it should have been. Good enough to make kids, but that was really just the mechanicals. Put the sperm here and let it run there and nine months later, the magic of life.

There should be more, shouldn't there? He'd always thought so. Some wild magic in the act itself. Surely God wouldn't have made it so pleasant if you weren't supposed to enjoy it. Get something out of it beyond the technical act of creation?

Face so slick. Sticky. Wet with tears. Tears?

So dark in the room. And Doris so quiet. It had been good. Even in the hollow, chilly letdown afterward, he knew it had been good. Maybe the best ever. The way she'd screamed out loud. But now it was dark, a red-tinged darkness, and his face was sticky.

Hands sticky.

So tired. Maybe it would better to sleep now. Sink back into the red dark and never wake up. Never hear Doris screaming again.

Never.

Oh God, what have I done?

8

Jim stared at the horror on the big holovid screen in the recreation room. The pseudo-leather of the recliner raised a film of sweat on his back.

The face reappeared. The man. His name was Harry. They'd put the cameras on him afterward, and his expression was peaceful. His eyes were closed, his lips slack. There were red streaks like welts down his cheeks where he'd clawed himself.

The newsies panning back, back, to take in what they all called the scene of the tragedy. Jim looked away when he couldn't stand it anymore. The forms, two small ones, two larger. Arranged about the bedroom beneath impossible splashes, as if some mad demon had taken his crimson paintbrush to the walls. Some mad demon.

Harry's face back on the screen. Except for the claw marks,

an average face. Receding hairline, broad forehead, a honker of a nose. Regular lips, a blocky chin. Could have been anybody, except for where he'd gouged out his own eyes.

A guy named Harry.

He hadn't used that name when Jim had sold him two packs of Heat the day before. He hadn't used any name at all.

And now he never would again.

9

"No, man, that's bullshit, and that's all it is." Kerry slapped the table for emphasis. An old guy and his wife looked up, like startled birds, from the other table in front of the small restaurant.

"Kerry, I sold him that shit. Two packs. He knew all about it, knew about the barf-bag dispenser. He was a regular."

"So? There are a lot of regulars. Who do you think pays the bills, anyway?" Kerry tensed, then visibly forced himself to relax. He leaned back in his chair. "So he went nuts. But there wasn't any connection." He shook his head. "You know how much of this shit we peddle?"

Jim shook his head.

"A lot. A *lot*. If there was something screwy with Heat, this whole damned ship would be a slaughterhouse." He leaned forward again, his expression intent. "And here's something else. I don't want you talking about this craziness. Crap like this gets out, it could be bad for business."

"Bad for business? I hope to God it would," Jim said.

"You're not listening to me, Jim. I swear on—" He looked around. "On my mother's grave, Heat doesn't have anything to do with this."

"Man, I'm telling you, I sold it to him. And twenty-four hours later he goes wackoid and murders his two little kids and his wife. And himself."

"You may know a lot, buddy, but you don't know much about this ship. You think he's the first one?"

Jim bit into his croissant, couldn't taste anything, put it down. "I don't know. So what? Isn't one enough?"

"There have been others. Some worse. You can look them up in NewsNet archives. But they know what causes it. Even have a name for it. 'The Rage,' they call it. It hits Plebs mostly. The shrinks say it has to do with the change in environment. Take a bunch of Plebs out of their cozy little Plebtowns and stick them into a giant tin can and shoot them off into space. For some of them, it's quite a shock to the nervous system. Maybe too much of a shock. And they go weird. You've heard about the Pleb Psychosis?"

"Sure, I've heard of it."

Kerry said, "I've got to pee." He stood up and vanished back into the restaurant.

Pleb Psychosis, Jim thought, suddenly uncertain. There wasn't much of that on Wolfbane, but some. A few stories. Plebs suddenly went violently nuts for no apparent reason. Not many, and not often, though he'd heard it was a hell of a lot worse on Terra. The experts thought it had to do with bad self-esteem or something. Plebs were social leftovers. They never went hungry, they were always given a decent roof over their heads, an adequate income. But they had nothing to do. There was no place for them in the dazzling world of high technology, and hadn't been for a hundred years. Plebs didn't work. Other experts said it was no accident that most of the colonists who went out came from the Pleb class. Out on the raw, new planets there were things a man could do with his hands alone. Most of the people on this ship were Plebs. So maybe . . .

"Anyway, I was saying," Kerry said as he sat down, "you got your head up your butt if you think Heat is a problem. Plebs are a problem. That's all there is to it."

"Is Pleb Psychosis this violent?"

"Can be. Some of the riots I've seen. The crowds pulled people apart. Just tore them up."

Jim tried to imagine it, and couldn't. He'd never thought he could imagine what he'd seen on the holovid either. Never imagined anything like Harry.

He took a deep breath. "It scared me, man. Maybe I made too

many connections. Ended up in the wrong place."

Kerry's pale blue eyes picked at his face. "You did, Jim. It isn't the Heat." He grinned. "It's that some people are just plain screwed. And most of them are Plebs." His grin was sour.

"Okay," Jim said.

"Then everything's cool?"

"Harry isn't, but . . ." Jim sighed. "It's too late for Harry."

"You want to send flowers or something? To the funeral?"

"There'll be a funeral?" For some reason, he hadn't thought of that.

"Sure. What do you think we are out here? Savages?"

Jim closed his eyes. "It's called 'The Rage,' huh?"

"Yeah," Kerry said. "The Rage."

CHAPTER NINE

1

They held the funeral two days later. There was a nice wreath, white roses and blue moonflowers, from the Cowboys, though their name wasn't on the ribbon.

Jim stood on the steps in front of the little chapel, a small crowd eddying around him, and watched the caskets go down. Stainless-steel boxes with rounded corners, polished to a nice sheen. The men and women who carried them looked like anybody. Two dozen of them, six to a coffin. Plus the rest of the mourners. A lot of people who cared about Harry and his little family.

The pallbearers loaded the steel coffins into a gravcar and slammed the rear hatch. The vehicle looked as if it had recently been painted black, not very well. A purple glimmer glowed through the sloppy job, and some ghostly letters: ABX—1228. It was a hearse today, but tomorrow it would be back on the job hauling steel or dirt or something just as dead as what it was carrying now.

He sensed somebody staring at him, turned, and saw an elderly woman wearing a shapeless brown dress, clutching a huge handbag, dabbing at her nose with a white hankie. Her eyes were red from weeping. He started to turn away, but she dropped the handkerchief, and said, "You. Boy. Come here."

He pointed at his chest. *Who, me?*

She nodded, the movement so sharp it set her gray hair, caught in a loose scarf at the back of her head, to swaying.

He edged through the crowd, which was already breaking up,

streaming down toward the hearse, until he stood next to her. She peered up at him, a fierce expression on her face. There were deep furrows at the corners of her eyes and running down from her nose.

She examined him for a long moment. "Who are you?" she said suddenly. "Why are you here?"

He didn't know what to say. "I'm a friend."

"You aren't no friend of them. She was my niece, Doris. I know all their friends. You aren't no friend of his, either. He didn't *have* any friends. The filthy murderer."

Jim stepped back without realizing it. "I'm sorry."

She glared at him. "You? Sorry? What are you? One of those freaks that likes to go to funerals? Like a vulture, feeding off other people's grief."

"Look, ma'am, I don't—"

"Oh, *ma'am.* Listen to him, *ma'am.* You talk pretty, boy, but I know what you are. I know what Harry was doing. And he got it from trash like you. My poor niece, she wasn't good enough for him. She wasn't *enough* for him. So he had to use his science. A pill for everything." She looked up at him again, her lips drawing back in a snarl of pure hatred. "And his pills got him *that!*" She wrapped her ancient fingers around Jim's arm and turned him, digging her nails in.

"*Look at him, boy. Look at them, my poor niece, her innocent children!*" she hissed. "*You did that! Your kind!*"

Jim threw his hands up. "I didn't—I can't—"

Chills rippled his spine. He was frozen in her witchy glare.

"I know what you are," she said in a voice that curdled his soul. "And I say you *did!*"

She spit in his face, turned, and walked away.

2

"Jeez, Sam, I just don't know. That little old lady. She was horrible. She didn't even know me, but she spit on me. Because of what she thought I was."

She seemed distant, preoccupied. Her set expression said she didn't want to hear about any of this. But Jim couldn't seem to stop himself from talking. There were ugly things floating around in his skull. Those four polished metal boxes, especially the two little ones. Harry's face, slack and still, with bloody holes for eyes. Harry couldn't stand to look at what he'd done, so he left it for everybody else to look at.

Harry the way he'd first seen him, a short, pudgy guy, bouncing up, looking to buy his Heat, not furtive at all. Happy, in fact.

"You the new guy?" he'd said, and Jim had nodded.

"Great. I need a couple, okay?"

"Sure," Jim said, and gave the signal. Ferrick was running stash for him. Jim watched him drift toward the barf-bag dispenser.

"Got your chip? It's twenty," Jim told the pudgy little man, who bobbed his head as he handed it over. Brisk and bored at the same time. A stone regular.

"You're all set," Jim told him as he handed the chip back. "You know—"

"Yeah, yeah, I know," the guy said. Harry said. "My belly gets to me all the time. Never know when I might have to heave it up." Then he grinned, bounced two fingers off his forehead like a captain boarding his vessel, saluting the peons, and ambled off toward the dispenser. And the next time Jim saw him was on the vid, but Harry couldn't see him.

"You've got to get over this," Sam told him. She was standing in front of a wide counter, examining a red-and-blue batwing. The clerk, a greasy guy with pimples and a wad of gum moving slowly in his bony jaws, leaned on the counter and examined her.

Asshole, Jim thought. "Hey," he said. "You. Show me something, too."

The clerk lifted his chin, his gaze turning smart-ass. "Yeah? What do you want to see?"

Jim half leaned over the counter. For some reason he was sure that smacking this wise-ass right in the mouth would make him feel worlds better. Smacking something, anyway, and this jerk was the closest thing handy.

The guy must have sensed it, or seen it in his eyes, because he suddenly raised both hands and took a step back. "Whoa, man. You want a wing, I'll get you a wing. But ice it, okay?"

"Yeah. Ice it," Jim said.

"You want any color in particular?"

"Whatever. . . ."

"Get red," Sam said. "Red would look nice, with your eyes and hair."

"Hey, what is this? A fashion show?"

She stopped. "It isn't gonna be anything if you don't lose that attitude. Unless you can explain to me why I should waste a whole afternoon kiting with a guy who can't do anything but smartmouth me all day long."

"Is that what this is? A waste?"

She pushed the wing back over the counter. "That's it. Don't call me, I'll call you."

She was ten feet away before he could think of anything to say. "Hey, Sam. Wait!"

Evidently that wasn't the right thing, because she didn't even look back, just kept on going, her butt a quivering study in indignation.

"Aw, shit," Jim said.

"Hey, buddy. You gonna rent this wing or not?"

Jim turned, looked back for Sam, but she was gone. He looked at the clerk, who had momentarily stopped chewing his gum. He scratched at a pimple instead. "Women," he said. "Can't live with them—"

"Yeah. Gimme the wing. But not that fracking red one. The black one."

"Yeah? How come?"

"It matches my eyes," Jim said.

"Huh? Your eyes are green."

"Just give me the damned wing," Jim said.

The clerk got a good squeeze and popped the largest pimple

on his chin. He checked the result on the tip of his finger as he watched Jim drag his wing off toward the launch area.

"Everybody's crazy," the clerk muttered. He wiped his fingertip on his pants, then reached into his pocket for a reload on the gum.

3

"Ouch! Damn. . . ." Jim stuck his index finger into his mouth, sucked, tasted blood. The cut was small, but nasty. The edges of the tiny circuit boards were the worst. He'd always had problems doing the really fine work.

Not that this was even close to ideal conditions. He was almost upside down, his feet up on his bunk, his head halfway under his desk. He could only work by the dim glow of the wall light, which wasn't aimed right in the first place. Luckily, the innards of the comm unit were fairly basic. Even working as much by feel as sight, he was able to find the security module. Getting it out wasn't difficult, just painstaking in the cramped quarters.

He took his finger out of his mouth and pulled the tiny module the rest of the way out. He got himself straightened up, sat down at his desk, and placed the module in the center of a white sheet of paper. The paper made for better contrast, and he needed all the help he could get.

He opened the compact case of electronics tools. He'd had the set for years. Carl had given it to him. He took out a small vanadium pick and leaned forward, squinting. Yep. There was a hardwired safety interlock protecting the module's core. He probed it with the tip of the pick, held his breath, then continued.

It wasn't all that complicated, but it would take a while to get it right.

4

Security on a colony ship with ten million passengers was less a problem than Jim had supposed. The reason was simple: Everything was under twenty-four-seven surveillance. The ship had been built that way. He doubted if the original intention was population management. More likely, it had to do with what the *Outward Bound* was: a ship in space. It might be twenty miles long and four miles thick. It might have its own interior weather. But beyond its hull was a trillion miles of vacuum. There were all kinds of things that could go wrong, in all kinds of unlikely places. You had to be able to watch it all the time. And when you built it from scratch, you could do that. Just add camera cells and feeds to the specs for everything. Then hook everything into a big computer.

The big computer made things even easier. Hack into it, and you could see whatever it saw. Which was pretty much everything.

He put an alert tag on the files for Kerry, Sam, Darnell, and Ferrick, and then he waited. He wasn't sure what he was waiting for, but something.

In the meantime, since he now had access, he began to rummage through other files. Honeg turned out to be what he looked like: a Pleb of uncertain background and a long history of petty crime. A brawler, a wirehead participant in three Pleb riots, suspected of several clumsy burglaries on Terra, convicted of three robberies aboard the *Outward Bound* before he got it into his thick skull that he wasn't still on Terra, and everything he did went into the security files.

Harry Osterlund was a different story, and given what had happened, an unsettling one. To start with, he wasn't a Pleb, nor were any of his family. He'd worked for a medium-sized nanotech developer on Terra, and signed up for the colonization effort apparently believing his future prospects would be better in the new colony. According to his file, he was probably right: His company was participating in the venture, and he'd gotten a nice promotion for signing on. He wasn't a wirehead, didn't even have the basic socket for it. No previous criminal history, no indications of mental instability. Just an average mid-class guy, going minor places at minor, but steady, speed. As ordinary as he looked.

His file contained scenes from the bedroom where he'd murdered his equally ordinary family, pictures that hadn't been on the public holovids. Jim couldn't look at those very long.

He knew one thing: Despite what Kerry had told him about Plebs and their problems, Harry hadn't suffered from Pleb Psychosis or any other obvious emotional dysfunction. He was just a nebbish kind of guy, trying to add a little excitement to his sex life. Yet something had turned him into a monster. The little old lady at the funeral thought she knew what it was.

Maybe she did.

5

"Hey, look, I'm sorry. I was an asshole," Jim said.

Sam was working a corner with Jenny. Jenny was dealing the dope and collecting the money, and Sam was handling the stash drop. They were using a big concrete pot that held a small willow tree. *Very pastoral,* Jim thought. *Two milkmaids out in the country with a pocketful of drugs.*

He'd given it three days for her to cool off, then went looking. He didn't find her right away and had to ask Kerry about it. Kerry thought it was hilarious.

"Lover's tiff," he chortled.

"Are you chortling at me?" Jim said.

"Huh. I guess I am. Damn. I never thought I'd chortle."

"Chortle this," Jim said.

When Kerry stopped laughing, he told Jim where Sam was staked out with Jenny. It was up near the agriculture decks, and it really was sort of like the country. If you could get used to countryside that had a whole lot more countryside hanging way up in the sky.

It smelled nice and clean, though. Jim noticed that right away, a dark, earthy aroma that reminded him of Wolfbane.

"Then you admit you were a jerk?" Sam said, but she didn't sound mad anymore.

"I was a jerk," he said. "No doubt about it, a one hundred percent jerk. Am I forgiven?"

She blinded him with a smile. "Let me think about it. . . okay," she said.

"Okay?"

"Okay, you're forgiven."

It must have been coincidence that a couple of robins in the willow tree burst into song just then. He turned toward the sound, and said, "Where late the sweet birds sang. . . ."

"That's pretty. Is it some kind of poetry?" she asked.

"Some kind, yeah."

Her expression grew wistful. "I wish I knew stuff like that. Poetry. They don't teach Plebs poetry. They don't teach Plebs much of anything, come right down to it."

They'd never talked much about her background. She'd change the subject when he tried. He'd checked her files, but they didn't say much. Mother dead, father abandoned her at the age of ten. Raised in a crèche until she reached adulthood at fourteen. He could have pushed it further with the computers, but looking into her life without her permission felt too much like treachery.

He moved closer, until he could smell raspberries mixed into the scent of the earth. "Nothing stopping you. From reading poetry, I mean."

She shrugged. "I don't read much."

The archived file on her educational records was one of the things he hadn't pushed into. A little snooping was one thing, but checking on her school grades was something else again. The thought struck him: *Can she read at all?*

He had just enough presence of mind not to blurt out the question, but it was a near thing. He felt a quiver when he realized how close he'd come, and covered himself quickly.

"I could read them to you. We could do it together."

She brightened. "That would be real nice. Romantic, like." She stared at him. "You really are different. From the other guys," she said. "I shouldn't get mad at you."

"No, you shouldn't."

"No, no," she said. "It's not like that. I mean the other day. You were all messed up about that dead guy. And bugging me about it. But I never stopped to think. Wherever you came from, dead guys, especially tore up like that, you probably didn't see a lot of that kind of shit, so it would mess you up. The guys I know, they saw the same things I did. So I probably treated you the same way I'd act with them, if they started moaning around about some dead guy they didn't even know."

"Dead guys were real common with you?"

She shrugged again. "Enough. I lived in a Plebtown." As if that explained everything. Maybe it did.

He knew he was stepping over a boundary, one he maybe shouldn't cross, but he had to know. "Did anybody ever love you?" he asked.

She tried a grin. "You do. Say you do, anyway."

"No, I mean when you were a kid."

"You mean before the Cowboys?"

"I guess."

She considered it, then shook her head. "No. Nobody ever loved me before I joined up."

"But afterward."

"Why do you think I joined up?" she said.

He looked away, hoping she wouldn't notice she'd just broken his heart a little. What a life, and she didn't even know. Took it for granted. She looked over his shoulder, and said, "Biz coming."

"Oh, sorry." He moved away, to give the john some room. Jenny had been watching them from a hundred yards away, not so far from the concrete planter, and she waved. He waved back and started toward her, but she motioned him off. Sure. The john would be heading in her direction next.

He turned back toward Sam just in time to see a short, heavyset woman with intense blue eyes walk past him purposefully, nearly running him off the walk in the process. She didn't seem to notice, just steamed onward, all her attention focused on the concrete pot. She wasn't a pretty woman by any means. A crooked scar about a quarter inch wide tracked from her right eyebrow down past the corner of her eye, like a thick white worm. Jim had seen scars like that. Some of the older kids in his martial arts class had sported them. They refused to have them fixed, wore them as badges of honor. He doubted the stocky woman thought of her scar as some kind of Heidelberg dueling memento. More like the mark of a bad memory of a bad night, and somebody's fist.

Sex. Hot sex. That was what she was riveted on, marching like a miniature tank toward the stash in the cement pot. That's what they all wanted. He'd been there. He knew.

"How much did she buy?" he asked Sam.

"Five," Sam said.

"God. A ton."

Sam smiled. "Yeah. She doesn't look it, does she?"

"Hard to imagine." He paused. "Most I ever sold at one time was three. Same thing, somebody you'd never think would use that much."

"I sold twenty-five at one time. I don't think it was wholesale, either. A skinny little guy with bulging eyes. Personally wouldn't touch him with *your* ten-foot pole, but"—she shrugged—"takes all kinds."

"What do you mean, wholesale?"

"If he wasn't buying it for himself. Planning to mark the stuff up, resell it."

"You mean like a dealer? Compete with us?"

"Sure, but not competing. He pays our price, if he wants to sell it again, he has to charge more. Where's the competition? Anyway, if there really was competition, Kerry would have to do something."

"Something?"

"We'd go to war. Like we used to with other stuff."

War. That was interesting. "You've gone to war before? The Cowboys, you mean?"

"Sure. Over turf, over distribution channels, over women." She grinned. "Sometimes just for the hell of it. You saw it."

"I did?"

"Uh-huh. Kerry told me. Hump and some other guys showed up at B Dorm looking for trouble." She glanced at him. "From what I hear, you gave them all they wanted." She pushed against him, looked up at him. Her long, brown eyelashes moved slowly up and down, almost a parody of the helpless maiden. Except there was a feeling of truth buried beneath her half-mocking expression, and his sense of it made him feel absurdly strong, protective. Like a knight or something.

Stupid. But irresistible . . .

"Where does the dope come from? We're in deep space, a million miles from nowhere."

She stiffened. She caught herself quickly and relaxed, but he felt it. *Careful,* he thought. *Watch yourself.*

"Something I said?" he asked.

She moved away from him, turned away so he couldn't see her face. "I dunno. What do you care, where it comes from?"

"No reason. Just curious. I'm selling the shit, after all." He wanted to take her by the shoulders, turn her gently back to him, put his arms around her. Hold her, kiss her. Without Heat.

"You should keep that in mind. What you're doing. All you're doing is selling it, you know? You're a salesman. Not into management, if you understand what I mean. You worry about selling, not about supply. Leave that for Kerry."

"How about you? Are you in management?"

"You're pissing me off again, Jim."

He could see it. Her spine had gone rigid, and she wouldn't look at him. He backed off.

"I'm sorry." He played a chuckle, like putting down a move in checkers. "Remember, I'm just some poor schmuck from a good family. Not an honorable rotten Pleb background."

She flinched, and he regretted it. His damned mouth.

"Is that what it was, Jim? A good family?"

He thought about it. "Not in the end."

6

Jim lay on his bunk and yawned. The alarm he'd set on Kerry's files had beeped him awake about eight bells of the middle watch. He thought about it as he rubbed the sleep from his eyes. One of the weird things about this world that was also a ship in space—they'd revived the practice of sounding the ancient ship's bells to keep track of the time. It wasn't anything like an actual bell ringing—more a soft, cooing sound, like somebody huffing gently across the top of a bottle. *Whoo-whoo*, and a pause. Repeated three more times for eight bells. It was four o'clock in the morning.

"Enlarge screen," he murmured. The holovid on his comm unit doubled in size. "Brighten," he said, and the picture suddenly became sharper, clearer.

He didn't recognize where they were, but he could make out Kerry, Sam, and Darnell easily enough. They were slinking. That was the only word he could think of to describe their careful, furtive movements.

Wherever they were, it was pretty dark. They moved from vague pools of shadow to other equally murky passages. Big, too. Jim got the sense they were in some vast enclosed space, somewhere out of the ordinary.

"Location," he whispered.

Numeric coordinates flashed redly in the upper part of the screen. After a moment, the voice of the computer spoke. It was a feminine voice, canned but soothing: "Secondary cargo bay, central launch fin."

Okay. Jim leaned forward. Getting somewhere now. The cargo bays were where he'd first come aboard. Huge, echoing chambers, not much used now. A few fast ships made the run back and forth between the lumbering *Outward Bound* and the planets she'd left behind. Not many, though. There was no need. The *OB* was mostly self-sufficient.

But if you were getting some special supplies from outside . . .

"Focus," Jim said. "Tight on main subject."

Obediently, whatever camera was trained on Kerry narrowed the field until only his head and shoulders were visible. In the shadowy light the veins in his high forehead stood out like ropes. His jaw was clenched, moving slightly, as if he was grinding his teeth without realizing it.

He stopped, looked at something off-screen that Jim couldn't see. He raised his hand and checked a small comm unit. His lips moved.

"Pick up sound," Jim ordered, barely fast enough to catch the last of it.

". . . lockout areas six five nine and six one zero," Kerry said.

Jim's holovid went dark. Evidently he wasn't the only one who knew about the computer that ran the cameras. But he knew where the secondary bay was. If he hurried, he could be there in ten minutes.

He reached for his socks, pulled them on, and started to hurry.

CHAPTER TEN

1

Jim could hear voices somewhere up ahead, but couldn't make out any words. He was well into the secondary bay, making his way through dimly lit spaces, past large, shrouded shapes. Everything there seemed to be mothballed.

What if it's an orgy? Everybody getting together to do some Heat? he thought suddenly. *I'd look like some kind of asshole then. . . .*

He didn't like to think about Sam that way, but it was a possibility. He had to keep reminding himself that the Cowboys lived different lives than he had. Than he still did, mostly.

The hum of their voices rose and fell, rose again. Sounded like they were arguing about something. He stopped behind a cargo hauler that was covered with protective sheeting and consulted the map in his head. He was near the center of the bay, and they were a hundred yards on. Far enough away he wouldn't be able to hear them at all except for the excellent acoustics of the huge enclosure.

What the hell were they doing? There was no reason for anybody to go to the bay. Just before he'd headed out, he'd checked the docking records for the day. No ships of any kind for the last three days, and none expected for another week.

So if they were meeting somebody, whoever it was wouldn't be coming from the outside. Unless . . .

Damn. No use guessing. The only thing was to see for himself. He glanced around, nerves jumping, then took a deep, silent breath and moved forward. Up ahead a light flared. He crouched lower and kept on going.

2

Kerry was waving his arms around in agitation, as Sam shook her head, and Darnell stood back and looked like he was trying to ignore the whole thing. Jim's curiosity about whatever they were yelling about paled, though, as he got a look at what they were standing in front of. A good-sized cruiser of alien design, four or five hundred feet long, a hundred fifty high. The flare of light came from an open port on the ship. Until that door had opened, the ship had been just another indistinct shadow. There was a gangplank extended, and the three Cowboys stood at the bottom, obviously waiting for somebody.

"This is bullshit!" Kerry shouted suddenly, then turned away from Sam and crossed his arms over his chest.

Jim still couldn't hear what was going on unless they started yelling again. Sam was talking to Kerry's back, but her words were only an imploring buzz.

Getting closer would be tricky. He was hunkered down behind a low grav-hauler. The next hiding place was a good twenty yards ahead, across that much open space. And though the light wasn't good, there was some backwash from the open port. He wouldn't be invisible, if one of them happened to glance in his direction.

Have to risk it. His pulse thudded in his throat as he scuttled forward, mental fingers crossed.

Made it. He ended up crouched behind a low metal wall that separated the gangway areas from the rest of the bay. He waited, breathing hard, until his heart stopped yammering, then peered gingerly over the top of the low wall. A shadow was moving in the light at the head of the gangplank. A *big* shadow.

Kerry and the rest of them turned to look. "About time," Kerry said.

The shadow solidified, moved forward with lumbering grace. Huge, at least eight feet tall. Long arms and . . . hair. Brown, silky hair, all over. A gorilla-like pug-nosed face, the skin bright orange. Oddly familiar—what was that ancient space movie? A Wokie, Walkie, something like that. . . .

Except Wokies were a fantasy, and this thing wasn't. Not unless fantasies had taken up smoking cigars. . . .

Jesus! What the hell is it? It seemed to be wearing gloves, and was carrying several large, sealed plastic packets.

He rose another couple of inches, straining for a better look. The gun barrel that gently touched the back of his neck just about stopped his heart.

"I've seen your moves, that martial-arts shit," Ferrick said. "So don't frackin' move, and I won't have to shoot your ass."

3

He felt like a complete idiot as he walked toward Kerry. All of them were watching him, including the Wokie, or whatever the hell it was. Maybe it wasn't going to be so bad. Kerry was actually smiling a little.

"Hold it," Ferrick said from behind him. Jim stopped five feet away from Kerry.

"Listen," Jim said, "it's not what it looks like."

Kerry nodded. Then he stepped forward, whipping his right hand up so quickly Jim never saw it coming. The punch twisted his head sideways and took his legs out from under him as if his spine had been cut. He hit the deck hard, felt something in his knee twist.

Kerry kicked him in the ribs. Something gave way there, too.

"No, no," Jim said, trying to bring his hands up. All that got him was bruised fingers, as Kerry kicked him again.

"I knew it was you, fracker," Kerry said. He still sounded cheerful. "All along." *Thud.* "Fracking asshole." *Thud.* "What the hell you think I am?" *Thud.* "Stupid?" *Thud.*

"Stop it, you'll kill him!" Sam yelled.

Jim was trying to roll himself into as tight a ball as he could. He was focused on a spot of white light deep in the darkness of his skull. The spot was growing smaller. But he heard what she shouted.

Kill me?

The thought echoed, and echoed. Finally, it faded away.

4

Waking up involved stages of growing pain. He knew he'd left the darkness because he was *aware* of darkness. But he felt disconnected, both from the dark behind him and the fuzzy vague glow that was rising around him. It was very quiet. Then he began to hear a distant, pounding roar, like waves crashing on a faraway reef.

The sound grew louder until it was thunder all around him, thunder that throbbed in his knee, his head, his ribs, his hands. That was when he realized he had all those things, and they were all damaged.

Déjà vu surged over him. He'd been badly hurt before, somewhere. Maybe had even died. Silliness. If he'd died, how could he be alive? But the feeling of familiarity was enormously comforting. Somehow it whispered to him that he would survive this, too.

The light came back all at once, almost as great a pain as his injuries. His eyelids came stickily open. A red film obscured his vision. He tasted blood in his mouth, moved his lips, spat. Something wrong with his jaw, too. The feeling of *déjà vu* faded.

"Ungh."

"He's coming out of it," Kerry said.

Jim flinched. "Don't hit me again."

Something soft and cool swiped across his eyes, wiped away the red haze. A faint stinging sensation, the smell of raw alcohol.

Vague shapes began to coalesce in the light. Sam. And Kerry, leaning close, still grinning. Jim would never think of it as a friendly grin again.

"I shoulda frackin' killed you," Kerry said. "I saw you coming from miles away. But we lost you there for a while, when you hacked the computers. I didn't make you for being good enough to crack the ship's machines."

Jim tried to look around, figure out where he was. His neck creaked, and he gasped at the agony of the movement. It was a small room, dimly lit by recessed overheads. The walls were some sort of dark material he'd never seen before, and looked soft and padded. The air smelled strongly of cinnamon and some other odor, sharp and vinegary, he couldn't identify.

Aboard the alien ship, then. . . .

He was lying on a bunk that was far too big for him. Big enough to hold—

A huge shadow shifted in the far corner, moved forward enough that Jim could see a pair of Ping-Pong eyes gleaming with purple fire, focused on him, glowing above a blue cigar about a foot long. Lot of yellowish teeth clenched on that stogie, too.

He ignored the pain and pushed himself up against the wall into a sitting position. He was in his underwear. A clear plastic cast was around his left knee. More clear gunk in a constricting band around his chest and ribs, and the fingers on his right hand were taped together.

"What the hell's wrong with you?" he said. He felt his jaw make funny ratcheting sounds as he spoke. "Are you nuts, like all those other psychos? Is that it?"

"Jim," Sam said warningly.

"Nah. I'm not crazy at all. I told you I saw you coming."

"What the hell is that supposed to mean? Saw me coming? Where do you think I'm coming from?"

Kerry sneered silently, shook his head. "You probably figured it out by now, that we're in the computers, too." He tilted his head toward Ferrick. "That's our guy. Doesn't look it, but he plays those machines like a virtuoso. He's kinda the Cowboys' intelligence capability, you know what I mean? One of the things we keep track of is the newbies. Run all the new colonists through the ringer, check them out. And your name popped up with big red lights and all kinds of bells ringing."

"Huh? My name?"

"Sure. What did you think? Whoever hacked you into the system at the last minute, there on Wolfbane, didn't have time to do much of a job. They tried to make it look like you'd been slated for the colony for a long time, but you hadn't. That was obvious right away. Just like your name. I don't know what your name really is, but it isn't Evanston." He paused. "So what is your real name, Jim? And who do you work for? The Colony Authority? The . . . Agency?"

"I don't know what you're talking about."

Kerry stared at him, the nasty grin flickering on his lips. "Have it your way. Man, you sure were stupid, though. I figured you might work it out, but you didn't."

Jim sighed, shook his head. "You still aren't making any sense, Kerry."

"You know a little about the Cowboys. About me, about what we do. Who I am. Didn't it ever occur to you it was a little strange, me being in the brig?"

Jim realized he'd never even thought about it. But Kerry was right. How did the leader of a powerful gang of drug dealers, with connections all over the ship, end up in a tank full of brawlers and drunks?

"Ah. Comes the dawn," Kerry said. "Of course I was there to take a look at you. And Honeg? Well, Honeg has a taste for Heat. He got his taste scratched, but good. He figured a busted nose was a small price to pay for a month in heaven." Kerry winked at Jim. "So did I."

They think I'm a spy, some kind of undercover agent. They thought so all along. They still *think so. . . .*

"So what's up now?" Jim said. "You going to kill me or not?"

5

Now that, Kerry thought, *is kind of a weird thing to say. No denials, no bullshit, just are you gonna kill me? Like the kid was expecting it or something.* It stopped him.

Because he hadn't really made up his mind. The whole secret-agent thing, it made sense. Sort of. But there were holes. Ferrick had pulled up Jim's name, mostly because of the way it had been inserted. Whoever had done the hack hadn't been all that good—or it had been a quick-and-dirty job. But if it was the Authority, hell, they owned the computers. If they'd done it, it would have been seamless, and Ferrick would never have seen it.

Almost the same thing with the Agency. Kerry had grown up in a Terran Plebtown, and was no stranger to the Agency's shadowy hands. That frackin' Delta guy, big mystery man, had his fingers in everything. A lot more than the average citizen knew, but Kerry had operated on the same fringes the Agency kept an eye on. And if the Agency had done it, they would have either used the Authority for the work, or brought in one of their own tame wizards. Either way, the job would have been a lot better than it was. It just didn't add up. In fact, it smelled more like a private job, something done in a hurry, slapped together on the run.

When it came right down to it, he didn't really know *what* Jim was. There was even the possibility the job had been made to look crude on purpose, to throw anybody off, anybody who might draw the conclusions he already had.

Christ. The simple thing would be to kill him, but . . .

"I don't like the simple things," Kerry said.

He watched the kid as he said it. Jim's chest flattened out a bit, as if he'd been holding his breath. So he was scared, which was the way he wanted him. But there was way too much mystery. How to find out for sure?

Kerry moved over, perched his butt on the edge of the huge bed. Jim flinched back, a tiny movement, quickly covered, but there all the same. Good. A taste of fear never hurt anything.

"Tell you what, Jim," Kerry said, and patted him gently on the knee cast, "we need to talk. Get things worked out." He grinned. "Right?"

Jim nodded.

"So now we'll talk, and if I don't like what I hear, I'll let Ferrick cut your head off."

"Let's talk," Jim said.

6

Jim said, "If you know anything more, don't tell me. Just listen, and see if everything fits up with what you already know. That way, if I don't know, I won't be able to make anything up."

Kerry nodded. "Go on. . . ."

Then Jim told them everything. He knew it was dangerous. Carl had warned him about the guy who had sent Commander Steele and a bunch of killers after his family, but what choice did he have? If he couldn't get out of this, it wouldn't matter about that guy. These guys would do the job.

Ferrick looked like he wanted to.

"So that's it," he said finally. "The story of Jim Endicott, and how he ended up on board the *Outward Bound.*"

There was a long moment of silence. Everybody looked at everybody else. Even the alien made a soft grumbling noise. It was like watching a family gathering, where everybody knew everybody else so well they didn't have to talk.

Oddly enough, it was Darnell who broke the silence. "Armored battle troopers? Man, that's crazy."

Kerry raised one hand. "It sure is. You got anything to back it up?"

"I can show you the letter my dad left me. I wish I could show you the gold, but it's gone."

Kerry glanced away. "No, it isn't."

"What?"

"I already told you. We were on to you from the beginning. You think it was an accident your bag got boosted? Just checking you out, Jim. And all that gold. Way too much for what you were supposed to be." He shrugged. "We took it. Just to throw a wrench in the works. I've read the letter, too."

He paused, thoughtful. "It could all be a plant, of course. But I don't know. I've been trying to work it out. All that other shit, too. The picture of your family. Your cute little spaceship. Why go to all that trouble, and then do such a crappy job with the computer hack?"

"'Cause there wasn't any time. That's all I can think of. I didn't know any of this was going to happen."

Kerry seemed to have calmed down a lot. Chewing on the puzzle had cooled him off.

"Okay. So let's say I buy it. Just for the moment. Then that raises a bunch of other problems."

"Yeah. I know," Jim said.

"Like why were you sneaking around here tonight?"

"Uh-huh."

"Well, why were you?"

Jim picked his words as carefully as he could. "Because I think Heat is some kind of shit that makes people into crazy killers, and I wanted to find out where you were getting it."

"That shit. You're nuts, man," Ferrick said. He glanced at Kerry. "Let me do him, man. This is all bullshit."

The chill in his voice transferred itself to Jim's spine, but before he could reply, Kerry said, "You really believe that?"

"Yeah. I do."

Kerry smiled. "Jim, meet Ur-Barrba. Ur-Barrba, meet Jim Endicott."

The big alien lumbered forward. Up close, it was even bigger than it first appeared. The cinnamon-vinegar scent billowed from the cigar and clung to it like a personal fogbank.

"Jim Endicott," it said, the voice a guttural roar.

"We get the shit from her," Kerry said.

7

Jim sensed that the emotional climate had shifted a bit. Kerry had backed off from his initial anger, though he was far from convinced. Darnell was a harder read. Jim thought the other boy wanted to be friendly again, but needed a solid reason. Ferrick was the scary one: He didn't like Jim, and nothing Jim had said had changed that at all. And Sam? He thought she was going both ways at once. They'd shared Heat together. That counted for something, but not enough.

At least they were all talking. For the moment.

"I know you've got this weird bug up your ass about Heat," Kerry was saying. "But I already told you. Plebs are weird. The psychosis."

"Harry wasn't a Pleb. Didn't wirehead, didn't do anything. Except Heat," Jim said.

"So? Does that mean he can't go nuts? There's ten million people on this can, Jim. Not all of them are Plebs. And not all of them are like totally sane, either. Man, how many times you hear it? Somebody goes off like Harry, and all the neighbors and family say that he was such a nice fellow. Such a quiet guy, just can't imagine him doing such awful things."

Jim nodded. It was true.

"Look. What about that other guy, the one who jumped me for no reason? I saw him eating his own fracking fingers! And he tried to kill me."

"Okay, that's two. I don't have the benefit of your fine education, Jim, but I read stuff. Even wild-ass stuff like basic statistics. You know anything about that?"

"Sure."

"Okay. So what do your stats say about a sample of two? Out of ten million?"

"I'm not saying I've got proof. What the hell you think I was doing crawling around in the dark here, sneaking after you? I was looking for proof." He raised his hands. "Okay, okay, so I didn't find any. But that doesn't mean it isn't out there."

He took a deep breath, trying to figure it out. "Maybe there's another way. Using those statistics. And Ferrick and me."

Ferrick didn't like that. Didn't want Jim bringing him in on it. He grunted.

"Sorry, but Ferrick has to be in on it. 'Cause it's computer stuff, and you wouldn't trust me by myself, right?"

Kerry nodded.

"So do it this way. We both go into the ship's computers, each checking the other. Kind of a fail-safe."

"All right," Kerry said. "What does that get us?"

"We look for this kind of stuff. Very specific. Psycho crap, extremely violent episodes involving murder, or that could have ended up as murder. Self-mutilation, too," Jim added, thinking about it. "Harry gouged out his eyes. That other one ate his own fingers. That's strange. It would stand out in the reports."

"And? If we find stuff like that?"

"Check it," Jim said. "Statistics. If there's an abnormal number for the population, then we know."

"Know what?" Kerry asked. "We know there's an abnormal number. We don't know if Heat's the cause."

He was right. But what else was there? "I know," Jim said. "But it would be a start."

Kerry chewed it over. "You're honest, at least. Tell me one thing. Why would I want to let you do this? Heat's how I make my living. How all of us do."

"I'm gambling," Jim said.

"What's the bet?"

Jim shrugged. "That you'd kill me if you had good reason. But I can't see you slaughtering lots of innocent people just to make a cred. Not if you know that's what you're doing."

Kerry stared at him for what seemed a long time. "Okay, you win your bet. For now. We'll do it."

"Kerry," Ferrick said.

"Shut up."

Ferrick subsided. Kerry glanced at the alien. "How about you, herbal? You selling us poison? Kill all the dirty humans?"

Ur-Barrba had been studying what looked to Jim like a translator disk of odd design. Now she looked up and began to rumble.

"Use the translator," Kerry said. "Too hard to understand you."

More rumbles, a couple of gestures with those huge, six-fingered hands. The voice came out high and tinny. "We don't run health studies and safety studies. If our product kills you, it's your problem. But if it does, we didn't know about it."

"Fair enough," Kerry said.

"Do you want this shipment or not?"

Kerry considered. "I'll let you know."

"Forty-eight of your small-time units. Hours. Can you cover my presence that long?"

Kerry glanced over. "Ferrick?"

"I'll hack the machines. Put this bay off-limits. Repairs or something. Nobody's due for a while. Should work."

"Yeah, you're covered," Kerry told the alien.

"Forty-eight hours," Ur-Barrba agreed. "Then I go. Whether you buy or not."

Kerry turned to Jim. "There's your timetable, pal. Is it enough?"

"It'll have to be, won't it?"

"Uh-huh," Kerry said. "After that, Ferrick gets you."

Ferrick grunted again. He liked that part.

8

"Why do you hate me?" Jim asked Ferrick.

The stocky boy shook his head. "Don't hate nobody. It gets in the way. You got to keep a clear head. A cool head." He stared at Jim. "You don't never want to kill anybody in hot blood. If you do, then you'll always wonder if you made a mistake. And you don't want to be wondering about that, not with killing. Like I said, it gets in the way."

That scared Jim about as much as anything. Ferrick's chilly, calculating gaze. As if measuring him for one of those polished-steel boxes. Once Ferrick had it worked out in his own mind that it was the right thing to do, he would kill Jim in an instant.

And his pulse probably wouldn't even skip a single beat.

Ferrick had a room in the clubhouse. Jim had never seen it before, hadn't even known it was there. Ferrick went through three different locks, all coded either to his palm or his password, to get inside. It was about the same size as the bedroom Jim had lived in while recovering from his injuries—and where he would no doubt be staying again to recover from his latest breaks, bruises, and contusions. He felt like an old man, stiff and achy, and he moved like one. He wondered if maybe he could take Ferrick in a fair fight, then decided it didn't matter. It wouldn't be a fair fight, not till he was recovered. Besides, he'd already seen Ferrick's gun. It wasn't anywhere as big as Jim's vanished .75, but it would do the job just fine.

"You know how to use that gun of yours, I guess," Jim said.

Ferrick nodded. "I guess."

"Well, we'd better get started."

The room was crowded with home-brewed comm equipment. Most of the cases were off, wires running everywhere, infrared data relays, some powerful-looking bubble processors. A lot of money involved, despite the crude appearances. No wonder Ferrick had been able to keep track of him. All the time he'd thought he was being so sneaky clever, the dark boy had been watching. And probably laughing at him. And getting his mind settled into the cool, calm state he required to kill him.

"What, exactly, are we gonna look for?" Ferrick said. "I need to know, for the search programs." Ferrick paused. "Are you any good at designing code modules? Tell me the truth. I'd like to split this up, make it go faster. But if you're just playing at it, I'll have to do it all myself."

"I'm okay. Maybe better than okay."

"I'll take your word. Your work was pretty good, using that rinky-dink dorm comm unit for the hack. What'd you do, override the hardwired security module by hand?"

"I thought you guys knew everything already," Jim said.

"Never looked at your room," Ferrick said. "Didn't care how you did it, just cared what you did." He wandered over to a bank of machines and began to energize touch pads. "I just want you to know, up front," he said.

"What's that?"

"I don't believe any of that shit you handed Kerry. Kerry's

okay, but sometimes he's a little soft. Lets the way he wants things to be influence how he sees things are." Ferrick shrugged. "He likes you. I don't give a crap one way or the other. What I think is, you're some kind of agent. And in the end I'm gonna kill you."

Jim limped over and joined him. "We'd better get started," he said. "How about you do the search programs, and I handle the statistics evaluation?"

"Suits me," Ferrick said.

Jim lifted a voice tablet and turned it on. His busted fingers wouldn't let him code by hand. "Where's that Ur-Barrba come from, anyway?"

Ferrick kept his eyes on the screen in front of him. "You don't need to worry about that," he said. "Far as you're concerned, it may never come up."

"Is that right?"

"Very right," Ferrick told him.

CHAPTER ELEVEN

1

They worked straight through, forty hours without a break. Jim plugged an electrostim into the cybersocket embedded beneath his ear to keep himself going and drank a lot of coffee. Ferrick popped some small green pills whenever he began to flag. The pills made his eyes glow like radioactive raisins, and he sweated a lot, but his fingers danced across his touch pad like a SWAT team of epileptic ants.

"Bingo," Jim said.

Ferrick yawned. He hadn't changed his clothes for almost three days, and it showed. Smelled, too. "Bingo what?"

"There's correlation."

"Explain that."

Jim pushed a sheaf of wrinkled printouts toward him. It was quicker to scan the annotated paper than bring the interesting bits up on a screen.

"That stuff I've underlined. You guys really got your operation rolling about a year after the *Outward Bound* was in space, right?"

Ferrick's exhausted gaze wandered away. "Could have been."

"It was, wasn't it?" Jim felt excitement begin to sprout through his foggy brain. "You can see it, right there. The *Outward Bound* started off with six million original colonists from Terra. It took maybe half a year to get them all loaded and settled. You guys came aboard then."

"Yeah," Ferrick mumbled. "I came up in the third month. It was a mess."

"Then the *OB* took off and hit five major established colonies and picked up another three million or so. That took another year, but by then you guys had started putting it together. And we've added the last million here and there, by freighter and barge. It's still going on, I guess. More people coming on board."

Ferrick nodded. "Okay, and so?"

"It's plain as—" Jim was about to say plain as the nose on your face, but with Ferrick's magnificent snout. . . "Plain as day. A year after launch, the *Outward Bound* had a population of seven million or so. Adjusting for population growth, I tracked the incidence of reported violent psychosis. You can't tell me my analysis is bullshit, 'cause I used the numbers you gave me."

Ferrick rattled the papers, rubbed his eyes, squinted. "Okay, I won't argue the numbers."

"Don't you see it?"

"I'm working, I'm working on it. . . ."

Jim reached over and jabbed at a block of print circled in red. "Right there, Ferrick. Those kinds of incidents were steady for the first year. About half a percent of the total population. At the end of the year they jumped, not just in number, but in percentage. Starting at the beginning of the second year, they went to two percent, and doubled to four by the end of year two. A four hundred percent increase starting at the end of the first twelve months, then another hundred percent the next year. That's huge, Ferrick. The rate of increase is holding steady, too. We're at the end of year three now, starting into year four, with three to go before arrival. Eight percent of the population, if your numbers are right, experienced a violent psychotic episode last year."

Ferrick's lips moved silently as he traced the numbers with a blunt finger. His forehead wrinkled. "Eight percent? That's . . . man, that's weird."

"You didn't give me the numbers for it, Ferrick, but it would be interesting to run a comparison study. Between your increase in the sales of Heat, and the increase in the violence over the same time line. Wouldn't it?"

"If you think I'm gonna give you that data—"

Jim shook his head. "I'm not asking for it. Run the numbers yourself. Then tell me."

Ferrick stared at him. Something was going on with his expression. Getting softer, collapsing somehow. Worried . . .

"I don't have to," he said. "I handle the books." He paused. "It's pretty close, Jim." It was the first time he'd used Jim's name since they'd caught him.

Maybe, Jim thought.

"So, what do you think?"

Ferrick shifted uncomfortably. "I didn't have any idea the numbers were so big. Eight percent? People would be yelling. It would be all over ShipNet."

"Not if the Authority was trying to keep it covered up. You hacked their security cores for your data. Is there any way to compare those private numbers with the ones they're putting out for public consumption?"

Ferrick grunted. "Give me half an hour."

Jim nodded. "I'm gonna get some shuteye."

Ferrick was back at work. "Crash in the chair there. I'll wake you up when I'm done."

"How come I can't use one of the bedrooms?" Jim stretched, felt his cracked ribs protest. "Man, I'm beat."

"So I know where you are. Until we get this shit straightened out, you're still mine."

His voice had gone cold again. "Okay," Jim said. "I'll crash in the chair."

2

Jim's first clue that Ferrick was really upset was when the other boy woke him up by kicking the legs of the chair and dumping him onto the floor.

"Jesus! Man, are you trying to kill me?" Jim mumbled, then realized what he'd said.

Ferrick stood over him, waving a fresh sheaf of printouts. His eyes looked like boiled plums.

"All right, wise-ass. You got it right. The Authority *has* been doctoring the numbers. Big-time."

He waited until Jim managed to crawl back into his seat, rubbing a couple of fresh bruises.

"So what is pissing you off so much?"

Ferrick slapped the printouts against his thigh. "I don't . . . know, damn it! I thought I had everything figured out, but . . ." He took a deep breath. "Something's really screwed up here, man. Screwed up big-time."

Jim wanted to say, "told you so," but decided maybe another time. From the way Ferrick was acting, it might earn him another punch in the mouth. He settled for, "Why do you suppose the Authority is fudging the numbers?"

Ferrick's eyebrows pinched together. "Who the hell knows? Keep everybody fat, dumb, and happy, I guess. They're a bunch of stuffed-suit frackers, their first move would be to cover their own ass."

"Yeah, that makes sense. Maybe they don't know where it's coming from. Kerry tried to tell me it was the ship. People having trouble adjusting, and going nuts. Maybe that's what they think is going on. And that would be a threat to the entire operation. *Outward Bound* is the first colony ship this big. If they're guessing the problem is caused by so many people crammed into one small space, they might try to hide it. Figure that it would be a temporary problem, that it would go away when we finally hit the new planet and folks start to get back to normal."

Ferrick whipped his arm, sent the printouts flying. "Shit, man. I can do the numbers as well as you. If that rate of increase keeps on—it's already at eight percent, if it keeps on doubling for another three years, that would mean . . . Jesus. Almost two-thirds of the population crazy as shithouse rats by the time we get there." He paused. "Which would mean we wouldn't get there. We'd all be dead."

"Uh-huh," Jim said. He'd already worked it out, too. "Heat makes screwing even more fun. So in the end, I guess we'd all be really screwed. What a way to go, huh?"

"I gotta talk to Kerry," Ferrick said.

"Maybe Kerry should talk to this Ur-Barrba thing."

"Yeah? About what?"

"About why she's trying to kill the *Outward Bound*."

Ferrick's dark eyes slowly widened.

Comes the light, Jim thought.

3

Kerry listened without saying much until they had both finished. He had a stack of printouts in his lap almost three inches high, but he never looked at them. Just nodded occasionally, and once or twice said, "Go on."

When they were done, he said, "Okay," stood up, and returned the pile of paper to one of the desks. Then he headed for the door.

"Okay?" Jim said. "That's all? Just okay?"

"What do you want me to say?"

"Well, for starters, what do you think?"

"I don't know yet."

Jim's frustration bubbled over. "What do you mean? We did all the numbers. You can't argue with them. Look at the correlations. You didn't even look at them."

"Don't need to. I know Ferrick's good, and if he says you're good, then you are, too. So if you both say there's correlation, then there's correlation."

"Okay. And . . . ?"

Kerry sighed. "Statistics, Jim. What's the first rule of statistics?"

Jim's brain, hammered by pain, by lack of sleep, by overstimulation, by fear, felt like a wad of overchewed bubble gum. "I don't get it," he said slowly.

"Let me help," Kerry replied. "Correlation doesn't equal what?"

Oh. Jim closed his eyes. The mantra had been one of the first things drummed into him in his basic statistics course. "Causation," he said tiredly. "Correlation doesn't equal causation."

Kerry nodded. "Now you're getting it."

Jim thought of the enormous work he and Ferrick had done to come up with the numbers. And now Kerry was just going to ignore all that? He couldn't stand it.

"God *damn* it, Kerry. You've got to at least look. You have to. It's too important!"

Even Ferrick looked uneasy. "Yeah, man," he said. "The numbers are real. Something's going on."

Kerry glanced at him. "I know that. The question is, what? And that's my problem, not yours." He headed for the door again. "You both look like hell. Get some sleep, let me work on it."

Just before he closed the door behind him, he turned and stared at Jim. "You aren't off the hook yet. But you're getting there. Stay iced."

The door closed. Jim glanced at Ferrick, who was staring at the door in a bleary-eyed daze.

"Iced," Jim said. "Stay iced."

Ferrick squeezed his eyes shut. "What else are we gonna do? He's the man."

"But if it's the Heat, if it's us killing all those people . . ."

"Shut up, man," Ferrick groaned.

"Yeah," Jim replied. "That's the right answer. Shut up. While innocent people die."

"I said *shut up*!"

He's still mad, Jim thought. *But maybe not so much at me anymore.*

Work with it.

4

Kerry wandered out of the clubhouse, his blue eyes hazy, his expression concentrated, deeply thoughtful. Buried somewhere beneath that expression was a war. One part of him wished that instead of setting Jim Endicott up with Honeg in the brig, he'd done that deal just a little differently and let the big guy beat the kid to death. If he'd done that—and he'd considered it—none of this would have come up. And it still wasn't too late to arrange something like that. Though he'd have to give it to somebody besides Ferrick. The numbers had changed

Ferrick. He might do Jim, but he would always wonder. That wasn't a good idea for the guy who ran the numbers on your dope-sales operation. To have him wondering.

On the other hand, a different part of him looked at that solution and turned away. It was too easy an answer, and Kerry had not become the success he was by choosing the easy answers. Sometimes he regretted that. What did they call it? He was a natural contrarian. He took the hard way just because it *was* the hard way, and screw them all if they couldn't take a joke.

This was dynamite, though. If Jim was right, he'd have to shut down the operation. And that wouldn't be easy. Too many people depended on it. The Cowboys were mostly Plebs. And they got more than money out of dope dealing. They got the gang, friendship, loyalty, self-respect. Without Heat, what were the Cowboys anyway? Just another bunch of guys hanging out, no power, no leverage. So it wasn't as easy a thing as Endicott thought it was. It was clear-cut for him, black-and-white, right and wrong. For Kerry, nothing had ever been clear-cut, not for his whole life.

Kerry scratched the side of his nose and looked up as he ambled across the plaza. Weather was brewing, a line of clouds that looked like a tube of dirty socks forming in the center of the ship, obscuring the other side. A whiff of ozone on the freshening breeze. When it was like this, he could almost imagine he was still on Terra, waiting for the rain.

He shook his head. Those weren't the best memories either. Scrabbling and hustling, fighting and clawing. Putting together the Cowboys was the hardest thing he'd ever done. He'd brought the nucleus up with him from Terra, where they'd already begun to scratch out a minor presence in the North American West Coast Plebtowns. Ferrick, Sam, Darnell, they'd all been with him from the beginning.

He glanced across the plaza and saw two guys looking back. Their fingers moved unobtrusively, a little hand jive. He gestured in response, and they went back to work.

Jim had no idea.

They'd kept him away from most of it. Endicott knew a few of them, because they'd let him know a few. The inner circle. It was a balancing act. He could give them up, cause real hurt. But the trade-off was they could watch him, keep him on a short leash. And if he turned out to be what he looked like in the beginning, well. One kid vanishing out of ten million wouldn't be noticed.

Jim hadn't been invited to the last initiation ten days ago. They'd beaten in seven new juniors, guys maybe thirteen, fourteen. That brought the total Cowboy membership over a thousand. A thousand guys, plus several hundred girls in the auxiliary, the Cowgirls. Sam ran that, had from the beginning. So the whole deal wasn't some little street-corner doping and fighting society. It was a big business, a hell of a big business. And more than a business, a family. The biggest family in the world, and he was the big daddy.

Jim didn't understand, because he couldn't. How could he know what it was like, having that much responsibility? Holding the hands of the young ones, slapping them on the back when they got scared. Making sure that anybody who got fracked up in some skirmish with another gang was taken care of. Making sure the pie got split up fairly, making sure the greedheads in the Authority got the necessary bribes, making sure the whole vast, sprawling mechanism functioned and kept on functioning.

Heat was at the very heart of it. Without Heat, where would they be? Where would *he* be?

He strolled on, looking good, looking *iced*, heading for the restaurant, wondering if Sam would be there. She was good to talk to, even if he couldn't tell her everything. Not yet. He couldn't tell anybody everything yet. Not until he knew.

He wondered: *Could I break it all up if I had to?*

Yeah, he thought, *I could. But I don't want to.*

5

"What's up?" Kerry said, as he scooted a chair away from the table and sat down. Sam looked like she hadn't been sleeping well. And Jenny, who didn't know much about any of this, not unless Sam had told her, and he doubted that very much, looked worried, too. So something was getting out, if only a whiff. A sense that there was a problem. If that sort of shit was getting out, that could be a problem all by itself. Sometimes it was worse when there was only a hint, some vague thing for rumor to feed on. That was when people started to worry about whatever they felt like worrying about. And things would get loose and hinky, and the fighting would start as other gangs picked up on it and looked to take a bite out of Cowboy hide.

Not much time.

"Hey, Jen," he said easily. "Me and Sam need to talk."

Jenny stood up. "I was just leaving." She turned and walked away.

"Bye," he said to her back.

When she was gone, he put his elbows on the table and leaned forward, until his face was only a few inches from Sam's. He could smell the raspberries about her, a fresh, happy-making scent. It had been a long time since they'd been lovers, but the feelings were still there. A little different, smudged and muted now, but still there.

"What did you find out?" Sam said.

"We could be in deep shit," he replied.

She closed her eyes. "I was afraid of that." For a moment she looked very young, and a little frightened.

If this goes down, I'll see a lot of that, Kerry thought.

"How deep?" Sam asked.

"Deep enough," he said, and told her what Jim and Ferrick had told him. She shook her head.

"Ferrick buys into this, too?"

"Yeah. I think so. Some of it, at least."

"I don't understand this correlation-causation bullshit."

When he finished explaining, she nodded. "Okay. So just

because we sell more Heat, and there's more of these psycho things, it doesn't necessarily mean that the Heat is causing it?"

"Yeah, that's right."

"But Jim thinks it is," she said.

"Uh-huh. He thinks so."

She looked away. "He could be wrong. But not because he's what you think he is. Some kind of secret-agent man."

Kerry leaned back. "I don't know if I think that anymore. Part of me does, maybe. If there was a real plot to put us out of the biz. If I wanted to shut down the Cowboys, this might be a good way to do it."

"You think he's that good? He'd have to be Agency then. The Authority would never come up with it, they're not smart enough."

He chewed that over for a minute. She was right. He knew the Authority. The fat cats who ran the ship. They were technocrats, and they had some smart people. But not smart that way. Not smart enough, at least. The Agency, on the other hand. He didn't know the Agency that well. Nobody did. Nobody still alive and on the outside, at least. But they were good enough.

"It doesn't fit," he said at last. "Endicott would have had to be a deep plant, right from the beginning. Sixteen years old. Which means they would have had to get started with him a long time before the Cowboys got going. Or the *Outward Bound*."

"They could have faked his records. They're good enough we'd never know. He came off a freighter. We don't know if he's ever even been on Wolfbane. He could have come straight from Terra."

Kerry shook his head. "We don't know everything about Delta and the Agency, but we know enough. If they knew that much about us, they wouldn't send a sixteen-year-old kid to take us down. They'd send somebody like that Commander Steele he told us about, and you, me, Darnell, Ferrick, and the others on the inside would suddenly get dead. Neat, clean, and quick. That's the way they'd do it."

She lifted her cup of tea, sipped, set it back down. Ran her fingertip across the tracery of damp cup-rings on the tabletop. "So if he's not Agency, and he's not Authority, what is he?"

"He's a problem," Kerry said.

"I know that. And what if he's right? What if it is the Heat?

What if it's *us* killing all those people?" She shook her head. "Kerry, I don't think I could deal with that."

"I know," he replied. "That's the biggest problem. I don't know if I could either."

6

"I took the shipment," Kerry said.

Jim's injuries were much improved. The marvels of modern medical science. Improved enough that he came up out of his chair with his fists balled.

"You what?"

Ferrick shifted in his own seat and said, "Settle down. Hear the man out."

Jim glared at him, but after a moment subsided. "I'm listening."

Kerry shot him a glance. "First thing is, you don't use that tone on me. I don't have to explain shit to you."

"Okay," Jim said.

"Second thing. I'm still not convinced. That's why I took the shipment. Ur-Barrba gave us forty-eight hours, and that's all the time we had. So I said yes."

"Why?"

"Because," Kerry said patiently, "I need more time. You don't know what's involved. Ferrick does, though. He understands."

Jim glanced at Ferrick. Ferrick nodded. "You saw the numbers," Jim said, getting hot all over again. "You know what they mean."

"I need causation, Jim," Kerry said. "I can't do anything unless I know there's a real connection." He fluttered his fingers. "I could, but I won't. That's what I mean."

"You won't. How many more people are gonna die?"

"I don't know. If you're right, that depends on how big a stash most folks have piled up. Since people tend to use what they buy right away, I'm guessing they don't keep a lot on hand."

Jim didn't get it. "What are you telling me?"

"I said I took the shipment. I didn't say I was distributing it. At the moment, there's something of a Heat shortage on the streets."

Ferrick's eyebrows jumped. "That's the first I heard of that."

"It'll start showing up in your numbers pretty quick. That's why I'm telling you in the first place. You'll see it first, and I don't want you wondering what the hell's going on."

"Who else knows?"

Kerry shrugged. "Him." He nodded at Jim. "Sam, Darnell, a couple of the others. You know who."

Ferrick nodded. "All right." He thought about it. "What's the word, then?"

"Shipment's been delayed. We don't know why. It's happened before."

"That'll hold, I guess. Not for long, though."

"No, not for long," Kerry agreed. "Long enough. I hope."

Jim stared at him. "Long enough for what?"

"Tests."

"What the hell does that mean, tests? We already know Heat's psychoactive. The sex thing, that's what it does. You can't just analyze the dope and come up with an answer right away."

"You can analyze some people *with* the dope," Kerry said mildly.

It took a few seconds for it to penetrate, and when it did, Jim's jaw dropped. "You're gonna test that shit on *people*?" He came out of his chair again. "*I can't let you do that!*"

Kerry rose to meet him. "Sit right frackin' back down, asshole. You don't have any frackin' choice in the matter."

They faced off, glaring at each other. Finally, Jim backed off, face red, breathing hard. "I just don't understand. What kind of a monster are you?"

"One who didn't kill you when he had the chance," Kerry said finally. "Don't make me think I made a mistake."

Jim collapsed in his chair, shaking his head. He looked over at Ferrick. "Is there anything you can say to him?"

Ferrick said, "You want to know, don't you?"

"Not this way," Jim replied.

7

Five days later, a well-dressed man about forty years old showed up at the clubhouse and was ushered into the room Kerry called his office. The man had a short, neat haircut, flecked with gray, was wearing a pretty nice suit that flattered his skinny frame, and a single gaudy ruby ring on his right hand.

"Hamilton," Kerry said, and gestured toward a sofa opposite his desk. "Get you something, a cola, some Heat?" He grinned.

Hamilton's muddy brown gaze jumped away from Kerry when he said that, the movement of a startled water bug. "No, nothing," he said. "I'm fine."

Kerry stood up, came around the desk, and perched on the low table in front of the sofa. "You don't look fine."

Hamilton reached into his pocket, brought out a data chip, tossed it on the table. They both looked at it for a second.

"What's on it?" Kerry said finally.

"What you were afraid of," Hamilton said. "You didn't give me much time. I can't say that's a real analysis. To know for sure, I'd want to do a complete study, analyze the substance, have three different cohorts, double-blind the whole thing, but—"

"Yeah, yeah," Kerry said. "So you don't have enough time to do it right. But you had enough time to do it wrong."

Hamilton nodded. His tongue came out and slithered wetly along his lips. "Even the preliminaries are bad enough," he said.

Kerry closed his eyes. "Tell me."

"We used ten people. Volunteers." Hamilton grinned sourly. "Not hard to find them. Free living, a cash bonus, and all the Heat you can eat? Shit. I might have gone for it."

"I know you like your Heat, Hamilton. But you say might have. Does that mean you wouldn't now?"

"It's cumulative," Hamilton said. "Screws with several different brain chemicals." He tapped the chip. "The details are all there."

"Screws with them how?"

"You want the long answer or the short one?"

"Short one."

"It makes people go crazy. Violent. Overdoses speed up the process, and we overdosed the crap out of those people."

"And?"

"If we hadn't been watching them every minute, we'd have lost four. As it was, we weren't fast enough with one of them."

"What happened?"

"Chewed off all the toes on his right foot. Spit them at us when we jumped him."

"Jesus."

"I'm never touching Heat again," Hamilton said.

Kerry rose to his feet. "First thing," he said. "Not one word. You got that? Not one."

Hamilton nodded.

"I'm serious. You let this out, you'll never touch anything again."

"I hear you." Hamilton's head was bobbing almost as fast as his Adam's apple.

"Number two. What about the test subjects?"

"The guy with the toes. He's still psycho. Don't know if we'll be able to pull him back or not. The rest came out of it. It's like a psychotic fugue. In the long term, with enough exposure, the changes may be permanent. We haven't seen them, because the first episode is usually the last. They try to kill everybody in reach, and then themselves. If they can't reach anybody else, they do themselves."

"Keep them locked up," Kerry said. "Do what you can for the one guy. Money's no problem, just take care of him."

"That makes me nervous," Hamilton said. "You tell me I'm dead if this gets out. But then you tell me to take good care of the evidence."

"That's exactly what I'm telling you," Kerry said. "Take care of those people like they were your own children. And don't start whining at me. Life's hard, and then you die. Now get out of here." Kerry scooped up the chip as Hamilton rose and headed for the door.

"Hamilton?"

"Yeah?"

"Don't frack this up. You wouldn't want to end up testing your own brain cells for damage. But you will if you mess with me. I'll pour an ounce of that crap down your throat and watch you eat your own dick."

Hamilton nodded. Kerry thought he saw him shudder as he closed the door.

He should, Kerry thought. *We all should.*

CHAPTER TWELVE

1

Kerry, Darnell, Ferrick, Sam, and Jim sat around the table at the restaurant. The sun bounced and jangled on the glittery things in Sam's hair. Everybody looked blurry and tired. Kerry had bags like suitcases under his eyes. Jim wondered when the last time was he'd slept.

"How much are you willing to risk to stop this thing?" Kerry asked.

"A lot," Jim said.

"Your life?"

Jim thought about it. Thought about the look on the face of the guy who'd tried to kill him. Who'd spit his fingers at him. Remembered the way the light had glinted off the two small coffins, Harry's dead kids, and the way the old lady had spit at him, too. Remembered selling the shit to Harry in the first place.

"Will it come to that?" he said.

"It could."

"If I have to, then," Jim told him. "If there's no other way."

Darnell was looking at Jim. He made a soft sound in his throat.

"What?" Kerry said.

"I said frackin' hero," Darnell replied. His voice was bleak with exhaustion. Jim wondered what Darnell had been doing. He hadn't been around for several days.

Kerry glanced at Jim. "I don't know. Could be. We'll find out, I guess."

Jim cocked his head and listened as Kerry told him how he'd worked it out. When Kerry was done, Jim looked at him. "That's the way it has to be?"

Kerry shrugged. "Unless you can think of something better."

Jim thought about it. "I can't," he said.

So they started.

2

Jenny ran the day-to-day with the Cowgirls. Sam met her for lunch at Scalio's, a nice restaurant near Ship's Center, where the big buildings were. The rain had stopped, and the clouds in the middle of the gravity well, two miles overhead, were breaking up. Sam couldn't tell if it was natural, or if they'd turned on some big fans or something. Ship's weather was a mystery to her. She knew they could control some of it, but not all. The only thing was, she didn't know which parts were which. In the end, she looked at it the way she'd always looked at the weather. Something that happened. You lived with it.

"What's up?" Jenny asked her, after they'd gotten themselves settled and given the human waiter an order for two of the fancy cocktails that had a lot of fruit and complicated stir-sticks in them. The human waiter was how you knew it was a good place. Usually they ate in the cafeteria-style places, or the ones with robot servers that looked like oversize garbage cans with rubber treads on them.

Sam thought Jenny looked worried. The rumors had been flying for at least a week, and Sam hadn't given her number two any help. Left her out there flying blind because Kerry said that was how it had to be. Everything had to look right for any of it to work. Sam wasn't sure it would work anyway, but she would do her part. It was a relief, though, to be able to fill Jenny in on some of it. Maybe after she did, she wouldn't feel like she was carrying around an ice-cold bowling ball somewhere in the neighborhood of her heart. It was scary, knowing her life was about to change.

She reached across the table and patted Jenny's hand. Jenny's fingers were as chilly as the two drink glasses the waiter placed on their table with an exaggerated, mocking flourish.

"You ladies ready to order?" he asked. Sam couldn't tell if he was sneering at them, or just in a shitty mood. His attitude irritated her, but she was a Pleb. Waiters in ritzy places intimidated her, and that made her even more irritated. She thought about mentioning the Cowboys—Heat was big in the restaurant-service community, they were all real dope hounds—but decided it wasn't worth it. Cheap thrills.

"Give us a few minutes," she told the waiter. He nodded, offered a half smile that looked about as sincere as the menu prices, then bustled away.

"What an asshole," Jenny said.

"Yeah. Forget him."

Their eyes met. Sam started to say something, but picked up her drink instead. Sucked on the straw, noticed it was smeared with salmon-colored lipstick when she took her lips away. "Good," she said. "Fruity tasting."

"Like the waiter," Jenny said, and giggled.

"You think so?"

"Oh, sure."

Kerry had been trying to teach Sam to act like a lady for years, or if not a lady, at least less of a Pleb. Not, as he explained it, because he didn't like the way she was, but because she could go farther if she knew how to fake the high-hat stuff. Some of it was interesting, and some of it bored her blind. She knew that the kind of bigotry exemplified by Jenny's remark was a typical Pleb thing, where ancient attitudes hadn't been modified to any great extent because nobody who could do anything about it cared enough to try. Plebs were Plebs, the thinking went. Why bother?

She sucked on the straw until the drink went dry and the straw made liquid rattling sounds at the bottom of the ice. The cocktail tasted mostly like fruit juice, but a slow, warm bomb was heating up in her stomach. It felt good. Some of the tension began to leak out of her muscles, and she settled back and sighed.

"What's going on?" Jenny asked suddenly. "You know the girls are all upset. Everybody's talking, nobody knows nothing. And there's no dope to sell."

"I know," Sam said. She moved her head back and forth, stretching her neck, listening to the gristle in there make tiny popping sounds only she could hear.

"I think there's gonna be some changes," she said. "Big ones. Pretty soon."

"Like what?" Jenny said, sounding even more worried than before.

"Kerry. Maybe he's gonna step down."

"Step down? What does that mean, step down?"

"You know. Quit. Leave the Cowboys."

Jenny was silent for a long beat. "Aw, shit. You'd better tell me the rest of it."

Sam leaned forward and did so, some of it at least. After that, they drank four more cocktails apiece and ate two aqua-farmed fish platters while they tried to figure out how to pull it off.

The waiter was really mean, in a snide, hard-to-pin-down way, while he served them. Just before they left, Sam fished in her bag, pulled out a ten cred packet of pink powder, and left it for a tip. But after they got outside, she turned around and went back in. He'd already picked up the dope, and he made her pay him fifty creds to give it back.

He was an asshole, but she didn't hate him. Not that much, anyway.

3

The word went out on the streets for two days: *top challenge*. Big Tiny Nero, a fourteen-year-old Pleb from the Atlanta region who weighed 250 pounds, was really excited about it. As far as anybody knew, Big Tiny hadn't spoken an intelligible word his whole life. He could hear and understand just fine, he just couldn't—or wouldn't—talk. He communicated by a complicated home brew of hand jive only his closest friends could understand. His hands went into fluttering overdrive as his friends explained as much as they knew about a top challenge: that somebody had challenged Kerry to a fight for control of the Cowboys. That the whole gang would have to be there, to see it. That the winner would be the new leader, unless the whole gang, by majority vote, overturned the results of the fight.

Big Tiny, a notable brawler already, thought that sounded just fine. He didn't worry much about all the other shit a leader had to do, because he didn't know about it. He judged things by his own experience, and he knew if you could take out an enemy with one punch, you were pretty hot shit. He had a healthy respect for physical force. So if the challenger, whoever it was, could kick Kerry's ass, then so be it. However things turned out, it would be okay with him.

If Jim had known about Big Tiny Nero, he might have thought about the Social Darwinism he'd learned in cultural-analysis classes, about the general proposition that might makes right. He might have recalled his once-naive belief that this was not a practical or effective way to structure a society, even a secret society engaged in a criminal enterprise.

But if he was honest, he would admit that grand social theories had a way of disintegrating in the face of reality on the street. And that guys like Big Tiny Nero didn't know dick about any Darwin dude, but they instinctively understood the value of a club to the side of the head. Terran civilization might be heading out toward the stars, but a lot of things about it hadn't changed much in ten thousand years.

"Darnell's pretty messed up about this," Ferrick said. They were in his computer room, both working the computers, getting ready for the changeover. They were spending so much time in the ship's systems that whenever they were able to snatch a couple hours of sleep, they dreamed in code.

"Yeah, I guess he would be," Jim said.

"You don't know shit about it," Ferrick told him.

"Oh?"

"No, you don't. You know what Darnell does?"

Jim shook his head.

"He's Kerry's right-hand guy. He's the organizer, the politician. He makes sure all the subgangs are set up right. He handles disputes. He holds the little guys' hands. Everybody knows him, they see a lot more of him than they do Kerry." Ferrick shrugged. "A lot of them, the dumber ones, probably think he's the leader."

Jim felt around the edges of it. "So he's really important. . . ." he said slowly.

"Yeah, he is. And you know what he'd have been without the Cowboys? He'd be shit. Just another useless Pleb rotting away in some Plebtown somewheres." Ferrick looked down at his blunt fingers. "And he's good at it. I couldn't do it. Long time ago I tried, but Kerry made me stop. He said I scared the younger ones. I don't know why."

Probably because they'd never seen a stone-cold killer before, Jim thought.

"Plebs. They don't get much respect, do they?"

"It ain't 'they,' Jim. It's me. And Kerry, and Darnell, and all the rest."

"People don't like you, is that it?" He was still reaching for it. "Or they're afraid of you?"

Ferrick shook his head. "It's more like they don't even know we're there. Oh, they do. They see the Pleb riots on the Nets and they probably think what a shame it is, but what can you expect? And then they flip the channels and go on to something else. It's not that the people who run things like us or hate us. They ignore us. We don't matter, because we don't do anything that matters. Not to them." He raised one hand, lowered it, examined his fingers again. "If we all went away tomorrow, none of them would miss us for a second. That's what all this colony bullshit is, you know. We're going away. Nobody's forcing us. But the ships are mostly Pleb. We're going away 'cause nobody cares enough to ask us to stay."

"Like the inner-city blacks back in the twentieth century," Jim mused.

"I don't know much old-time history."

"It doesn't matter," Jim said.

But it did matter. He just hadn't seen it before. No reason to, really. But the pattern was there, once you knew what to look for.

Marginalization. If the members of a subclass somehow lost their essential value to the system, then they became invisible to the system. If they couldn't contribute in some coin the system valued—labor, ideas, art, whatever—then, if the system wasn't totally heartless, it might feed, clothe, and shelter them, but otherwise it would utterly ignore them. That was what had happened to the twentieth-century urban black populations, the ones left behind when their brothers and sisters had abandoned the inner cities and fled to the suburbs. Those who had something to offer.

And then the great wheel of technology had spun and spun again. Suddenly a huge proportion of the population, because it lacked the highly specialized abilities or talents a mature technical society demanded, found itself useless to the brave new world coming into existence. They were the Plebs, a shadow culture united by perceived uselessness, a perception even the Plebs themselves shared. Because everything that mattered in the world told them it was true.

"You didn't have anything to *do,*" Jim said softly. "And you knew you never would."

"You know what Plebs stands for?" Ferrick said.

"No."

"When they first realized that there were a lot of unemployable people around, they set up a system to take care of them. It was called "Provide Low-Energy Basic Systems." That's what we got. Low-energy, and basic, 'cause that's what they figured we were. And they were right."

His expression looked like paper, carefully smoothed. "Anyway, that's what Darnell's messed up about," he continued. "Kerry gave him something to do. Now he's afraid it's all gonna go away. So he's scared." Ferrick glanced at Jim, his eyes flat as mirrors of black ice. "Plebs are always afraid. That it's all gonna go away, anything we do that matters."

"Jesus," Jim said. "That's harsh."

Ferrick shrugged. "That's life."

A search program they were running in the innards of the Authority's main security database beeped softly, and they dropped it for a while. But later, after he'd thought on it some more, Jim said, "What about you?"

"What about me?"

"How do you feel about this?"

"Better than Darnell."

"How come?"

"I got skills. I didn't go to no fancy schools, but I understand computers. If we ever get the colony going, I'll find a place. Won't be much but Plebs around, so I'll stand out." He grinned, a bitter, twisting flash. "And I got some other things I'm good at."

Jim thought: *like killing.* But how bad was that, when you came down to it? He had always wanted to become a starship captain. But the starships fought, and sometimes they killed, too. And that was too easy. The starships didn't kill, any more than the .75 Jim had used on Commander Steele killed by itself. No, men were the killers, and that skill had served them well over their entire existence. Jim doubted the necessity for it would go away anytime soon. So it was a matter of how somebody like Ferrick was used. Handle him, control him, use him like the weapon he was, and what he did could be turned toward the good.

He thought he would need somebody like Ferrick. If he was able to pull it off.

"What if you could find something besides the colony? Some other kind of work?"

Ferrick's dark gaze sharpened just a bit. "Like what?"

"There could be something," Jim said.

4

The public gyms were well equipped, but they were like gyms everywhere. Darnell and Jim found a small one, back in a leafy suburb, far away from the center of things.

The place had a pool and weight machines, and a mat room for floor gymnasts and martial-arts nuts. Darnell led the way in. Both boys were wearing sweats. The place smelled of dirty socks and body odor. Good light streamed in from a bank of high windows. The mats had yellow streaks on them, and a couple of rusty brown spots.

"Nice," Jim said. "Somebody takes good care of it."

"Probably a Pleb," Darnell said. "A Pleb doing Heat."

They squared off and started. Jim's injuries had healed, but he felt rusty and out of shape. It was good just to move, to throw the punches and the kicks, feel his heart pound and taste the sweat running down his face.

"Uh," Darnell said when they stopped for a break. He went to one of the fountains and let the water splash on his face, then drank some and shook the moisture out of his hair. His long, sallow face was flushed. "You're good," he said.

"I'm not at full speed," Jim told him.

"I wouldn't want to mess with you," Darnell said.

"I studied this shit all my life," Jim said. "My dad said it was important. That I know how to do it. He never told me why, but I liked it, so I kept on. Anybody can learn it. You know some."

"Yeah, some," Darnell said. "I don't know if it's enough."

"We'll keep at it," Jim said, thinking of the challenge to come. Everything hinged on that. It had to look legitimate. Kerry would fight. Maybe not to kill, but he wouldn't spare anything. Wouldn't pull his punches. And accidents could happen. Best to be ready for anything.

"Let's go," Jim said.

They went another ten minutes. Darnell was picking it up fast. He was a natural fighter, snake-quick and smart. He didn't look like it, but some of the best fighters Jim had ever seen didn't look like it.

Kerry didn't, really. Though Ferrick did. But Ferrick wasn't really a fighter. He was a killer, and there was a difference.

They were both blowing hard when they took another break. "Your dad made you learn this?" Darnell said.

"Yeah."

"Because of that guy, huh? The one who sent the killers after you?"

"I guess," Jim said.

"How'd he know?"

"Maybe he didn't. Maybe he hoped it wouldn't happen, but if it did, he wanted me to be ready."

Darnell nodded. "Must have been hard on him. Knowing what

could happen, trying to make a life for you anyway. I wish I had somebody cared about me like that."

Jim turned and looked at the other boy. He had never thought of it in exactly that way. It hit him like a hammer.

"You're right," he said, surprised at how choked his voice sounded.

Darnell glanced at his face, looked away. "Are you crying?"

"Naw, man. Just some sweat got in my eyes."

Darnell nodded, got up, ran a towel over his head. Threw it aside, went back to the mat and stood there, bouncing in place, his hands raised in loose fists. "You ready?"

"Yeah."

Jim felt a gnawing sense of urgency as they worked. Not much time left before the challenge, and it had to be right. Too much at stake to screw it up now.

5

The timing was tricky and very delicate. Kerry and Jim worked on it together, because everything had to happen all at once. Like throwing a jigsaw puzzle into the air and having all the pieces come down together to form the picture.

Kerry had an enormous amount of street smarts. He instinctively understood power relationships, even if he sometimes couldn't articulate them with any precision. He would, Jim thought, have made a fine general.

And Jim brought his own skills to the mix, knowledge gained from a thorough education. They were in Kerry's office, Kerry sprawled on the sofa, staring up at the ceiling, his eyes closed. Jim wondered how he could look so relaxed.

Jim was sitting in the fat chair from his recovery room, his feet up on the low table. Sam had wandered in a few minutes before, hung out a little, then left. The scent of raspberries still drifted in the air.

After she left, Kerry started explaining some of the methods he used to keep the Cowboy operations running smoothly. He used crude words and street descriptions, but suddenly Jim understood what he was hearing, because he'd heard it before. Kerry was saying how he never touched the girls down at the street level, restricted himself to a few private relationships outside of the gang.

"Yeah," Jim said, the quotation suddenly floating in his mind. "'Hatred, as I said before, he will most readily engender by being rapacious and seizing the property and the women of his subjects. These he must not touch.'"

Kerry opened his eyes and looked at Jim. "You pulling my dong? Making fun of me?"

"No, no. I didn't say that, I was quoting another guy."

"The guy talks funny."

"Yeah, he lived almost a thousand years ago."

Kerry's eyebrows rose. "Huh?"

"His name was Machiavelli. Niccolo Machiavelli. He wrote a book titled *The Prince.*"

"A thousand years ago? And he said you should keep your hands off the women?"

"Yeah."

Kerry settled back. "He knew his shit, then."

"He knew a lot. He also said, 'Men are less concerned with offending someone they have cause to love than someone they have cause to fear.'"

Kerry opened his eyes again. "He said that, too? Man." He shook his head. "You say he wrote this stuff down, in a book or something?"

"Sure. You want me to download it? I'm sure it's in the ship's library somewhere. It's a classic."

"They taught you this stuff in school?"

"In ethics class."

Kerry said, "No wonder the Plebs have such a hard time of it. Your average Pleb figures he can probably kick any Tech's ass, but they teach you guys in school the stuff we have to learn the hard way. So we never get it right the way you people do."

"Hey, they don't teach Machiavelli as the way to do things. Actually, the opposite. He's supposed to be a bad guy."

Kerry eyed him. "Ethics. Sure." He rolled away, spoke to the ceiling. "Jim. That guy who sent the killers after you. You think he was studying the Bible or something, or this Mack-a-what'shisname?"

Jim's eyes widened. "Out of the mouth of babes."

"That from him, too?"

"No, it's just a saying."

"Well, I ain't no babe." He slapped his chest. "No tits, see."

Jim burst out laughing.

"What? What?" Kerry said.

But he read the downloaded copy of *The Prince* and even printed out a paper copy of his favorite parts, which he thumbed through whenever he had a spare moment. "The old guy knew his stuff, Jim," he would say. "You could learn a lot from him."

"Shit," Jim told him. "Maybe I better introduce you to Socrates. For balance."

"Who's that?"

"Another dead guy," Jim said.

"Maybe later. I don't have much time for reading now. If we screw this up, we're gonna have a lot of guys as dead as this Socrates. And I don't think many of them wrote any books."

"You've got a point," Jim said. He thought of something else that needed checking. "When will the ship be there?"

Kerry sighed. "On schedule," he said.

6

Jim hadn't expected to be awed by it, but he was. The Cowboys drifted in alone or in small groups. The Cowgirls came in, too, their usual bright chatter muted. The vast space of the secondary cargo bay felt like Jim imagined a cathedral would: dim, high, solemn.

Everybody had brought a light of some kind, pencil flashes, laser pointers, something. As they settled down, pressing together, the last dregs of conversation went silent. Then the lights began to come on, thin lances that looked like firefly trails.

Jim stood with the rest of the leaders, at the edge of the crowd. At their back the high wall of Ur-Barrba's ship loomed like a black-steel cliff. Ferrick had hacked all the computer data about the secondary bay early in the morning. As far as anybody in the Authority knew, the bay was empty and locked. The alien vessel was, as Kerry had promised, right on schedule.

Kerry glanced at Darnell. "Is that about all of them?"

Darnell licked his lips and nodded.

"Okay." Kerry took a shallow breath, stepped forward into the rustling shadows, and raised his hands for quiet. He told them that he'd been challenged. He explained that it was because he'd lost the connection, that there would be no more Heat coming in. That brought a collective gasp that sounded like storm winds hustling over the horizon.

He said that he'd accepted the challenge, and that if he failed, he wanted them to recognize the winner as their new leader. He said he had no hard feelings about it, that it was being done by the rules they all understood. When he said that, some of the people nearest him began to stomp on the floor. The sound quickly spread, until the deck began to vibrate.

"Challenge, challenge, *challenge*!" they chanted. Jim saw eyes glitter in the gloom. There was bloodlust out there.

Ferrick, standing next to Jim, handed him a package. "Kerry said this was yours," he whispered.

Jim fumbled with it, unwrapped it. It was his Styron und Ritter .75. He slipped the heavy pistol into the waist of his pants. "Thanks," he whispered.

There was a stir in the ranks of the leadership. It was time for the challenger to make himself known. He stripped off his shirt and stepped forward. His appearance brought a few scattered cheers and some awkward applause, quickly stilled.

Kerry stripped off his own shirt as he watched the challenger approach. "Are you ready?" he said, when his foe stood facing him.

Jim felt a chill wrap his spine. It was like some ancient ritual, old bone and blood. His body knew. Even at a distance, watching, his body was scared.

Darnell, the challenger, crouched forward, hands extended in front of him, and nodded. "Let's do it," he said.

CHAPTER THIRTEEN

1

Jim watched the beginning of the fight, long enough to see that all the coaching he'd done with Darnell hadn't gone to waste. Kerry didn't look like he was holding anything back. He was moving, throwing those rattlesnake punches, right, right, left, right again, but Darnell was holding up okay. The smaller boy slipped and dodged, slid under another punch, and landed a belly kick of his own.

That had been one of the biggest problems. "If it isn't about nine hundred ninety-nine percent for real, they'll smell it," Kerry had told Jim. "Some of those guys are real fighters, and they'll sense a fake. I'm gonna do almost my best to kill Darnell, and you know how that can go. I miss once, or hit the wrong spot, and I might wipe him by accident. Same with me. He's fast, Darnell. Catch me in the throat or something, he might end up doing me. The point is, we don't want either thing to happen, him or me. The idea is we both walk away from it, or at least crawl. So you work with him, get him up to speed on that fancy shit you know."

Jim watched them dance around each other, heard their raspy breath, the sharp, meaty slap of fist meeting flesh. Saw blood start to run, smelled the sour-coppery odor of it on the thick air. So did the crowd. They were screaming now, waving their arms, mirroring the punches. You could spot the ones with the laser pointers, thin green or red lances smearing tiny dancing dots on every surface.

It looked real enough to him. He hoped the experts watching

would think so, too, or if they had doubts, they'd be uncertain enough to keep them to themselves.

"You ready?" he whispered to Ferrick.

"Yeah." Ferrick moved sideways, slipping away from Sam and the rest, Jim sliding in his wake. Nobody noticed them leaving, and that was part of it, too.

They moved silently down the side of the big bay, vanishing into the shadows. Jim wore black jeans and a dark red pullover. Ferrick was all in dark brown. It was the best they could come up with for dark-time camouflage.

"I don't see them," Jim murmured, hanging close to Ferrick's broad back.

"Good. You aren't supposed to—ah. Hold it, we're here."

He stopped suddenly, and Jim ran into his shoulders, bounced as if he'd hit a brick wall.

"Hey," Ferrick said, not talking to Jim. "We're on."

Somebody said: "Let's quit fracking around and go, then."

Jim was suddenly surrounded by bulky, jostling shapes. Thirty of them, handpicked by Ferrick. Some of them were fighters, but most of them were killers. Ferrick knew how to find that kind.

One of them slapped a floppy weight at Jim's chest. "Vest," he said, the tension making his voice hoarse. "Better wear it. It won't stop one of the big blasters, but it'll slow the light stuff down."

Jim nodded, strapping it on. The vest was a dull, flat black, and made him even harder to see. "Ferrick? You wearing one?"

"Nah. I'm the bait, remember? It would look kinda funny. Those big apes might not know it's not just a fashion statement, but why take the chance?"

"Yeah, I guess," Jim said doubtfully.

Ferrick slapped him on the back. He seemed happy. Maybe he was, with the prospect of killing something. "Don't sweat it, man. You can't think about it, you just have to do it."

Good advice. Jim tried to clear his mind and follow it. It was hard, though.

2

Ur-Barrba's ship was buttoned up, almost invisible in the murk. Only the firefly jitter of the laser pointers flickering across its steel hide showed that something big was there.

The ship's gangplank was withdrawn, the port dogged shut. Ferrick's little army flowed silently around him, splitting and passing him like a dark river rushing past a stone.

"You two," Ferrick said, and yanked a couple of guys out of the crowd. "Give me a hand."

The cargo bay was set up to handle all kinds of vessels. Some had their own gangplanks, some didn't. Ferrick pointed. "Push it forward. No, slower. It frackin' squeaks." He turned to Jim. "Damn it, I forgot to check. Should have sprayed the rails with graphite or something."

"Don't worry about it," Jim told him. "It either works or it doesn't."

Ferrick nodded, then turned back toward the ship, directing the two with the portable stairway toward the silent ship. The tall metal structure struck the hull with the soft thud of padded bumpers. Jim watched the rest of the team spreading out, concealing themselves around the base of the ladder.

Ferrick looked over his shoulder, gestured with his right hand. *You, too.*

Jim bobbed his head and scrambled over to the base of the stairs, hid himself beneath the risers. He was wedged in against other sweating bodies, hot breath murmuring harshly in his ears, the thick, bitter stink of boys scared enough to fight, to kill, clogging his nostrils.

He licked his lips, pulled the .75 from his waistband, checked the loads by feel. Everything felt right. But he hadn't stripped the weapon since the firefight back on Wolfbane. Unless Kerry had done something to it, it should be okay. He wished he knew for sure. Hell of a thing, to go into battle holding a weapon you didn't know wouldn't blow up in your hand. . . .

The heavy steel ladder thrummed as Ferrick slowly mounted the stairs. They were well away from the action with Kerry and

Darnell, which was still going on. Cheers and shouts rolled across the room in waves that echoed and bounced before losing themselves in the upper reaches. The lights made a show of it, a flickering, gleaming blood sport. Only someone very observant, who knew what he was looking at, would notice that some of the lascr pointers had their spots fixed unmoving on certain specific spots along the ship's hull, most of them near the main entry hatch.

Observation lenses. Overamping from the focused radiation of several beams of coherent light, blinding the ship to the bodies hidden beneath the ladder.

Jim had identified the vessel type. It had been built in a Hunzzan shipyard, probably modified for Ur-Barrba's people. The Hunzza would sell military equipment to anybody, even their enemies. They didn't give a shit, figured they could use their own stuff better than anybody else, and in the meantime, why not make a cred at it?

Jim raised his hand, checked the tiny face of the nailtale set into his thumb. Time now. Suddenly the comm bead buried in his right ear hissed alive, and he heard Ferrick's husky breathing. He couldn't see Ferrick from his own position, but he knew what was going on. Ferrick was standing right outside Ur-Barrba's front door, sending recognition codes from a portable unit. The aliens might be nervous, what with all the noise and shouting from the fight, and they'd be watching that. Jim hoped they'd think it was an accident when they discovered the low-powered laser beams had disabled the observation nodes nearest their main port. And they knew Ferrick, or at least Ur-Barrba did. On occasion he'd picked up dope shipments by himself. And as far as the aliens knew, a pickup was on the schedule for tonight. Jim wondered what they were making of the bloody carnival a couple of hundred yards away.

"Open the door," Jim muttered, not realizing he was talking out loud until somebody jammed an elbow in his ribs and hissed, "Shut the frack up," into his ear. He crouched down a little lower and waited, breath hitching in his chest, sweat burning into his eyes.

He felt it before he heard it, a faint vibration that came from the ship and moaned through the steel deck plates. Then a sharp pop, a sudden hiss as the hydraulics kicked in, and he knew the hatch was sliding open, Ferrick stepping forward to block the port with his own body, give them the four or five seconds that were all they needed. . . .

Ferrick's voice roared in his ear. *"Move!"*

"Go go go!" Jim shouted.

3

They clattered up the steps, Jim scrambling to keep in the lead, his boots slipping, grabbing on the corrugated metal. He roared up to the top and flung himself through the hatch, which was already half-closed.

A few feet beyond, Ferrick was wrestling with an alien twice his size. The alien grabbed him by the throat, picked him up, and slammed him hard against a bulkhead. Jim saw Ferrick's head bounce, saw him come down shaking his head, his eyes glazed.

Whirled and found the second alien, big as the first, holding down a large red button on a panel next to the hatch. Closing the door. Jim brought the .75 up, swept the snout across the alien's broad chest, pulled the trigger.

A sound like a cathedral bell tolling a single great stroke shattered the confined space, hammered against his ears like a blow. The alien's chest vanished from shoulders to rib cage as the force of the rocket shell blew him backwards in bloody rags. The hatch stopped closing. More Cowboys poured through, whooping, their eyes the color and size of hard-boiled eggs. High on adrenaline and fear.

Jim spun back toward Ferrick, bringing the muzzle of the .75 up again. Saw the alien stagger backwards, holding his belly, saw Ferrick flash a grin like the wink of an ivory billiard ball as he plunged a twelve-inch bowie knife again and again. . . .

Jim lunged toward him, grabbed him. "He's dead, you killed him, come on," he yelled.

The rest of the Cowboys had slowed, waiting for somebody to tell them where to go, what to do. Ferrick's eyes lost their blank sheen and focused again. The entry chamber reeked of blood and the stench of the .75's propellant. Somewhere deeper in the ship a siren began to hoot.

Jim yanked a small tablet out of his pants, flicked it on, examined the schematic on its little screen. "Straight through," he said. "We'll hit a main corridor. We want to go right. The comm facilities and the bridge. Bridge first, if we can." He stopped, thought about it. "This ship has emergency blast doors. They'll probably try to close them, seal us off."

"Let's go," Ferrick grunted.

A Cowboy piled through the outer hatch and ran up to Ferrick. "Here," he said, and thrust a scatterblaster into Ferrick's hands. The thing was about as long as a baseball bat, with a ring of barrels like an ancient Gatling gun. Weighed a ton, dealt an enormous amount of firepower. Ferrick hefted it, flicked that switchblade grin again. Jim noticed his teeth were bloody. Had he *bitten* the alien?

"That's more like it," Ferrick said. He turned, thrust through the team. Pointed a finger at three of them. "You three. Stay here, keep the hatch open, but douse the lights."

They nodded, split away as Ferrick peered out the port. He turned back to Jim. "I don't think anybody's noticed yet. They're all still watching the fight."

Jim nodded. "We got to get moving."

"Right." Ferrick brought one hand up, like a cavalry leader signaling the charge. "The rest of you, follow me," he roared. "No mercy! Kill everybody."

Jim said, "Hey! That's not the plan!"

But Ferrick was gone. A couple of seconds later, the gunfire began.

"Shit!" Jim said, and took off running.

4

It began to fall apart about halfway through.

Ferrick and his gang poured through the corridors of the ship like hot lava, screaming, leaping, killing. The carnage was appalling. The aliens didn't seem to have much heavy weaponry, at least not the portable kind. But some of them did have small energy weapons. They were huge, strong as two men, and they used that, too. Jim passed one body that looked so strange he stopped for a second, trying to figure it out. Then he realized: The head was gone, twisted or chewed off.

He found two more bodies scorched beyond recognition, and another kid, a small, brown-haired guy, whose face looked like it had been roasted in a microwave, the skin crusted, blackened, and oozing in red-meat fissures. The kid was barely conscious, moaning and twisting. Jim, his stomach lurching, knelt next to him, touched his shoulder, said, "Hang on, you're gonna be okay, you're gonna be fine."

The kid didn't seem to hear him, and Jim went on, a wad of bile big as a doughnut choking his throat. The ship had gone eerily silent, except for the mournful hooting of the alarm. Smoke drifted in the corridors. Shafts of orange light dropped like glowing pillars from the ceiling, outlined in the haze. One Terran Pleb kid, his hair hanging in his face, muttered that the place smelled like a Kansas City barbecue joint as Jim went past him.

He found Ferrick and several of the others crouched behind a makeshift barricade, a pile of oversize alien furniture, some equipment racks, a couple of huge barrels. He slid in behind Ferrick's shoulder, tapped him. Ferrick jerked, turned, stared at him.

"Oh. Okay," he said. He sounded vaguely disoriented, not all there, not connected

"What's going on? Why did you stop?"

Ferrick gestured with the barrel of his blaster. "Keep your head down," he said. "They managed to get one of the blast doors shut. There's still a couple on this side, and they've got guns. We've been potshotting back and forth."

"That's trouble," Jim said.

"Yeah. I sent some of the guys looking for another way in. This can't be the only way into the bridge and the comm section."

"Hang on," Jim told him. He pulled out his tablet and lit it up. He traced the schematic with his fingertip. As he worked it, he felt an odd itch, like a rash on the back of his neck. "There's two other passages, one an emergency gangway back to the engine room, the other a ventilator and cable tube." He squinted, tapped the screen, read what came up: "The ventilator shaft is ten inches wide. No help."

"What about the emergency thing?"

"They'll have it blocked off by now. Besides, it's pretty small, only wide enough for one of them to squeeze through at a time. Just one guy with one of those hand beamers could hold it against us forever."

"And we ain't got forever," Ferrick said. "Okay, I was afraid of that." He glanced forward, chewing on his lower lip. "We got to go through there, in other words."

"Yeah."

Ferrick closed his eyes, thought about it some more, sighed heavily. "Okay, then," he said. "It's trade-off time."

"Huh? What—"

"Shut up and watch, Wolfbane boy."

"Ferrick, what are you gonna do?"

Ferrick racked the slide on the scatterblaster, arming it. "Send a bunch of the guys over the top to draw fire. They'll either get the apes." He lifted the blaster slightly. "Or I will."

Jim stared at him in horror. The other boy had been hot. Now he was cold as ice again. Jim could almost feel the chill blowing off him, like leaning too close to the open door of a freezer. "Jesus, Ferrick, you'll kill a bunch of our own people."

"You want through that blast door or not?"

"We can't—"

"Sure we can. I can," Ferrick told him.

As Jim groped for an answer—*Jesus, I can't let him just kill those guys*—he felt the itch again, stronger but still somehow phantomlike. A ghost itch. His fingers moved toward the back of his neck. Stopped.

"Oh, frack," he whispered.

"What?"

"Can't you feel it? Like an itch on your skin?"

"What about it?"

"They're starting the engines. The drive. But they're still docked, inside the *OB*'s hull."

Ferrick rose into a crouch, peering forward. "Then I'd better—"

"No! If they light their torch, they'll destroy the whole colony!"

Ferrick settled back down. "That true?"

"Yeah."

"Shit," Ferrick said.

"Shit what?" Kerry asked.

5

Kerry looked like he'd stuck his face in a garbage disposal. He held his left arm gingerly, at an awkward angle.

"Damn," Ferrick said, sounding as close to awed as Jim had ever heard him. "That little fracker really worked you over."

"You oughta see what he looks like," Kerry said.

"It's over, then?"

"Yeah, it's over. Darnell sent everybody home after they ratified the change. He's the new top-kick now." Kerry sounded a little sad. "It was hard. There at the end, I could have taken him. I thought about it, but—" He shrugged. "So what's the problem here? From my understanding of the plan, it looks like you're a little behind schedule."

Jim explained about the drives. "They haven't fired them up all the way. But they've started the countdown."

Kerry raised up a little, grunted, and peered over the barricade. "Huh," he said. He sank back down, looked at Ferrick. "You know we can get through that door. At least those guys in front of it."

"Yeah, I know. I told him how." He tilted his head at Jim.

"So what are we waiting for?"

Ferrick exhaled. "I was gonna do it, but Jim's right. It might be enough to spook them into lighting off their torch. If they think they're all gonna die anyway, why not take the chance? If they pull it off, get out into space, they can decompress the rest of the ship. Turn us all into vacuum-dried people-jerky."

Kerry thought about it, finally nodded. "So it's a standoff."

"For the time being," Jim agreed.

"Well, it can't stay a standoff for very long," Kerry said.

"What do you mean?"

Kerry made an exasperated clicking sound. "Think it through, genius. They've started firing up their drive. You think our little computer hacks are enough to keep that away from the Authority? We can make this bay look empty to the computers. But we can't hide a fracking space drive clearing its throat back here."

"Oh, God," Ferrick said. "I didn't think of that."

"Yeah," Kerry said. "There's probably an army of proctors steaming for this bay right now."

Ferrick groaned. "Oh, shit. A sandwich."

"Uh-huh," Kerry replied. "That's right, a shit sandwich, and we're the ones gonna be eating it. Right in the middle."

6

"By the way, Sam says hi," Kerry said.

Jim was concentrating on his tablet, pummeling his tired brain, trying to figure a way through. "Um-huh," he muttered. Then, suddenly, he looked up. "She's not here?"

Kerry nodded. "She changed her mind at the last minute. Decided to come along for the ride. I left her at the entry hatch. Didn't want to bring her in till I knew what was up."

"Damn, Kerry. You gotta get her out of here. This whole thing could blow any minute."

Kerry shrugged. "Get her out where? If it does blow, it won't matter whether she's here on the ship, or out in the colony. We all eat it, right?"

Jim closed his eyes, shook his head. "Actually, she might be safer here. This frackin' ship is a converted Hunzzan light cruiser. And I'm not sure how converted it is. Got good armor, anyway."

Ferrick had left to recon the situation. Jim and Kerry had left a small team to keep the two aliens bottled up in their hidey-hole in front of the blast door, and retreated to a cabin farther back. They were close enough they could get back to the action if they had to, but in the meantime, they could come and go without worrying about somebody getting his head blown off.

Ferrick walked through the door, his dark eyes shadowed beneath half-lowered lips. His throat was bruised and swollen from the first fight with the alien who'd choked him, and he was stiffening up a little from being slammed against the bulkhead. His hair stuck out in odd places. He ran his fingers through it.

"They're out there," he said. "About a million of them. Got loudspeakers and rifles and all that shit."

"What are they doing?"

"Not much. We've got the hatch cracked maybe an inch, just enough to keep an eye on them. They keep yelling about giving ourselves up. I dunno if they mean us or the Kolumbans."

Jim glanced at him. Kolumbans. That was the first he'd heard of that. He made a mental note, filed it away.

"They probably don't know themselves," Kerry said. He uttered a short, barking laugh. "They must be pissing their drawers out there, trying to figure out how a deep-space cruiser showed up in their empty cargo bay."

"Yeah, well, that may be so, but they're gonna stop pissing pretty soon and try to do something about it."

Jim looked up again. "You guys would know better than me. What can they do about it?"

Ferrick scratched his head. "Hm. Hard to say, exactly. The colony isn't heavily armed. Just peacekeeping stuff, you know, like for crowd control and routine police work. We weren't set up to fight no wars. Definitely not against any space cruisers, anyhow. That scatterblaster of mine, that's about as heavy as anything they got."

"Huh. Can't do much against a foot of reinforced armor plate with that," Jim said. "Not to mention the force shields."

"Well, we don't control the force shields," Ferrick said. "As it was, I had to physically cut the hardwiring to the main entry hatch. Those frackers on the bridge kept trying to open it."

"So how are you gonna move it, if you have to?"

"The old-fashioned way. Brute force. Just shove it back and forth."

Jim thought about it. "I don't know if we can get a good seal that way, just shoving it closed."

"So what?" Kerry said. "So it leaks a little. There's oxygen on both sides of it."

"Right now there is," Jim agreed.

Ferrick stared at him. "Uh-oh," he said.

"Yeah," Jim replied. "It would be a real bitch, but it might work. Maybe."

Kerry was shifting his gaze back and forth between them, a suddenly worried expression on his battered features.

"What are you two assholes talking about?"

Jim and Ferrick glanced at each other. "There's one thing we could try," Jim said.

7

"I wish we had our computers," Jim said.

He and Ferrick were arm deep in a cable junction. They'd ended up ripping out a big piece of bulkhead to get at it.

"I dunno if they would do any good," Ferrick said. "Machine language incompatibility, probably."

Jim gestured at the squiggly, serpentine markings on the nest of wires. "This is all Hunzza stuff, their kind of writing," he said. "They probably modified all the user IDs to whatever these—what'd you call them, Kolumbans?"

Ferrick nodded absently, his concentration fixed on a junction box he'd cracked open and from which he was carefully separating multicolored wires.

"So everything out where they can use it is Kolumban language, whatever that is, but the hidden stuff is still Hunzzan. Probably the computer system, too. The Hunzzans build good computers, from what I know. I studied their code once."

Ferrick turned his head. "These Hunzza. Lizards, right? One of the big-time alien powers? Got an empire or something."

"Yeah, one of them. And the Albans."

"Those are the dog boys?"

"Uh-huh."

"I don't guess they told us much about them in school." He chuckled sharply, an almost-hysterical sound, and Jim suddenly realized Ferrick wasn't as icy as he seemed. "Didn't get that much school, either."

"Well, it doesn't matter now. Just that the Hunzza are good, and they sell to just about anybody with money."

"So they sold the apes this ship?"

"Looks like it."

Ferrick stuck his tongue in his cheek. "I never give the apes much thought. Dealers is all. The only thing you worry about with dealers is the quality of the dope. And whether they try to rip you off."

Jim nodded, reached into the opening, and pulled out another length of thick, multicolored cables. "These Kolumban guys honest crooks?"

"Yeah. Always gave accurate weight. Showed up when they said they would, never tried to change the price. Honest enough."

"How'd you get started with them? I mean, the dope. Dealing it. How'd you make the connection?"

Ferrick looked at him. "You sure you're not working for somebody? That curiosity of yours."

Jim started to laugh. It was thin, and stopped after a couple of seconds, but it was laughter. Weird. That you could be deep in the shit like this, and still laugh.

"Yeah, I'm a secret agent, man. Hang on a second, I'll get out my comm, call up the fleet to rescue us."

"Funny," Ferrick said.

"No, I'm just wondering. We're all probably gonna die, I'd sorta like to know the details of why."

"I don't really know," Ferrick said. "Kerry came up with it, but he never explained. You know Kerry."

"Yeah."

They both fell silent, working with the cables. "You think this will work?" Ferrick asked.

Jim didn't look at him. "A lot of stuff has to go right. And I'm probably no better at guessing what the aliens might do than you are."

"I know one thing. They know they're dealing dope. They know it's illegal here on the ship, the kind of quantity they're bringing in. They won't talk to the Authority unless they have to."

"Maybe they can cut a deal. The Authority won't want the colony blown up."

"Yeah, give them both enough time, they'll probably work something out. But we don't plan to give them enough time."

Kerry wandered up, looking as tense and bored as a guy with a face like chopped hamburger can. "How's it going?" he asked.

"We're getting there," Jim said.

CHAPTER FOURTEEN

1

"Sam, you take a crew and search the ship. Locate all the food and make sure it's guarded."

Sam looked tired, a pallid stretchiness to the skin at the side of her eyes, and two vertical lines incised at the bridge of her nose said she was scared, too. But hiding it well, Jim thought, wishing he could touch her, run his fingertips across her honey-colored cheek. . . .

She nodded as he went on. "I don't think they can break out of the bridge area. We've got their food, and they should be getting hungry pretty soon."

"They're vegetarians," Ferrick said. "Nothing but weeds in the food-storage lockers."

"All the better. Vegetarians need to eat a lot."

Kerry said, "These are alien vegetarians, remember."

"Sure. But just because they're aliens doesn't mean they can violate the laws of physics. There's less available energy, pound for pound, in vegetables than in meat."

Kerry lifted his eyebrows. "Is that so?"

"Uh-huh. What do you think the meat you eat—like cows and stuff—eats? Vegetables and grains, that's what. You can think of people who eat meat as eating concentrated veggies."

"Score another useless fact for formal education," Kerry muttered.

"Not so useless. It means we know the Kolumbans will get hungrier quicker than if they ate meat. And they're less likely to have a few tons of hay stored in the bridge for snacks. That goes for those two holed up outside the blast door, too. They'll be getting real hungry, real soon."

"All right," Kerry said.

Sam got up and left the room, leaving the three boys together. They were gathered around a Kolumban table, too tall for them, and were perched like small children on thick printout ledgers placed on the chair seats. The tabletop was littered with more printouts and scraps of paper on which Jim had scrawled things as he thought of them.

His tablet was open in front of him. He leaned forward, worked the controls, found what he was looking for. "Here's some more formal education," he said.

"Oh, boy," Ferrick said.

"No, you'll like this, Ferrick. Lot of killing involved."

Ferrick's eyelids flickered. A glint appeared in his bleary gaze. "Killing? Yeah?"

"Uh-huh. You ever heard of Caesar?"

"Scissor?" Ferrick shook his head. "Nope. What is it, some kind of fancy knife?"

"Not a knife. An old-time guy from Terra. Long time ago." He spelled out the name for them.

"He any relative of that Machiavelli guy?" Kerry asked.

Jim shook his head. "But he was from the same people, except he lived about a thousand five hundred years before Machiavelli."

"Who the hell is Machiavelli?" Ferrick wondered.

"An old gang consigliere," Kerry told him.

Ferrick brightened. "He know his shit?"

"He knew it."

Ferrick looked over at Jim. "So what about this Caesar? Another old-time advisor?"

"No, he was one of the greatest generals who ever lived," Jim said. "That's the killing part I told you. Caesar fought a bunch of wars against the enemies of Rome. They were known as the Gauls. Barbarians."

Ferrick tasted the unfamiliar word. "Barbarians?"

"The Techs probably think the Plebs are barbarians," Jim told him.

"Oh. I get it. So Caesar killed a bunch of barbarians? How

does that help? Looks to me like we're the barbarians in the current picture."

"Whenever he won a battle, Caesar wrote down everything about it. It's still around. Even the guys at ConFleet study his battles. You learn about them at the Academy." Jim paused. "I. . . wanted to go to the Academy once. So I started learning about all this stuff. To get ready, you know?"

"I guess," Ferrick said.

"Anyway, I've got every major battle ever fought stored away in my tablet. I can look them up. And this deal here? With us caught in the middle? Caesar fought a battle just like it. It was called the Battle of Alesia, and it's one of the most famous fights in human military history."

"He was caught just like us? Surrounded on the outside and the inside? So what happened?"

Jim grinned. "He kicked their asses. All of them. Just like we're gonna do."

Ferrick looked down at the table, stirred his blunt fingers through the mass of paper. "I dunno, Jim. Some guy from a long time ago when they fought with spears or whatever. I don't see how that helps us."

"Tactics and strategy, Ferrick. When you get right down to it, there isn't a hell of a lot of difference between a spear and a scatterblaster. You can use either one to kill somebody up close. You got a hole through your chest, it doesn't matter whether it got there from my .75, or your bowie knife."

Ferrick understood that. "Okay. That makes sense."

"You need some education, you ignorant asshole," Kerry said, but he grinned as he said it, to take the sting out.

"Yeah, yeah. Tell you what. If this Caesar fracker helps us get out of this, I'll give it a whirl. Jim? You teach me?"

Jim felt a bit of heat kindle in his belly, and thought he might pull everything off yet. If he was lucky and good. Although lucky might end up playing the bigger role.

"Count on it," he said.

Then he told them about Caesar and the Battle of Alesia.

2

A younger boy named Elwood knocked on the doorjamb of the small storeroom Ferrick had converted into his command post. "Yeah. Come in," Ferrick said.

Elwood entered. He was seventeen, tall, and very thin, still getting his growth. His Adam's apple stuck out and bobbed when he talked. Ferrick had once seen a nature vid about some earth snake, maybe a python, eating a goat. The goat would go down the python in jerky little jumps. Elwood's Adam's apple reminded him of that.

Elwood had curly hair the color of carrots, cut close on the side, blooming in a pile of tight curls on top. His ears stuck out, and his nose was a first-class honker. It was easy to underestimate Elwood. Ferrick had never made that mistake. Elwood never seemed to get too hot or too cold. It was hard to describe just what he did get. Ferrick had groped around for it once, finally decided the best description of Elwood was . . . interested.

Nothing ever seemed to upset him, but you didn't want to get him interested. He'd have that alertly placid, *interested* expression on his kisser while he sawed your head off. Probably watching to see what came out of the hole in your neck. He even scared Ferrick sometimes. But he was about the smartest guy Ferrick knew, besides Jim and Kerry, and he knew how to follow orders. They'd been noodling around with the idea of Ferrick teaching him about computers. Elwood was interested in them, too, and Ferrick had given some thought to the possibility of transferring Elwood's interest to something a little more productive than outright murder. Not that outright murder didn't have a place sometimes. . . .

Ferrick was stroking the edge of his bowie on a thin strip of whetstone, one slow, careful scrape after another. Elwood watched for a few seconds—he liked knives, found them interesting—then hunkered down next to Ferrick, and said, "Sam's doing a good job."

"Tell me," Ferrick said.

"She's been playing around with that Kolumban shit, their

food. She defrosted a bunch of it and figured out how to use their galley equipment. Been trying to cook it so it don't taste as bad as it looks."

"Is that what that bowl of brown shit was?"

"Yeah, I guess. Mine was yellow and blue," Elwood said. "How'd yours taste?"

Ferrick glanced up from his work. "Like brown shit."

Elwood nodded. "I don't think there's no such thing as yellow-and-blue shit, but if there was, that's what mine tasted like, too."

"Did it kill anybody?"

"Nah. Nobody even got sick, last I heard."

"Good. Jim said we could eat it okay."

Elwood settled down until his legs stuck out in front of him and his back was against the wall. "About this Jim guy," he said, and then stopped.

Ferrick's knife stopped moving. "What about him?"

"Uhm, don't take this wrong, okay?"

"Spit it out, Elwood."

Elwood knit his long, knobby fingers together, stared down at them like they were of intense interest. Like maybe he would eat them or something.

"I know you top guys, you and Kerry, seem to kiss his ass a lot. But you know, he ain't even been beat in yet."

Ferrick leaned back, closed his eyes, exhaled, the movement causing his lips to flap softly together. Bronx cheer, though he'd never heard of the Bronx.

"So you think maybe we're dealing too much with somebody we don't know exactly how strong his loyalties are? Somebody not a real Cowboy?"

Elwood looked away. "You the one said it, not me."

Ferrick set the knife aside, began to pull absently on his lower lip. He'd been afraid this would happen, been expecting it, actually, but he'd hoped not this soon. Still, now that it had come up, he'd have to deal with it.

He knew that Elwood wasn't dumb, just ignorant. Ignorant meant uneducated, and didn't have anything to do with how smart you were. He'd educated himself about computers. Some other stuff as well, things he'd decided he should know more about. So he was still ignorant, but not as ignorant as Elwood.

He thought everybody was probably ignorant about a lot of things, though Jim came closer to not being ignorant, in a general way, than anybody else he knew. Jim, with his education and his natural smarts, always seemed to know at least something about almost everything.

He tried to think how to explain this to Elwood, who understood his world on an instinctive level, though not really on an intellectual level. Elwood sort of knew how things should work, without having much of a clue why they worked that way. Ferrick had taken the trouble to learn about the why, at least about some things. He figured it gave him an advantage. Besides, when he was in the mood, he liked learning shit. It made him feel powerful, somehow, to know stuff other people didn't.

It was called sociology. It was an actual science, like physics or something, though he got the idea it wasn't quite as tight as, say, mathematics. You could add two and two and always end up with four, but when you tried to do the same thing with people, the answers were often different. But allowing for that, there was a lot of stuff out there about how people interacted with each other. There was even a subset of sociology called "gang studies," and he'd spent a lot of time boning up on that.

So make it a little exam for Elwood. See whether he was fooling himself, or whether Elwood actually had real possibilities.

He picked up the knife again, started stroking. "Elwood, what do you think a gang is for?"

Elwood blinked. "Huh? What do you mean?"

Ferrick gestured with the knife. "Why do you think gangs exist? You think about it, it's sort of stupid, eh? Bunch of kids stick together, start doing illegal shit, fight all the time. Hump the girls, tell their own families to screw off, at least the ones who have families. So why? How come it happens that way?"

"You're serious, aren't you?"

"As a bullet in the brain, Elwood."

"Ho. Um, well." Elwood scrunched his forehead, working it. Finally, he said slowly, "I was gonna say it's just natural that it happens. But that isn't quite it. The most natural thing is families. The way people stick together. Mom and Pop and the kids. They're all related, see? Got the blood. And the . . . I dunno, the instincts."

"That's good, Elwood," Ferrick said. "Keep on going."

Elwood warmed up. Now he was *interested*, and his eyes, the shifting gray colors of a spring storm cloud, began to glow. "So if you take kids away from their families, which they'd naturally be a part of if things was normal, then they miss them."

"Why? Why miss them?"

"'Cause you get shit from being with your family." Elwood looked down at his hands again. "Not just like money or food or stuff, okay? But like closeness. Loyalty. Uh . . . like . . ." He stopped, embarrassed.

"It's okay, you can say it," Ferrick told him. "I won't rank you." He snorted. "I'd be the last one to do that."

"Yeah," Elwood said, his cheeks dusting with pink. "Love. Kids want to be loved, right? I did. Didn't you?"

"'Course I did, Elwood. So if you don't have a family where you get all that shit, the closeness, the understanding, loyalty and . . . love, what do you do?"

"Maybe you go look for it. See if you can find it somewhere else." He brightened. "Like the Cowboys." Abruptly he reached up and slammed his fist against his chest. "The Cowboys are *my* family."

"They are, huh?"

Elwood went on, really rolling with it now. "Sure. Even better than a family, 'cause people understand me. Everybody's like me, knows the same shit. Not like parents, all the time trying to make you do useless shit, never understanding what life is like."

Ferrick eyed him, surprised to find his own interest ignited. "But the Cowboys tell you what to do. We got rules, you break them, we mess you up a lot worse than Mommy or Daddy would ever do."

"Sure. But I don't mind. Nobody minds. 'Cause it's fair. The rules are part of the game, and we all know them. We all agree to them."

"Some don't. A few."

"Sure, but there's always assholes. And when that happens, we kick them out."

"Just like some kids get kicked out by their own families."

"That's different."

"Is it, Elwood? Is it really?"

Elwood's blush deepened. He thought he'd made some kind of

mistake, made himself look stupid. His first reaction was to get mad, but he looked up and saw Ferrick staring at him calmly. Like he was really curious. So he dug a little deeper, looking for the answer.

"I think so," he said. "See, you don't get a choice about your family. You're born into it, nobody asks you. Or asks them, either, maybe your family would rather not have you. So nobody gets a choice. But you have to choose to join the gang. And . . . the gang has to choose you!"

"Long time ago, in the old cities, some people used to say everybody belonged to a gang because, well, everybody belonged to a gang. It was the thing to do. They called it peer pressure."

Elwood stared at him. "Sounds to me like somebody didn't know shit about gangs, then."

"Oh?"

"If everybody could be in a gang, what would be the point? It would just be part of the way things were. Like breathing. No choice. Not for you, not for the gang."

"That's really it, isn't it? The choice? And that not just everybody can choose? Or be chosen?"

"Yeah, yeah, that's it. Peer pressure, that's bullshit."

Ferrick shifted. He'd been leaning slightly forward, listening intently, and now his bruised back protested. He leaned back, trying for a more comfortable position.

"Well, I'll tell you a little secret, Elwood. It isn't *entirely* bullshit."

"Sure it is. You know it."

"Not after you make your choice. Not after you get into the gang. There's more than a thousand Cowboys. And most everybody follows the rules. How come that is? What keeps them in line?"

"Well, people like you, Kerry, Darnell. Maybe a little ass-kicking here and there." He grinned. "You know I've done my share with my own crew."

"But could me or Kerry kick everybody's asses?" Ferrick shook his head. "Not hardly. We don't need to, though. 'Cause if somebody starts acting like an asshole, breaking the rules, *everybody* will kick his ass. 'Cause everybody agrees on the rules, and agrees we should all follow them."

"Uhm . . . yeah. I guess you're right. I never thought about it that way exactly."

"That's peer pressure, Elwood. Peer means equal. Your equals put the screws on you if you mess up. And in the Cowboys, first thing is, we're all equal. We're all Cowboys."

"Okay."

"Which is why Jim makes you nervous. Or did you know that already?"

Elwood gave his head a little puzzled shake. "I don't follow."

"The first thing you said about him was he hadn't been beaten in."

"Well, yeah. And it's true, ain't it?"

"Sure. But Kerry and me, we aren't bothered. We deal with the guy. You trust us, right? So how come you still got a bat up your butt about it?"

"'Cause you treat him like one of us. Like a real Cowboy, and he ain't one. Not yet."

"Ice out, Elwood. You ain't wrong. In fact, you're right."

It surprised him. "I am?"

"Course you are. You may not know"—Ferrick tapped his own forehead—"up here, exactly why, but you *are* right."

"So tell me."

"'Cause Jim hasn't chosen. Kerry chose him, so the Cowboys chose him, but Jim himself hasn't made his own choice. It's not two ways yet. And until Jim accepts our own rules, goes through the initiation, gets beaten in, whatever, he's not a peer. He's not an equal. He's not a Cowboy. And until he is, you're right not to trust him."

Elwood fell silent. After a while he looked up. "Do you trust him, Ferrick? From what I hear, you guys are depending on him pretty heavy."

Ferrick had stopped whetting his blade. Now he started again, the steel making slow scritching noises against the stone.

"I trust him for some things," Ferrick said slowly. "The things he knows about." He looked up, and for a moment his eyes were very cold, like raisins after a frost. "But trust him like a Cowboy, like family, like a brother? He knows a lot of shit, but he doesn't know about us. Not really. So, hell, no, I don't trust him that way!"

Ferrick gave the blade a final vicious swipe and stopped. He grinned, and somebody who didn't know him might have thought it was a cheery expression. But Elwood knew him.

"And I won't, not until I've personally busted him in the mouth a couple of times, and he's an official, beaten-in Cowboy."

"That's good enough," Elwood said.

"Better be," Ferrick replied. "It's true."

3

Elwood left a couple of minutes later. Ferrick heard him mumble something just beyond the doorway, talking to somebody, then Kerry walked in. He stood for a second, looking down, grinning at him. Then, slowly, he raised his hands and began to clap, his grin growing wider.

"What the frack's that for?" Ferrick asked.

"I stood outside, couldn't help listening to your little speech."

Ferrick's gaze darkened. "Yeah? You got a problem with what I said or something?"

"No, no, not at all. You surprise me sometimes, Ferrick." Kerry came over, squatted. "You really do."

"Why? 'Cause I'm not a total dumb-ass all the time? Frack you, Kerry."

"Hey. I didn't mean it that way. You were right. Not everybody really understands the . . . dynamics . . . of something like the Cowboys, but you got it down."

Ferrick bobbed his head, still not sure whether to be pissed or pleased. "All right."

"But you left out one thing, and I'm curious. Whether you did it on purpose, or hadn't thought about it."

"What's that?"

"For us, for you and me—and for Elwood, too, though he

might not quite have it figured out yet—there ain't any more Cowboys. The Cowboys are dead and gone for us, they belong to Darnell now. I don't know what we are, but we aren't Cowboys. Not any longer."

"I know," Ferrick said.

"But you didn't say anything to Elwood. How come?"

"'Cause it don't matter. We may not be Cowboys, but if we get out of this shit we'll be something. We'll still be a gang. And the same rules will apply."

Kerry eyed him somberly. "Will they, Ferrick?"

Ferrick looked up in surprise. "What the hell are you saying, Kerry?"

"Something you should consider," Kerry replied. "Something you should think about." Then he tapped him once on the knee, nodded, got up, and left.

4

Jim's brain felt like somebody had spread it out and gone roller-skating on it. They were into the third day of the standoff now, and he'd made all the adjustments he could think of. He hadn't mentioned it to Kerry and Ferrick, but Caesar had known a couple of other things, too: the main thing being that in a battle, no matter how good your plans were, you could always count on something going wrong. Which wasn't much help, unless you knew exactly what one thing would go wrong, and you never did.

Their plans to take the ship had foundered on one insignificant item: The Kolumbans had managed to get a blast door closed with two of them on the wrong side of it. So until they removed those two, they couldn't just rip the wall open over the control panel and open the door from the outside.

One little thing, and it had screwed the whole deal. He'd spent the last three days coming up with a different way. Who would have thought he'd need a good cook to make the new plan work?

The good cook turned out to be a pudgy, slow-moving kid named Hunky. Hunky had a button nose, watery hazel eyes, and an earnest, peering look to him, like he was always just about to ask a question. But he had a way with cooking, a natural talent. He could just smell something and have a pretty fair idea if it was any good. He was a little out of his depth with Kolumban recipes, though. After trying a couple of ideas, he'd told Sam it wasn't working. Early this morning Sam had told Jim.

"But I don't know much about cooking," Jim said.

"No, but maybe you can figure out this Kolumban writing. I found something that looks like recipes in a computer in the galley, but I don't know for sure."

"Oh. All right, I'll take a look."

Now he, Sam, and Hunky were all gathered around a holovid terminal as impenetrable squiggles danced across the screen.

"Can you read this shit?" Sam asked.

"Nah. Neither can my tablct." Jim waved the small unit. He'd established an infrared relay between the tablet and the terminal, but without a Kolumban database, the tablet couldn't translate.

"Then we're screwed," Hunky said. He was sweating. The galley was the warmest place on the ship.

"Maybe not," Jim said, running his fingers across an on-screen touch pad of menus. "Well, okay. Look there," he muttered.

"What?" Sam said, peering over his shoulder.

"Those are Alban characters. Let's see if they've got an Alban translator function built in." He fiddled with the controls a bit, tapping one icon, then another, and finally the entire screen changed.

"There we go," he said. "Wait a minute." He switched to his tablet. "Okay. This may not be perfect." A printer underneath the terminal whirred into action, then spit out a sheet of thin, plasticized paper. Jim picked it up, looked at it, nodded.

"They use smart type. Just tap the corner of the paper when you want a new recipe. Like I said, it may not be perfect—it's been translated from Kolumban to Alban to English—but Sam says you're a talented guy, Hunky. You'll figure it out."

Hunky's plump cheeks turned the color of ripe strawberries. "She did?" he said, his voice rough, husked with wonder. He wouldn't look at her.

Oh, Jesus, Jim thought. *She's got another one in love with her.* He felt some sympathy, but it was tempered with a certain jealousy. He slapped the other boy on one meaty shoulder.

"How soon can you come up with some stuff?"

Hunky was holding the sheet in one greasy hand, scanning it. "This looks pretty simple. I think I know what most of the ingredients are. We've been through this galley pretty good."

"If you run into any markings you can't understand, let me know, and we'll try the dual translation thing again. Cook up something that smells good, Hunky."

Hunky nodded. "This afternoon be okay?"

"Yeah. That would be great."

Jim wondered if Caesar had ever hinged an entire battle on something as unwarlike as a delicious-smelling home-cooked meal.

Maybe not, but if he'd had to, he would have dealt with it. Not many people understood, but that was the real lesson Caesar taught. Whatever it was, deal with it.

CHAPTER FIFTEEN

1

On the morning of the fourth day, Kerry woke Jim up, and said, "Something's happening with the Authority. You'd better come."

Jim sat up, blinking, his back aching from the makeshift bed he'd cobbled together out of some cargo rugs they'd found. His mouth tasted like a pigeon graveyard: Thank God you couldn't die from morning mouth.

"Come on, come on," Kerry said, snapping his fingers nervously. "This ain't nursery school."

Jim climbed to his feet, groaned, ran one hand through hair that felt like a nest of greasy straw. "What are they doing now?"

Kerry was halfway out the door. He paused, looked over his shoulder. "I think they're getting ready to fire on the ship."

"Slow down, wait for me," Jim said.

2

Ferrick was waiting for them at the entry port, with a squad of three heavily armed boys. He scowled, cradling his scatterblaster as he squinted through the inch-wide opening they'd left when they pushed the outer lock shut.

"Anything new?" Kerry said, as he and Jim came up.

"No. They're still milling around out there, screwing with that cannon thing." He stepped back from the door and motioned for a very tall, extremely thin boy to take his place. "Keep an eye, Elwood. If somebody gets too close, shoot them."

Elwood nodded. Jim thought he looked like a jug-eared geek, like he couldn't hurt a flea. Then he looked again. There was something unsettling about Elwood's mild gray eyes, a weird calm that didn't fit the tension of the moment. He looked like he might find shooting somebody, or a whole lot of somebodies, quite interesting. In a detached sort of way, like stepping on bugs.

Jim moved up next to Elwood and took a look. About two hundred yards away were gathered half a dozen blue-uniformed proctors, in front of maybe a hundred uncomfortable rankers who looked way out of their depth. Breaking up fights or cleaning up after accidents was one thing. An alien ship appearing out of nowhere was another. They all stared nervously at the ship, as if it might blow up at any moment.

Hell, it might, Jim thought.

In their midst was a square, squat, aluminum-colored shape with a heavy, bell-shaped barrel. The wide end of the barrel was aimed directly at the door—to Jim, it was like looking down a chrome-plated well. He stared at it a long moment, trying to figure it out.

"You should have got me up," Jim said, as he and the other two retreated several paces from the door.

"The doofus we had watching the door didn't notice anything out of the ordinary until they started yelling at us with a loud hailer," Ferrick said, disgusted. "By the time he sent somebody for me, and I sent for Kerry, and Kerry had a look for himself . . ." He shrugged. "You know the drill. Screwups all around." He shook his head. "Too late to worry about it. What do we do now?"

"First thing, we stay cool," Jim said. "I'm not sure that thing is really even a cannon. It doesn't look like one. Kerry, you said you had a pipe into the proctor armory. They have any cannon?"

Kerry shook his head. "But they've had three days, and

they've got all the manufacturing capability in the world out there. Maybe they built one."

"Yeah, I guess they could have. But it can't be a cannon. You're not gonna get through a deep-space hull by lobbing steel balls at it. No matter how fast you toss them."

"Huh," Ferrick said. "That's right. I never thought of that."

"Don't get me wrong," Jim said. "They probably cobbled *something* together, unless that thing is a total fake that's just supposed to scare us out."

"That'd be pretty stupid, even for proctors," Kerry said.

"You said they were yelling something through a loudspeaker. Anybody think to record it?"

"I doubt it," Ferrick replied. "I'll go get the kid who heard it." He rubbed his chin. "He's not the hottest chip in the processing unit, though."

Jim waved him off. "That's okay. It doesn't really matter. We knew they'd make a move eventually, counted on it. So the first thing to find out is if this is their move. And what kind of move they think it is."

"What are you gonna do, just ask them?" Kerry said.

"That's usually the easiest way, yeah," Jim replied.

3

"Careful," Ferrick told Elwood. "Watch those frackers."

Elwood nodded, edged back from the door a bit, leveled his heavy-duty battle laser at the widening opening. Ferrick joined him, the huge barrel-snouts of his scatterblaster also seeking targets beyond the door.

"Open it just wide enough for them to see me, and for me to get in and out," Jim said. "If they're gonna shoot at us with that thing, whatever it is, let's give them as few targets as we can."

"The main one being you," Kerry said. "You sure you want to go? It really ought to be me."

"If we're gonna negotiate, the more respect we get, the better off we are. They know you. Far as they're concerned, you're a crook. Hell, you probably been paying off half those guys out there."

Kerry spread his hands. "What can I say? A little more than half, actually. Of the honchos, at least."

"You said I didn't act like a Pleb, or sound like one. Maybe that will be an advantage. A small one, but something."

"I think those guys want to shoot somebody, and they won't be real concerned about your social standing if that somebody turns out to be you," Kerry observed. "They gotta be going nuts by now."

Jim quirked his lips. "So let's give them something to really worry about."

Kerry slapped him on the back. "I'm behind you one thousand percent." He paused, grinned as he gauged the distance from the ship to the proctors. "And about two hundred yards."

"Good enough," Jim said. "Let's see what they have to say."

4

Almost twenty-five hundred years before Jim found himself surrounded from the inside and the outside, Julius Caesar had faced a similar situation with the great Gaulish leader Vercingetorix, whom he'd pinned up in the fortress town of Alesia.

Jim had known of the battle, but hadn't really studied it until he realized just how many similarities there were between his current situation and the problems the first of the Caesars had faced—and dealt with.

He doubted if many people had ever heard of the great Julius Caesar—the man who had made his own name come to mean "leader"—or especially of his finest military moment, at Alesia. The aliens wouldn't know Caesar, and it was a fair guess the proctors hadn't studied him either. Worse for them.

They hadn't pulled the lock-door quite wide enough, and he had to turn sideways to get past it. As soon as he got on the other side, standing on top of the mobile boarding ladder, he felt as if he'd moved into the center of a naked target.

The Authority had brought up lights, lots of them, high-powered spotlights that gave the dark steel walls of the bay a washed-out look; they'd turned on all the banks of overheads as well. The whole vast area looked like the biggest stage in the world. Jim felt as welcome as a cockroach on a wedding cake.

Two of the half dozen blue uniforms gathered around the cannon had a lot of silver braid on their shoulders. As soon as Jim stepped out onto the boarding stairway and looked down at them, they began to yammer rapidly at each other. They both got red in the face and waved their arms around before finally reaching some sort of agreement. The larger of the two, an unctuous bald man with a gray fringe and a pitted nose who looked like a debauched preacher, out of place in a military uniform, left the group and lumbered hesitantly forward until he stood a few feet away from the bottom of the stairs.

He held a holocube in his hand. He looked down at it, up at Jim, then back down. "James Evanston," he said finally.

"That's me."

"No, it's not. We've figured out that much. What we haven't figured out is who you really are."

"Okay," Jim said. "Got me."

"So who are you?"

Jim shrugged. "That's not the real problem, is it?" He turned, waved one hand toward the alien ship at his back. "This is the problem, right? What's your name?"

The question threw the preacher-general off a little. He was used to asking questions, not answering them. He blinked. "Uh, call me Colonel Brian," he said.

"Call me Jim."

Keep pushing him. Don't let him think, Jim told himself.

"Yes, uh, well." Colonel Brian's gaze wandered, as if he'd forgotten for a moment why he was there. He caught himself and started over. "Listen, whoever you are—"

"—Jim," Jim said.

"—uhm, yes, Jim. All right. Enough of this. You are to leave that ship immediately and surrender to the Authority, you and the rest of your gang. Surrender to me. The aliens aboard the vessel, too. Whoever they are."

"It doesn't matter, does it? Who they are? Who I am? I'm not the problem, this ship is. The aliens want to leave, and you've got their ship locked in."

"We can do something about that," the colonel said.

"You'd better think about it before you do anything. What do you think the situation is?" Jim asked.

"Well." Brian jerked a thumb in the direction of the small army of Authority proctors drawn up behind him. "We've got you outnumbered, for one thing. And surrounded."

Ah, Alesia, Jim thought. But he didn't say it, just nodded. "That's true," he agreed. "But that's sort of like saying you've got a hydrogen bomb surrounded and outnumbered, isn't it?"

The colonel's face seemed to take on a slightly greenish tinge in the harsh lights; he licked his lips and cleared his throat. "Maybe so. We've been monitoring the radiation from the drive. But if you try to light that torch while you're in this bay with the entry locks closed, you're in the middle of the bomb, too. And you don't look suicidal to me."

"Appearances could be deceiving," Jim said. "You ever think of that?"

Colonel Brian flipped his hand back and forth. "If you're going to kill yourselves—and us along with you—then there's nothing we can do. Nothing to talk about. I might as well give them the order to shoot you now, and take our chances."

"Yeah, that would make sense. If we were both that suicidal. But what if I told you that we aren't in control of the ship. Of its drives? That we're, ah, caught in the middle, so to speak."

The colonel's eyes bulged slightly. He looked at Jim, then at the ship, then back to Jim again, his returning gaze now colored by a certain horrified fascination. "Is that so?" he said.

"Yeah, that's so," Jim told him.

5

"What's going on?" Kerry said when Jim came back inside.

"With them, the Authority? I don't know. I don't think even they know. I shook that fat guy up, though, told him we weren't in charge of the ship. He thought maybe we should let them come in, let them handle the aliens. And surrender ourselves, of course. He promised us light terms in the brig. That's what he said, light terms."

"Colonel Brian," Kerry snickered. "I know him."

"Yeah, he gets real nervous whenever your name comes up."

"He should. I've been doubling his Authority paycheck almost since I came aboard. He's director of public security."

"What does that mean, exactly, director of public security?"

"Head cop and chief bagman," Kerry said. "He collects the bribes for the rest of the bigwigs."

"So the last thing he needs is you getting arrested in a big deal he can't sweep under the rug? Something where the temptation for you to spill your guts might become overwhelming? Huh. I bet your term in the brig would be real light. Just until you croaked in some unfortunate accident."

"Something like that. I hadn't quite thought of it that way, but from his point of view, me getting suddenly dead wouldn't be a bad deal at all. For him, at least. . . ." Kerry said.

"Probably the rest of us, too. His idea of the best solution would be if we all died resisting arrest."

"Well, we're gonna resist," Kerry said.

6

Ferrick was halfway into another wall they'd ripped down in a corridor that had been badly torn up in the initial attack. Insulation billowed from the ceiling and hung down like gray Spanish moss. The pungent odor of burnt plastic and fire suppressant hung heavy in the air. Somebody had found a couple of portable emergency lights and focused them on the hole in the wall, giving the whole scene the flat, chill glare of an operating room.

"Any luck?"

Ferrick, stripped to the waist, pulled out of the hole. His face was streaked with grime, his hair a gooey mass plastered flat on his large skull. He swiped at his eyes, sniffed, wiped his nose on the back of his arm, shook his head. "Nah. I thought we could tap into their comm by cracking the hardwiring, but whatever they're doing, they aren't using the ship's interior systems. Hell, maybe they're tapping Morse code on the hull or something."

Jim stuck his head in the cavity, peered around at the tangle of scorched wiring, shook his head. "What a rat's nest. What do you think? Worth keeping at it?"

"Probably not," Ferrick said, shaking his head. "But it would be nice to know what the apes are saying to the Authority. If they're talking at all."

"Unless the Authority opens up the bay and lets them go, their choices are somewhat limited," Jim said.

"So are ours," Ferrick said dourly.

Jim clapped him on the shoulders. "Don't give up yet. Remember Alesia."

"Huh. I never heard of Alesia before you brought it up."

"Well, let's hope the apes and the Authority haven't either."

A deafening clap of thunder rolled down the hallway, a shock wave so powerful it sent them both staggering. Jim went to his hands and knees, head down, shaking his head. His nose began to bleed.

Ferrick grabbed him by one arm and dragged him to his feet. "Come on, let's go," he said. "It's started."

7

By the time Jim ran into the galley, he had gotten himself together. Sam, her hair and eyes wild, was frantically ladling some hot green sludge into a pair of large bowls, while Hunky steadily piled onto oversize plates something that looked and smelled like runny pig shit.

"What was that?" Sam yelled. "I felt it, then Kerry came running in and told us to get everything ready."

Jim groped for an answer. The explosive force, the vast sound . . . he remembered something . . . got it. "The Authority must have built a sonic cannon," Jim said. "As long as the shields are down, the hull will actually amplify the sonar force. It won't kill us, but they can rattle us around like peas in a blender."

As if to punctuate his thought, another blast came rumbling through the ship. It felt to Jim as if somebody was slamming a pair of anvils over his eardrums. Sam dropped the bowl she was working with, scattering the foul-smelling gunk all over the deck.

"Shit!" She whirled. "Hunky, is there more soup? No? Okay, we'll split the big bowl into two smaller ones and hope it works." She looked at Jim. "I'm sorry."

Jim patted her shoulder. "Nothing ever works perfectly," he said. "It's not really a sit-down dinner. All they have to be able to do is see it and smell it."

Sam looked down at the mess on the floor and wrinkled her nose. "They'll be able to smell it, anyway."

Ferrick stuck his head around the corner. "Sam! Move it! Jim, Kerry's at the front lock. He wants you to meet him there." He paused. "Plug your ears with something. The noise is worse up there."

"On my way," Jim said. Ferrick pulled back into the corridor. Jim heard him racking the charger on his scatterblaster as he raced away, a harsh, metallic sound. A killing sound.

Sam headed for the door, a bowl of sloshing alien sludge in her arms. She stopped, leaned over, gave Jim a peck on his cheek. "Don't worry about me, I'll be fine," she said breathlessly. "And you be careful."

Jim started to reach for her, but she spun away and was gone. "You be careful too, Sam," he yelled after her.

Hunky pushed past him and vanished. Jim stood in the silent galley as a wave of paranoia more devastating than the sonic blast washed over him. What if it didn't work? What if he'd fracked up totally?

A lot of innocent people might be dead, that's what. Ten million of them.

A third sonic boom, this one not quite as painful as the first two, jarred him out of his funk. He took a deep breath and started to run.

8

Jim came skidding around the corner into the front airlock, where Ferrick and Elwood were taking potshots at the proctors outside.

Ferrick looked up when he arrived, nodded a terse greeting. Jim sucked in some air, and said, "What's going on?"

"They've got two more of those sonic cannons set up," Ferrick yelled. He was talking loud, like a deaf man. "They're firing them off one after the other. If you feel a really solid jolt, it means they've fired two of them at the same time." He grimaced. "I can't wait for them to do all three."

Elwood paid them no attention, except to say, "Better keep back unless you've got protection. It's enough to scramble your brains head-on." He didn't look up from the gunsight of the high-powered battle laser resting against his shoulder.

He was wearing a bandage of some thick, absorbent material wrapped around his head, covering his ears. He pulled the trigger twice. The sound of the laser was like someone burping a buzz saw. Elwood's demeanor was about as Jim had figured it:

no emotion on his features beyond a calm interest in what he was doing. He might have been watching a fascinating holovid episode instead of what he was actually doing: burning large holes in the deck plating two hundred yards away.

"He's right," Ferrick bellowed. "Here." He handed Jim another set of head wrappings. "Sam rigged these up out of blankets and some Velcro fastenings. Just wind them around your head, pretty snug. They'll hold. You got earplugs?"

Jim shook his head.

"Take these. They're made out of wax. Just push them in."

Jim followed the directions, just in time to ride out another sonic boom. Though the plugs and wrap muffled it, it was still strong enough to push him back. Elwood swayed, but before the vibration had fully dissipated, he began firing the laser rifle again.

"Good man, Elwood. Steady," Ferrick roared, but now it sounded as if he was speaking in normal tones.

Jim peeked over Elwood's shoulder. The masses of proctors had vanished. He could see what looked like heads popping up, then ducking back down, at makeshift barricades set up on the far side of the bay, as far away as they could get from the ship. The sonic cannon were closer, also masked behind mounds of junk steel.

"We're not doing much damage," Ferrick said. "Even my blaster spreads too far at that range. But nobody out there's in much of a hurry to rush this frackin' door."

"How long can you keep it that way?"

Ferrick shrugged. "Until they get a sharpshooter good enough to pick us off through that opening. One with enough stones to stand up and let Elwood and me shoot at him while he shoots at us." His lips drew back from very white teeth, like a man revealing a concealed razor. "It'll be a while, in other words."

"Okay. Soon as you get the word, really start burning them. Shake them up. Get them firing those sonic cannon for all they're worth. Make it plain they aren't getting through that door, no matter what they try, till they take you out."

"We'll let them know, Jim. Ain't none of them gonna want to run right into a scatterblaster."

Jim nodded. "I'd better get going."

He paused, stuck out one hand. "If it doesn't work out, Ferrick, it's been nice knowing you."

The other boy grasped his hand, squeezed, nodded. "Gotta say one thing about you, Jim. Life has a way of getting interesting with you around."

He hefted his scatterblaster, licked his lips, nodded. "We'll hold them," he said. "Long as you don't take forever on the rest of it."

"We won't," Jim said.

9

"You got it done?" Jim asked Sam.

"Yeah, we made six bowlsful. You think it will be enough?"

"I hope so," Jim said. He peered into one of the bowls filled with sticky goo, wrinkling his nose at the stink. "Whew."

"I know. Maybe it would be better to take our chances."

He took her hands. Her fingers felt cool, but not cold. She didn't seem frightened. He wasn't sure if that was a good thing or not. "No, it wouldn't. I don't know how long the vacuum will last, but trust me. You wouldn't want to test it. Not without a suit."

"All right," she said. "I think we've got enough plastic sheeting. There are only six ventilator openings, and we've pasted all of them shut. Take a look."

She led him over to the nearest wall and pointed up at the ceiling. A square vent a foot on a side had been covered over with a thick plastic sheet glued in place with the adhesive mixture.

"That goop won't dry, but it's sticky enough to hold the plastic in place," Sam observed.

"Don't worry, then. When the rest of the ship decompresses, the air pressure here in the galley will press the plastic even tighter against the holes. Same thing with the doors. They have pretty tight seals in the first place. Smear them good with that gunk, and they oughta be airtight, too. At worst, they won't leak very fast. Enough time for us to know, one way or the other."

The galley was filling up with most of the Cowboys who'd taken part in the initial raid. Only a few would remain outside. Jim watched them as they ambled in, cracking jokes, grinning, chatting. Cool as penguins. They had to be scared, but they weren't showing it.

"You'll be okay," he said to Sam, as they walked toward the main entry.

She touched his shoulder. "I want a kiss. If we don't . . ." Her voice trailed off. Suddenly she took him, pulled him close. Put her lips on his . . .

She wore a crooked smile when she stepped back. "Not the best final clinch," she said. "But not the worst, either."

Jim took a breath. "I promise I'll do better. Later."

She moved him gently out the door. "If there is a later," she said softly, "I'll let you try."

She closed the door, leaving him staring at the other side. A moment later he heard a liquid brushing sound, as they started on their makeshift sealant around the edges.

"God, Sam . . . "

A huge sonic blast boomed down the corridor and sent him spinning. When he picked himself up, he could taste the blood running from his nose down across his lips and chin. A few more of those, and he wouldn't be good for anything at all.

10

"Careful," Kerry hissed. "Keep your frackin' head down. Just push them out as far as you can."

He and a dark, slender, almond-eyed boy named Saranji were using long metal poles to push the bowls of steaming alien goodies out across the no-man's-land before the blast door that led to the bridge.

Jim crouched behind their hasty barricade, watching. "That's good enough," he said. "Either they will or they won't. If they don't, then we have to do it the hard way. Ferrick's way."

Kerry and Saranji dragged their poles back, leaving the bowls and plates about halfway between their position and the makeshift alien defense nest by the far door.

Kerry pulled out a hand laser. "It would be a shame," he said, "to go through all this if they'd gotten really hungry and croaked. Haven't heard anything from them in a long time. 'Course we haven't poked them, either."

"What are you gonna do?" Jim asked.

"Poke them," Kerry said, as he rose into a half crouch and fired a fusillade of sizzling beams at the door.

As soon as he stopped firing a pair of bright purple blasts came blazing back at him.

"That answers that," he said.

Jim nodded. "Okay. You ready? Saranji, everybody?"

Saranji ran his tongue across his lips, nodded. Kerry blinked. "Hell, I was born ready. Do it."

Jim took a small two-way dedicated comm unit from his pocket, raised it to his mouth. "Ferrick?" A tinny reply, short and sharp, crackled softly in the air. Jim glanced at Kerry. "Here we go," he said.

He brought the communicator up again. "Hit them," he said.

CHAPTER SIXTEEN

1

"Elwood and Ferrick must have really stirred up those proctors!" Jim yelled.

Kerry didn't bother to answer. The proctors were firing their trio of sonic cannon one after the other. It was like being trapped inside a bell getting the crap slammed out of it by John Henry, the steel-driving man.

"Pull back now?" Kerry mouthed.

Jim nodded. He put his lips close to Kerry's ear, trying to make himself heard through the protective headgear. "Let them see us go," he said.

Kerry raised one hand, waved it in a circular motion. Saranji and the other two boys with him rose, crouched, scuttled away. After a moment Jim and Kerry did likewise. Jim risked a glance backward as they pulled out. He thought he saw an apelike orange face peering out at him.

They pulled up just around a bend in the corridor and hunkered down, grimacing as the sonic bombardment rose to a skull-banging crescendo.

"Now what?" Saranji asked.

"Now we wait," Jim told him.

2

Kindra, of the clan Ar, stared at the steaming bowls and plates only a few feet away. "Ur-Barbba says they're a compassionate people," he muttered. "Evidently they can cook, too." He was half out of his mind, feverish and weak. In his condition, it didn't seem strange that the inexplicable humans had put out a food offering and then run away.

Lallup, also of the clan Ar, was foaming at the mouth, faint with hunger. Neither of the Kolumbans had eaten in four days. Ar-Lallup was close to death. Ar-Kindra, his branch brother, was not much better, though he was still able to move about, still had some of his wits about him, though starvation fog had dulled him. He fought the fog in his brain now, tried to force himself to think.

"It's probably a trick," he said.

Ar-Lallup groaned. "I don't care," he said. "If I don't get food, I'm going to die. You, too," he said, trying to raise himself.

Ar-Kindra soothed him back down. "Our tree brothers don't care. If they did, they would have let us through the door. We could have made it if they'd opened up and given us covering fire."

Ar-Lallup shook his big head back and forth. "Prop me up so I can see. Whatever that horrible thunder is, it's driven those humans away. Who knows when they'll come back? Get the food, branch brother. With food we can hold out longer. Without it, we'll die soon." He grunted, trying to hitch himself closer to their barricade. "I'll try to shoot them if they come back."

"It still smells like a trick."

"Poison?"

"Maybe," Ar-Kindra said.

"Then we die. And if we don't eat, we die. But how would they know what would poison us? They don't know our metabolism. They couldn't be sure. Would they be that reckless?"

Ar-Kindra thought about it. "I don't know."

"Get it, branch brother. Please."

Ar-Kindra nodded. He helped Ar-Lallup lean against the barricade, stretched his hand out, positioned the laser pistol. "Just pull the trigger," he said. "Don't worry about trying to hit anything. The blast itself should be enough cover for me to get back."

Ar-Lallup nodded. Pink foam was drooling from the edges of his mouth. "Hurry," he whispered.

Ar-Kindra took a deep breath, nerving himself, gripping his own laser more tightly. Then he lunged around the barricade and headed for the food. The sudden movement dizzied him and, overbalanced, he fell. Got up, kept on going, his skin quivering beneath his pelt in anticipation of the human's guns. But nothing happened. He reached the first bowl, plunged his face into its steaming contents and, ignoring the burning pain, sucked down several mouthfuls.

"Ar-Kindra. . . ." Ar-Lallup whispered behind him.

It took enormous physical and mental effort for Ar-Kindra to pull his snout out of the bowl. He was accustomed to eating nearly a sixth of his great weight a day, just in order to maintain normal energy levels. Four days of starvation had turned him into a gigantic bag of bones, with his skin hanging off him like oversize, badly fitting clothes. He felt barely strong enough to lift the large bowl, but he did, and headed back to the barricade. He handed the bowl across. Ar-Lallup took it, dropped his face to it, moaned at the heat, but didn't stop slurping.

Ar-Kindra lurched around, went back for the rest of it.

The bowls were filled with *pookub*, the plates with *ulrishi*. Both tasted pretty much as they should have. Ar-Kindra, no gourmet, put down any difference to the fact that humans had cooked them. Probably used recipes from the galley, he thought, as he gnashed and snarled and swallowed. But it was rich and filling, and as he and Ar-Lallup licked the plates and bowls clean, he thought maybe they might live after all.

Then the Heat began to hit them.

3

The sounds were audible even over the proctors' cannonade. A thin, high-pitched snarling that cut through the air like a bloody knife.

"I'm gonna take a look," Kerry shouted.

"Keep your head down."

Kerry nodded, already creeping forward on his hands and knees. He bobbed around the corner, ducked back, then looked again, slower this time.

Jim rapped him on the shoulder. "What?"

Kerry stood up, hefted his weapon. "See for yourself," he said, and stepped out into the main corridor. Jim, Saranji, and the others followed.

The two aliens had rolled out of their enclosure, scattering plates and bowls. They looked like eight-foot-tall scarecrows draped in hairy rugs as they swayed back and forth, grappling with each other. One of them still held a hand laser, but he had forgotten about it, falling back in his frenzy on older skills of tooth and claw.

They yowled as they tore at each other. Jim stared, awestruck at the violence of their battle. Kerry was frozen, too. They glanced at each other.

"It hits them quicker and harder than it does us," Jim said.

"God, yes," Kerry breathed. "You guessed it right. From the gloves they always wore, and the way they vacuum-sealed the packets. They were afraid of it." He looked back at the two screeching, spitting aliens. Then he raised his laser.

"No!" Jim said. "They're helpless."

"We don't have any time," Kerry answered. "And one of them has a gun." Then he cut them both down, with no more emotion than if he'd been swatting flies.

4

"Get that cover plate off," Jim said.

They'd pushed the two scorched alien corpses to the side of the corridor, out of the way, then pulled their makeshift barricade back from the blast door. Now Jim and Kerry stood before the control panel.

Kerry glanced at him, then quickly punched every button on the panel. Nothing happened.

"Don't bother with that," Jim said. "They've turned it off from the inside. We need to get the panel off, short-circuit the hard-wiring. And they have to know we're doing it."

Another series of booms thundered through the ship. Kerry flinched. "Jesus."

"As long as the Authority is still pounding us, they're not inside. And that's the way we want it. Let's get burning."

Kerry raised his laser pistol, set the aperture on high-powered hairline, and began to etch a groove around the edge of the outer panel. Saranji handed Jim another pistol, and Jim added his own efforts. Thirty seconds later, the metal turned red, then yellow, then white. It began to hiss and drip.

A muffled hooting sounded beyond the blast door.

"They know what we're doing. They know we're coming through," Jim said.

Suddenly his skin began to itch. A quiver ran up his spine. He glanced over, saw Kerry looking back at him. Kerry's face was pale as uncooked dough, the skin at the corners of his eyes pinched.

"They're firing up the drive," Kerry said. "Here we go."

"One way or the other," Jim replied, and turned back to his work. "Hurry."

5

Colonel Brian bounced up for a quick look, then slammed back down as one of Elwood's sizzling bolts nearly parted his balding skull.

"Frack!" The bay had turned into chaos. The *chucka-chucka* chatter of Ferrick's scatterblaster had done as much damage to their nerves as Elwood's focused sharpshooting had to their barricades. Brian, along with the other proctors, was wearing proper headgear, and so the continuous bellowing of the sonic cannon hadn't bothered them much. He tried to imagine what it must be like inside the ship, and shook his head.

Lieutenant Hasbendorffer, commanding the detachment of proctors, edged over from his own outpost. "What do you think?" the lieutenant said.

Hasbendorffer had a sanctimonious air about him that Brian had never much liked. The slender little man with the black crew cut worked out every day, and Brian thought that he was the source of the jokes about Brian's weight that made the rounds with uncomfortable regularity. Those jokes had the same sneering tone Brian believed he detected in Hasbendorffer's own speech, which Brian thought often verged on the insubordinate. Not that the lieutenant allowed his self-righteousness to interfere with taking his own share of the Cowboy loot.

What the hell was going on with those people? This Jim what'shisname, where had he come from? And why had the Cowboys shut off the flow of Heat? And this alien vessel . . .

Brian had told his own people to go over the hacks in the Authority computers. There were so many it looked as if some of the Cowboys had taken up virtual residence in the main cores. But the pattern was plain. This ship, or one like it, had visited the colony many times, and each visit had been carefully concealed by altering the computers themselves. The computers were a weak point that nobody had figured. They made a perfect cover for the alien visits. And those visits, once his own experts had analyzed the pattern, correlated perfectly with upsurges in the supply of Heat, so the aliens were probably the source of the dope. But what had gone wrong this time? Why was the ship still here?

So many questions. Too many. And no time to find answers. Not everybody in the Authority was on the take. If this went on much longer, the danger of his own corruption being discovered would rise exponentially. And he had enemies, powerful enemies, who would know how to use the knowledge. They would destroy him. Maybe it was time to think about making his own unscheduled departure. . . .

"We're not gonna be able to kill those frackers," he muttered to Hasbendorffer. "We can't even get past that airlock." He ran nervous fingers across the top of his head. "Damn. Why didn't the Authority stock a few mobile battle platforms in the armory?"

When Hasbendorffer replied, for once he didn't sound supercilious, he just sounded dazed. "For what? To blast holes in the colony walls? Nobody ever thought . . . Christ, Brian, that's a Hunzzan warship there."

Colonel Brian didn't keep up with galactic politics—or military capabilities—as well as Hasbendorffer did. What the lieutenant said stunned him.

"Hunzzan? Jesus, you think those are Hunzza aboard?"

"Hell no. If it was, if that was the Hunzzan navy there, they'd just send out a squad of marines and go through all those"—Hasbendorffer waved one hand at the huddled proctors—"like molten steel through your guts."

Colonel Brian shuddered faintly. Neither the thought of Hunzzan space marines, nor Hasbendorffer's vivid imagery, was very reassuring.

He shook his head. "We're gonna have to let them go."

"Leave those assholes out there doing God knows what? Are you crazy? With what they know, they've got our balls in their back pocket."

"Yeah, yeah, but what—"

Brian stopped, a look of horror suddenly blooming on his pasty features. "Did you feel that?"

Lieutenant Hasbendorffer looked like he'd swallowed a bad egg. "Oh, God—"

"—they're firing up the drive again," Brian finished. "Shit, it feels like somebody dipped my nerves in poison ivy!"

"What are we gonna do?"

Colonel Brian started knee-walking toward the portable shielded comm unit. "What the frack you think I'm gonna do? I'm gonna open the fracking bay doors!"

6

The air outside the blast door reeked of fried metal, of scorched Kolumban, of human sweat. Kerry had his arms around Jim from the back, bracing him against the bulkhead while he worked on the wiring behind the melted faceplate. The other three boys, clutching their weapons, watched tensely.

"Damn, I can't tell," Jim said. "They may have shorted out the whole damned thing from the other side. Or we may have melted something when we cut our way in."

Kerry gritted his teeth. The Kolumbans were still running their main drives through the ignition checklist, bringing the massive grav thrusters up to full ready status. The electronic blowback, rippling invisibly through the ship, made Kerry feel as if he'd been dipped in a nest of fire ants.

"They're gonna blow us outta here, or blow us up, one or the other," Kerry said. "Better hurry."

Jim sliced open the edge of his right hand on a piece of sharp metal as he reached for a new batch of wires. Blood from his nose had crusted on his lips and chin. Sweat flooded into his eyes, burning like hot oil. And he itched.

"I'm going as fast as I frackin'—"

The ship shifted. A moment later they felt the entire vessel vibrate. It was a different sound than the sonic cannons, sharper, heavier. As if in response, the cannon fell silent.

"They're opening the bay doors," Jim breathed. He swiped at his eyes, spattering his face with fresh blood. "Better hang on."

"You got it figured out yet?"

"No," Jim replied.

"Then we're gonna be—"

"—hang on," Jim said again.

Kerry grunted with effort as the ship lurched, then lifted off at what felt like full-grav thrust. He staggered, but he hung on.

7

Silence. That was the first thing, the sudden onrush of silence. They'd grown so used to the bellowing roar of the sonic cannon that when it ceased, they stopped and stared at each other, stunned.

"We're out of the bay," Kerry breathed.

Jim unwrapped the protective gear from his head. His ears rang, a weird tinnitus caused by the cessation of noise, an aural hangover.

"What?"

"I said—" Kerry stopped, unwrapped his own skull, shook his head. "Sorry," he said, in a normal tone. "Still yelling, I guess."

The motion of the ship had steadied out. Somewhere in the distance something clanged, heavily. "What was that?"

"Don't know," Jim said tensely. "If they're gonna do it, they'll do it now."

"Decompress the ship."

"Yeah, like killing rats. That's what they probably figure us for, rats infesting their ship. So blow the air out on our side of this door and sweep the bodies out later."

Another clang, and then a sudden, sighing hiss. Kerry reflexively gulped in air, though there was as yet no noticeable change in the pressure. His already pale features turned the color of fresh paper.

"We're not gonna get that damned door open in time," he said.

Jim reached down, grabbed the butt of the .75, and yanked the big hand weapon from his belt. "Yes we are," he said.

He stepped back, pushing Kerry out of the way. "If they've frozen the circuits, that's what's holding the door shut. So if there aren't any circuits anymore—"

"Just do it," Kerry hissed. "Shoot the damned thing."

Jim nodded, lifted his pistol, aimed, and pulled the trigger.

The vast, bell-like tone, louder in the enclosed space than anything the sonic cannon had achieved, blew them all the way across the room. The guts of the control panel vaporized in a white flash, half-blinding them.

Jim recovered first, blinking, shaking his head. He couldn't hear anything. But the greasy smoke billowing from the panel told him everything he needed to know. Instead of hanging in the air, it was flowing with increasing speed back down the corridor like a ghost being sucked down a drain.

"They've got a lock open somewhere," Jim said. "Hope you like breathing vacuum. Remember what I told you." Then he flung himself at the blast door.

8

Ferrick and Elwood pushed at the front airlock, trying to shove it closed, trying to shut the last half inch of clear space. Air roared past them, tugged at the wrappings on their heads, made an odd, low-pitched whistling sound, like blowing across the neck of a bottle, as it rushed out into the vacuum of space.

"Push, damn it," Ferrick grunted.

"I'm pushing," Elwood replied, his voice odd, high, and frightened.

"Push harder, then."

"Did I ever tell you my worst nightmare? Had it since I was a little kid. That I drowned, that my lungs fill up with water, and I couldn't breathe. . . ."

"Shut up," Ferrick said. "Just frackin' shut up."

And the wind roared.

9

"Push, damn it, push!" Jim yelled. He felt his ears pop as the air pressure lowered. Like climbing a mountain, going higher and higher, the air getting thinner. . . . Except at the top of this mountain there was no air at all.

Suddenly his nose was bleeding again. He ignored it. His bloody hand slipped, and he almost fell. He steadied himself and grabbed the long emergency bar set into the middle of the blast door. It was the only leverage they had.

Kerry grunted, saving his breath, and pushed.

Now a low, moaning sound filled the chamber and began to rise higher. Like holding the neck of a balloon and letting the air out.

"Remember, don't take a deep breath. Empty out your lungs. If we get full vacuum, and you've got air, your chest will explode!" Jim said. "Exhale and keep your mouth open to equalize the pressure. That will give us a few more seconds!"

"Yeah, yeah. . . ."

Jim bit his lip, tasted more blood. His vision was turning black at the edges, and white dots had begun to dance in the center of things. The world was dimming out. His skin felt stretched, tight.

"Exhale!" he shouted, but it came out as a squeak, barely audible. He felt Kerry's breath hot on his neck, blowing out.

Full vacuum came like a fire on the skin, like a thunder in the ears. Jim closed his eyes before all the moisture boiled off his eyeballs. They had maybe thirty seconds, and then the moisture inside their bodies would begin to vaporize, and cells would explode. . . .

Push push push push push. . . .

He felt the sound through his palms. Had to, because sound didn't travel in a vacuum. A soft, gritty scrape, then another. The blast door gave the tiniest of hitches, and he felt another scrape, longer this time.

Push!

A sharp, grinding scream as the door, frozen in place for

almost four days, finally began to slide in its tracks. And kept on sliding, sliding, sliding all the way open.

Oxygen rushed out from the other side, a vast torrent of precious air, filling the corridor, filling the ship. Jim staggered, his chest heaving. He felt Kerry hanging on to his shoulders, heard him gasping.

"Uh, huh. Huh!"

Kerry hugged him, squeezed like a drowning man clinging to the last life preserver. Hell, he was a drowning man. Had been.

"We made it," Jim said. "We made it."

He almost blacked out, but kept enough of consciousness to see the first huge form come rushing up from the other side. Saw the laser pistol in the big ape's hand, felt the incandescent knife of coherent light sizzle past, a finger away from his skull.

He lifted his .75. He was weak. It felt as if the pistol weighed a hundred pounds. Another laser blast hissed by, a foot over his head. More huge shapes appeared, screaming some sort of ululating battle cry. He felt Kerry yank him back from the door, out of the line of fire.

"Here they come," he yelled. "Everybody, here they come!"

10

In the end, it wasn't much of a fight. Jim shot the first Kolumban down the corridor, and the .75's rocket shell blew the big alien back almost ten yards. Kerry stepped up, a laser in each hand, a twisted grin on his face, firing like some old-time gunslinger at the O.K. Corral.

Saranji and the other two added their own firepower. The aliens might have put up more resistance, but they'd been weakened almost as much by starvation as the two they'd marooned on the far side of their blast door. And they were heavily outgunned, especially when Ferrick arrived with his scatterblaster and Elwood with his battle laser.

"We have to hold that door, we can't let them take it back," Jim said to Kerry as they advanced. "As long as we have it, they can't decompress the ship."

Kerry saw a flicker of movement at the far end of the corridor, raised one laser, fired. "They won't take it back," he said grimly.

Ferrick came running up, followed by Elwood. Their faces were bright red, as if they'd been staked out on some desert beneath a burning sun. Their skin was blistered, already beginning to peel. *Vacuum burn,* Jim thought. But he was never so glad to see anybody in his life. Without thinking, he grabbed Ferrick in a bear hug.

"Uhf. Let go," Ferrick grunted.

"I see you made it," Jim said.

Ferrick nodded. "Yeah. Barely. We both blacked out. But we got the airlock shut. When the air came back, so did we."

Jim shook his head. "Too close. Way too close."

Ferrick shrugged. "Close enough." He glanced over at Elwood. "Elwood thought it was interesting."

"I did," Elwood agreed. "You're an interesting guy, Jim. I think I like that."

"Yeah, sure," Kerry said. "Enough with the love poems, okay? Jim? The engine room, right?"

Jim took out his pad, brought up the schematic of the Hunzzan vessel, and showed it to Ferrick. "There's another door between us and the bridge, but it isn't a blast door. We can crack it easily enough if they try to hide behind it. But the engine room's on this side, and there's a backup set of controls for the ship. Ferrick, I showed you how to override the bridge controls?"

Ferrick nodded. "Don't worry about it." He hefted his blaster. "Come on, Elwood. Got some more interesting shit for you."

Elwood stared at him calmly. "Interesting is good," he said.

Ferrick rounded up four more Cowboys from the crowd that had arrived from the galley, and they all set off, whooping and yelling.

"I missed all the fun," Sam said.

Jim jumped, whirled. "Sam!"

"Uh-huh, that's my name." She was smiling at him.

He wrapped his arms around her, crushed her to him, her

raspberry scent filling his nostrils, working its dizzy magic on his brain.

Unlike Ferrick, she didn't push him away. After a long moment he released her, stared into her eyes. "I was so afraid," he whispered.

"It was boring, in a way. Nothing happened. There was this weird whapping sound when the air pressure dropped outside, and all the plastic shields flattened out against the ventilator ducts. But there wasn't much leakage." She grinned. "I was more worried about dying from the stink of all those sweaty boys."

A mind picture floated into Jim's skull, the small galley packed solid with terrified Cowboys, their bowels and perspiration glands all working overtime.

"I'll bet," he said. "Must have been horrible."

"I hate to interrupt you two," Kerry said. "True love is always so touching." He tapped Jim on the shoulder. "But there are a few minor details. Like however many Kolumbans are still holed up in the bridge."

"Okay. Just a second," Jim said, and turned back to Sam.

"Is that what it is?" Sam said softly. "True love?" There was a luminous light in her eyes.

Jim leaned forward, put his lips on hers. "I don't know," he murmured. "But I'd like to find out. What do you think?"

"I think I already told you," she answered. "I like learning new things."

"Come on, come on, let's go," Kerry said.

Jim kissed her again, and *then* they went.

CHAPTER SEVENTEEN

The largest space on the Kolumban ship was the main cargo hold, and they all gathered there. Jim, Kerry, Ferrick, and Sam stood in the center of a loose semicircle of the rest of them, who sat cross-legged or sprawled on the deck. Maybe forty, Jim estimated. Two had died in the initial attack on the ship. He felt a scratchy, persistent guilt about that, one that wouldn't let him alone.

His fault. It had been his plan, all of it. And it was still going on, though nobody, not even the other leaders, knew that part of it. And wouldn't, not until it no longer mattered. He didn't know how long that would be.

It was a restive crowd, all male, young, cynical. Uneducated and ignorant, but not dumb. Ferrick had called them the best of what they had, and then added, with a bitter tang on the tail of his words, "although that probably isn't the definition of 'best' you'd use, Jim."

Ferrick would be a problem. He still wasn't convinced, maybe never would be. But that wasn't his fault. Jim couldn't blame him for it. Ferrick was what he was. And he'd worked hard to become better than what he was. Most of all, despite everything, Ferrick was his friend. Could he betray him, after everything?

Should he?

The kids in the audience coughed, chattered, laughed, offered biting comments out of the side of their mouths. This wasn't the leaders dictating to the troops. This was equals, some of whom happened to be more equal than others.

He wondered if he could change that. He knew he would try. Because if he couldn't, then the rest of his plan wouldn't work.

Secrets. Secrets that felt like treachery. He wondered if he would ever be able to tell any of them the whole story. Sam, maybe, someday. And maybe not.

"Let's get this show on the road," Kerry muttered. "Those assholes . . . look at them."

"But they're our assholes," Ferrick said.

"Yeah, that's true." Kerry turned to Jim. "I'll give them a general rundown. Some of them still don't know the real details, and there's a lot of rumors. Then we'll decide what to do."

"Okay," Jim said.

Kerry nodded, then stepped into the center of the semicircle and raised his hands for quiet. After a moment or two the hooting died down. "Yo, Kerry," somebody at the back yelled. "Big dude! Cowboys forever!"

Kerry grinned, nodded, waited it out. When he had silence, he told them all about it. About what Heat really was. About where it had come from. About his suspicions why the Kolumbans had brought the dope to the *Outward Bound* in the first place.

"They weren't trying to make money," he said. "They were trying to kill the colony."

A rustling mutter swept through the crowd. Attentive faces looked up, waiting for more.

"How do you know that?" Elwood said. He was seated near the center of the circle, his own squad around him.

Kerry shrugged, turned, motioned for Jim to come forward.

"Ask him," he said. "He's the one who figured it out."

Jim took them through the rest of it, step by step. "When we realized that Heat was deadly, knew what it would do to the ship, knew it would eventually kill us all, we knew we had to do something. But what? Cowboys depended on dealing the shit. Everything we did was based on it. We had to stop it, to stop dealing Heat, but we had to do it so the Cowboys survived. Kerry had too many connections with the Authority, so he couldn't keep on leading. That's what the challenge was all about, to set up the Cowboys in a different way. To start over. But then we had to go."

From the rear, a derisive hoot. "What's this 'we' shit, *kemo sabe?* You ain't no Cowboy."

Jim nodded. "Maybe not. But it doesn't matter. You aren't either. Not anymore."

Another shadowy rustling, this one sharper, more urgent. "What you mean, asshole? We're Cowboys. Cowboys are forever!"

Jim shook his head. "The Cowboys are back on the *Outward Bound*. Darnell has them now, you saw it. Kerry lost the challenge, and now the Cowboys are Darnell's gang. You guys want to go back, join up again? I bet the proctors would like to see you."

More mutters. They knew they were outcasts. But it hadn't quite sunk in yet. It had started as an adventure. Take over the alien ship, hijack it. Now it was becoming permanent. Becoming real. Some of them didn't like it.

Jim rode over them. "Look, we did it, and now it's done. Elwood, you asked how we knew for sure about Heat, about the Kolumbans wanting to destroy the *Outward Bound*. Why we had no choice."

He turned, nodded at Ferrick. There was a stir at the main door, and then a huge figure, shepherded by two armed boys, entered, lumbered forward until it stood silently just beyond thc ring.

"One survivor," Jim shouted. "She locked herself in a cabin and waited till the fighting was over. Then she surrendered to Kerry, because she knew him. And she told him what she knew. She told him we guessed right, that Heat was designed to drive humans nuts. Kill them. Destroy them. Destroy us!"

He pointed. "Meet Ur-Barrba. One of the Kolumbans who designed Heat in the first place!"

The mutters grew to a roar. "Kill the ape!" somebody yelled.

Jim shook his head. "No, there won't be any more killing. Ur-Barrba surrendered. She's told us what she knows, and it's even bigger than what we thought. She gave us the answer to our biggest question—why? Why would some aliens we never heard of try to destroy a Terran colony ship?"

He paused, letting it sink in. Predictably, it was Elwood who finally responded. He sounded interested again.

"Okay, tell us. Why?"

"They were hired," Jim said softly. "Paid to do it. By another alien race. Called the 'Communers.' The Communers hired them to design the dope, gave them human specifications, DNA samples, everything they needed. And the Kolumbans did it. They'll keep on doing it. We captured one ship. Now we've got to take on a whole planet!"

Elwood stood up. "That's ridiculous. We're just kids. Plebs. Cowboys. How are we going to deal with a planet full of orange apes?"

Jim stared at him. "I can show you how," he said softly. "If you're interested."

Elwood stared at him for what seemed a very long time. Jim felt it hanging in the balance, wondered what he would do if Elwood shot him down.

Elwood shook his head. "You got balls, I'll say that. Okay, I'm interested."

Everybody chewed on it some more, but after Elwood, it was pretty much decided. When they voted, made it official, Jim felt a darkness rise from his mind, turn golden, vanish.

He'd won. For a while, at least. He stood and faced them again, this time with Ferrick, Sam, and Kerry standing with him.

It felt like a moment, a big one. Felt even more like one when Elwood slowly began to applaud. When everybody else joined in.

Almost everybody. The voice from the rear shouted a final time, as the applause faded away.

"What about the Cowboys?" it shouted. "What about the gang?"

Jim glanced at the others, then faced the group at large. "We aren't a gang anymore," he told them. "We're a crew. We're a starship crew."

Kerry stepped forward. "And the first order of business, crew members, is the most important." He raised his hands for quiet, so they could all hear.

"The first thing we do," he said, "is choose our captain. The captain of the free starship *Endeavor!*"

They liked it. Even Elwood smiled.

Kerry waited until the cheering died. "And then we're gonna go kick some alien butt! Are you with us?"

Jim listened to the fresh round of cheers ringing in his ears. He had them now. The plan was still on track. But for how long?

I guess I'm about to find out, he thought. And with the

thought came the remembering whisper, the déjà vu, the secret knowledge that came from within, that he had been in a place like this, done this, *known* this.

Overwhelming, perfectly certain, but formless, without detail. Just the knowing—I've been here before.

But where? When?

The moment passed, and he went on.

"You're smiling," Sam whispered.

"I must be happy," he told her. And it wasn't a lie. He was.

BIBLIOGRAPHY

Humankind has always been a traveling race, a race of adventurers and colonizers. It is no accident that, come what may, one of the abiding dreams of the human consciousness remains the vast realms of space and our eventual role there. Nobody doubts that we plan to go. The only questions are when, and how.

There is a wealth of books that try to answer both questions. For the best, see:

The High Frontier by Gerard K. O'Neill, 1976, Bantam Books/SSI Press, ISBN: 0–9622379–0–6

Colonies in Space by T. A. Heppenheimer, 1977, Warner Books, ISBN: 0–446–81–581–0

Toward Distant Suns by T. A. Heppenheimer, 1979, Stackpole Books, ISBN: 0–449–90035–5

The Millennial Project by Marshall T. Savage, 1992, Little, Brown & Company, ISBN: 0–316–77163–1 and 0–316–77163–5

Space Colonies edited by Stewart Brand, 1977, Penguin Books, ISBN: 0–140–04805–7

2081: A Hopeful View of the Human Future by Gerard K. O'Neill, 1981, Simon & Schuster, ISBN: 0–671–24257–1

Space Trek: The Endless Migration by Jerome Clayon Glenn and George S. Robinson, 1978, Warner Books, ISBN: 0–446–91122–4

The High Road by Ben Bova, 1981, Pocket Books, ISBN: 0–671–45805–1

A Step Further Out by Jerry Pournelle, 1980, Ace Books, ISBN: 0–441–78583–2

The Illustrated Encyclopedia of Space Technology, 2nd ed. by Kenneth Gatland, 1989, Orion Books, ISBN: 0–517–57427–8

There is also a plethora of information on the World Wide Web. Start with the wonderful Space Settlement FAQ, written and maintained by Mike Combs. The bibliography above is taken in part from that FAQ, as well as the web sites listed below:

Space Studies Institute: Founded by Gerard O'Neill, this non-profit organization funds research into space manufacturing. Features the SSI slide show and several good articles.

http://www.ssi.org

Space Settlement: Web page maintained by Al Globus, features pictures of space habitats.

http://www.nas.nasa.gov/NAS/SpaceSettlement/

The Living Universe Foundation: Founded by Marshall Savage, author of *The Millennial Project*. Dedicated to expanding life into space.

http://www.luf.org/

The PERMANENT Web Site: PERMANENT is an acronym for Program to Employ Resources of the Moon and Asteroids Near Earth in the Near Term. This web site goes into deeper detail on many of the subjects of this FAQ.

http://www.permanent.com/

Island One Society: Group emphasizing the political freedom that may be possible in space habitats.

http://www.islandone.org/

National Space Settlement Design Competition: Academic contest for students to design their own space habitats.

http://space.bsdi.com/index.html

The Artemis Society: Devoted to a return to the moon with an emphasis on commercial development.

http://www.asi.org/

Moon Miners' Manifesto: Required reading for all lunar prospectors.

http://www.asi.org/mmm/mmmhome.html

The Space Frontier Foundation: Pushing for the opening of the high frontier to the average citizen and cheap access to space.

http://www.space-frontier.org/

Military history might seem an odd subject to call a science, but that is exactly what it is, a division of the larger classification military science. In our day and age, where high-tech smart bombs send us video pictures before slamming into their targets, one could wonder what value the battles of Julius Caesar might hold for the warriors of the future.

Quite a bit, actually. As Robert Heinlein and many others noted, for all the glitz and glitter, one still has to take the ground and hold it. For that you need battle tactics, and almost nobody has done better at it than Gaius Julius Caesar, though two thousand years have come and gone since he conquered the Gauls and noted in a phrase learned by every school-age Latin scholar that "*Omnia Gallia in tres partes divisa est.*" (All Gaul is divided into three parts.)

Alesia is generally considered to be Caesar's finest military hour. For an excellent, though fictionalized account, read:

Caesar: A Novel by Colleen McCullough, 1997, William Morrow & Company; ISBN: 0–688–09372–8.

For another approach, this one delineating six of the greatest generals of history—Caesar, Alexander the Great, Ulysses S. Grant, Horatio Nelson, Napoléon Bonaparte, and Georgi Zhukov—see:

The Great Commanders: Alexander, Caesar, Nelson, Napoleon, Grant and Zhukov by Phil Grabsky and David G. Chandler, 1995, TV Books Inc; ISBN: 1–575–00003–2.

Street gangs, even, or especially, those involved in the drug trade, have highly evolved, complex social structures. For further discussion, see:

Delinquent Boys: The Culture of the Gang by Albert Kircidel Cohen, 1971, Free Press; ISBN: 0–029–05770–1

Chinatown Gangs: Extortion, Enterprise, and Ethnicity (Studies in Crime and Public Policy) by Ko-Lin Chin, 1996, Oxford University Press; ISBN: 0–195–10238–X

Always Running: LA Vida Loca: Gang Days in L.A. by Luis J. Rodriguez, Reprint edition, 1994, Touchstone Books; ISBN: 0–671–88231–7

8 Ball Chicks: A Year in the Violent World of Girl Gangsters by Gini Sikes, Anchor edition, 1998, Doubleday; ISBN: 0–385–47432–6